OLIVER TWIST

Published by Priory Books,
© Peter Haddock Publishing,
United Kingdom, YO16 6BT.

OLIVER TWIST

CHAPTER 1

Among other public buildings in a certain town there is a workhouse. In this workhouse was born the item of mortality whose name is prefixed to this book.

For a long time after it was ushered into this world of sorrow and trouble, by the parish surgeon, it remained a matter of considerable doubt whether the child would survive to bear any name at all.

Being born in a workhouse was the best thing that could have happened to Oliver Twist. There was considerable difficulty in inducing Oliver to breathe. For some time he lay gasping on a little flock mattress, poised between this world and the next. Now if, during this brief period he had been cared for by loving grandmothers and experienced nurses and doctors, he would most certainly have been killed in no time. There being nobody but a pauper old woman, who was rendered rather misty by beer; and a parish surgeon who did such matters by contract – Oliver and Nature fought out the point between them. The result was that, after a few struggles, Oliver breathed and sneezed. He then set up as loud a cry as could be expected from a male infant who had only existed for three minutes and a quarter.

As Oliver gave this first use to his lungs, the patchwork coverlet on the iron bedstead rustled and the pale face of a young woman was raised feebly from the pillow. Her faint voice whispered, "Let me see the child, and die."

The surgeon had been sitting facing the fire, warming his hands. He rose, and advancing to the bed's head, said, with more kindness than might have been expected, "You must not talk about dying."

"Lor' bless her heart, no!" interposed the nurse. "Think what it is to be a mother, there's a dear young lamb, do."

The patient shook her head, stretching her hand to the child.

The surgeon put it in her arms. She kissed it passionately on its forehead, fell back – and died. The blood had stopped forever.

"It's all over, Mrs Thingummy!" said the surgeon at last.

"Ah, poor dear, so it is!" said the nurse. She stooped to take up the child. "Poor dear!"

"You needn't mind sending up to me, if the child cries, nurse," said the surgeon, putting on his gloves with great deliberation. "It's very likely it *will* be troublesome. Give it a little gruel if it is." He put on his hat, and, pausing by the bed on his way to the door, added: "She was a good-looking girl, too; where did she come from!"

"She was brought here last night," replied the old woman. "Found lying in the street. She had walked a distance, for her shoes were worn to pieces; but where she came from, or where she was going to, nobody knows."

The surgeon leaned over the body, and raised the left hand. "No wedding ring, I see," he said, shaking his head. "Ah! Good night!"

The medical gentleman walked away to dinner; and the nurse sat down on a low chair before the fire, to dress the infant.

Wrapped in the blanket, Oliver might have been the child of a nobleman or a beggar. But now that he wore the old calico robes, he was badged and ticketed – an orphan of a workhouse – to be buffeted through the world – despised by all, and pitied by none.

Oliver cried lustily. If he could have known that he was an orphan, left to the tender mercies of churchwardens and overseers, perhaps he would have cried the louder.

CHAPTER 2

For the next eight or ten months, Oliver was brought up by hand. He was despatched to a branch-workhouse some three miles off, where twenty or thirty other juvenile offenders against the poor-laws, rolled about the floor all day, without the inconvenience of too much food or too much clothing. An elderly woman received the culprits for sevenpence-halfpenny per small head per week. Sevenpence-halfpenny's worth per week is a good round diet for a child, quite enough to overload its stomach, and make it uncomfortable. The elderly woman knew what was good for children and she knew exactly what was good for herself. So, she appropriated the greater part of the weekly stipend to herself, giving the rising parochial generation a smaller allowance than was originally provided for them.

This system of farming will never produce a luxuriant crop. Oliver Twist's ninth birthday found him a pale thin child, somewhat diminutive in stature, and decidedly small in circumference. But he had a good sturdy spirit inside him that had had plenty of room to expand, thanks to the spare diet of the establishment. On this, his ninth birthday, he was celebrating in the coal-cellar with two other young gentlemen. They had been locked up for atrociously presuming to be hungry. Meanwhile, Mrs Mann, the good lady of the house, was unexpectedly startled to see Mr Bumble, the beadle, at the wicket of the garden-gate.

"Goodness gracious! Is that you, Mr Bumble, sir!" said Mrs Mann, thrusting her head out of the window. "(Susan, take Oliver and them two brats upstairs, and wash 'em directly.) Mr Bumble, how glad I am to see you!"

Now, Mr Bumble was a fat man, and gave the little wicket a tremendous shake.

"Lor, only think," said Mrs Mann, running out, for the three boys had been removed by then, "I had forgotten that the gate was bolted on the inside, on account of them dear children! Walk in, Mr Bumble, do, sir."

"Do you think this right, Mrs Mann," inquired Mr Bumble, grasping his cane, "to keep the parish officers a-waiting at your garden-gate, when they come here upon porochial business connected with the porochial orphans?"

"I'm sure, Mr Bumble, that I was only a-telling one or two of the dear children as is so fond of you, that it was you a-coming," replied Mrs Mann with great humility.

Mr Bumble had a great idea of his oratorical powers and his importance. He had displayed the one, and vindicated the other. He relaxed. "Well, Mrs Mann," he replied. "Lead the way in, for I come on business."

Mrs Mann ushered the beadle into a small parlour and deposited his cocked hat and cane on the table before him. Mr Bumble glanced complacently at the cocked hat, and smiled. Beadles are but men and Mr Bumble smiled.

He took out a pocket-book. "The child that was half-baptised, Oliver Twist, is nine year old today."

"Bless him!" interposed Mrs Mann.

"Notwithstanding an offered reward of ten pound, afterwards increased to twenty pound," said Bumble, "we have been unable to discover anything concerning his mother or father."

Mrs Mann raised her hands in astonishment, but added, after a moment, "How come he has any name at all, then?"

The beadle drew himself up with great pride, and said, "I inwented it. We name our foundlings in alphabetical order. The last was a S – Swubble, this was a T – Twist. The next one as comes will be Unwin, and the next Vilkins. I have names ready made to the end of the alphabet."

"Why, you're quite a literary character, sir!" said Mrs Mann.

"Well," said the beadle, delighted by the compliment. "Perhaps I may be, Mrs Mann. Oliver is now too old to remain here, I have come to take him back into the house. Let me see him at once."

"I'll fetch him directly," said Mrs Mann, leaving the room. Oliver, having by this time been scrubbed, was led into the room by his benevolent protectress.

"Make a bow to the gentleman, Oliver," said Mrs Mann.

Oliver made a bow, divided between the beadle and the hat on the table.

"Will you come with me, Oliver?" said Mr Bumble, in a majestic voice.

Oliver caught sight of Mrs Mann, behind the beadle's chair. She was shaking her fist at him. "Will *she* go with me?" he asked.

"No, she can't," replied Mr Bumble. "But she'll see you sometimes."

This was no great consolation to the child. Young as he was, he had enough sense to pretend to feel regret at leaving. Mrs Mann gave him a thousand embraces, and, what Oliver wanted a great deal more – a piece of bread and butter, lest he should seem too hungry when he got to the workhouse. With the slice of bread in hand, and the little parish cap on his head, Oliver was then led by Mr Bumble from the wretched home. Yet he burst into an agony of childish grief, as the gate closed after him. He was leaving behind the only friends he had and a sense of loneliness in the great wide world sank into his heart for the first time.

Mr Bumble walked on with long strides; little Oliver, firmly grasping his gold-laced cuff, trotted beside him. At the end of every quarter of a mile, he inquired were they "nearly there?" Mr Bumble's replies were short and snappish.

Oliver had been within the walls of the workhouse a quarter of an hour, and had scarcely eaten a second slice of bread, when Mr Bumble informed him it was a board night, and that he was to appear before it forthwith.

He was taken to a large whitewashed room, where eight or ten fat gentlemen sat round a table.

"Bow to the board," said Bumble. Oliver brushed away two or three tears that lingered in his eyes; and seeing no board but the table fortunately bowed to that.

"What's your name, boy?" said the gentleman in the high chair. "You know you're an orphan, I suppose?"

"What's that, sir?" inquired poor Oliver.

"The boy is a fool," said the gentleman in the white waistcoat.

"Hush!" said the gentleman who had spoken first. "You know you have no father or mother, and were brought up by the parish?"

"Yes, sir," replied Oliver, weeping bitterly.

"Why are you crying?" inquired the gentleman in the white waistcoat. "You are here to be educated, and taught a useful trade. So you'll begin to pick oakum tomorrow morning at six o'clock".

Oliver bowed low and was then hurried away to a large ward, where, on a rough, hard bed, he sobbed himself to sleep.

The room in which the boys were fed, was a large stone hall. The master, dressed in an apron ladled the gruel at meal-times. Each boy had one porringer, and no more. The bowls never wanted washing. The boys polished them with their spoons till they shone again. This operation never took very long, as the spoons were nearly as large as the bowls. They would then sit staring at the copper, sucking their fingers most assiduously, with the view of catching up any stray splashes of gruel. Boys have generally excellent appetites. Oliver Twist and his companions suffered the tortures of slow starvation for three months. A council was held; lots were cast who should walk up to the master after supper that evening, and ask for more; and it fell to Oliver Twist.

The evening arrived, the boys took their places. The master served out the gruel. A long grace was said. The gruel disappeared. The boys whispered to each other, and winked at Oliver. He was desperate with hunger. He rose from the table and advanced to the master, basin and spoon in hand.

"Please, sir, I want some more," he whispered.

The master was a fat, healthy man, but he turned very pale. He gazed in astonishment on the small rebel. The assistants were paralysed with wonder; the boys with fear.

"What!" said the master, faintly.

"Please, sir," replied Oliver, "I want some more."

The master aimed a blow at Oliver's head with the ladle; pinioned him in his arms; and shrieked aloud for the beadle.

The board were sitting in solemn conclave, when Mr Bumble rushed into the room, and said, "Mr Limbkins, I beg your pardon, sir! Oliver Twist has asked for more!"

"For *more!*" said Mr Limbkins. "Compose yourself, Bumble. He asked for more, after eating the supper allotted by the dietary?"

"He did, sir," replied Bumble.

"That boy will be hung," said the gentleman in the white waistcoat.

An animated discussion then took place. Oliver was ordered into instant confinement. A bill was pasted on the outside of the gate, offering a reward of five pounds to anyone who would take the boy off the hands of the parish.

"I never was more convinced of anything in my life," said the gentleman in the white waistcoat, as he knocked at the gate and read the bill next morning, "that that boy will be hung."

CHAPTER 3

Oliver remained a close prisoner for a week. He cried bitterly all day; and crouched in the corner at night, trying to sleep, waking with a start and tremble, and drawing himself closer and closer to the wall.

It was nice cold weather, and he was allowed to wash, every morning under the pump, in a stone yard, in the presence of Mr Bumble, who prevented his catching cold, by repeated applications of the cane. And for society, he was taken every other day into the hall where the boys dined, and flogged as a public warning.

The board took counsel together on the expediency of shipping off Oliver Twist, in a trading vessel bound to an unhealthy port.

Mr Bumble was despatched to make inquiries, when he encountered at the gate, Mr Sowerberry, the parochial undertaker.

Mr Sowerberry was a tall, gaunt man, in a suit of threadbare black.

"I have taken the measure of the two women that died last night, Mr Bumble," said the undertaker.

"You'll make your fortune, Mr Sowerberry," said the beadle, tapping the undertaker on the shoulder with his cane.

"Think so?" said the undertaker. "The prices allowed by the board are very small, Mr Bumble."

"So are the coffins," replied the beadle. Mr Sowerberry was much tickled at this: as of course he ought to be; and laughed.

"By the bye," said Mr Bumble, "you don't know anyone who wants a boy, do you? A porochial 'prentis? Liberal terms, Mr Sowerberry!" He raised his cane to the bill, and rapped upon the words "five pounds".

"Gadso!" said the undertaker, "that's just what I wanted to speak to you about. You know, Mr Bumble, I was thinking that if I pay so much towards poor rates, I've a right to get as much out of 'em as I can; and so – I think I'll take the boy myself."

Mr Bumble led the undertaker into the building. Mr Sowerberry was closeted with the board for five minutes; and it was arranged that Oliver should go to him that evening.

Oliver was taken before "the gentlemen" that evening; and informed that he was to go, that night, as general house-lad to a coffin-maker's; and that if he complained of his situation he would be sent to sea.

Oliver heard the news in perfect silence and, having had his luggage put into his hand – a brown paper parcel – he pulled his cap over his eyes and once more held on to Mr Bumble's cuff.

As they drew near to their destination, Mr Bumble looked down, to see that the boy was in good order for inspection by his new master.

"Oliver!" said Mr Bumble. "Pull that cap off your eyes, and hold up your head, sir."

Although Oliver did as he was desired at once, he left a tear in his eyes when he looked up at his conductor. As Mr Bumble gazed sternly upon him, it rolled down his cheek. More followed. The child made a strong effort, but was unsuccessful. He covered his face with both his hands and wept.

"Well!" exclaimed Mr Bumble stopping short. "Well! Of all the ungratefullest boys as ever I see, Oliver, you are the – "

"No, no, sir," sobbed Oliver, clinging to the hand which held the cane, "no, sir; I will be good, indeed I will! I am very little, sir, and it is so – so – "

"So what?" inquired Mr Bumble in amazement.

"So lonely, sir!" cried the child. "Everybody hates me. Oh! sir, don't pray be cross to me!"

Mr Bumble regarded Oliver's helpless look with astonishment for a few seconds; hemmed three or four times huskily, and, after muttering something about "that troublesome cough," bade Oliver dry his eyes and be a good boy. Then, once more taking his hand, he walked on with him.

The undertaker, who had just put up the shutters of his shop, was making entries in his day-book by the light of a most appropriate dismal candle, when Mr Bumble entered.

"Aha!" said the undertaker: looking up from the book, and pausing in the middle of a word, "is that you, Bumble?"

"No one else, Mr Sowerberry," replied the beadle. "Here! I've brought the boy." Oliver made a bow.

"Oh! That's the boy, is it?" said the undertaker: raising the candle to get a better view of Oliver. "Mrs Sowerberry, will come here a moment, my dear?"

Mrs Sowerberry emerged from a little room behind the shop, a short, thin, squeezed-up woman.

"My dear," said Mr Sowerberry, deferentially, "this is the boy from the workhouse that I told you of." Oliver bowed again.

"Dear me!" said the undertaker's wife, "he's very small."

"Why, he is rather small," replied Mr Bumble, looking at Oliver as if it were his fault. "There's no denying it. But he'll grow, Mrs Sowerberry."

"Ah! I dare say he will," replied the lady pettishly, "on our victuals and our drink. I see no saving in parish children for they always cost more to keep, than they're worth. However, men always think they know best. Get downstairs, little bag o' bones." With this, the undertaker's wife opened a side door, and pushed Oliver down a steep flight of stairs into a dark, damp stone cell. It was the "kitchen" next to the coal cellar.

Mrs Sowerberry gave the boy some of the cold bits that were put by for the dog.

Oliver's eyes glistened at the plateful of coarse broken victuals set before him. He tore at them and ate them swiftly.

"Well," said the undertaker's wife, when Oliver had finished. She thought of his future appetite. "Have you done?"

There being nothing eatable within his reach, Oliver nodded.

"Then come with me," said Mrs Sowerberry, taking up a dim and dirty lamp, and leading the way up stairs; "your bed's under the counter. You don't mind sleeping among the coffins, I suppose? Doesn't much matter whether you do or don't, for there's nowhere else. Come, don't keep me here all night!"

Oliver meekly followed his new mistress.

CHAPTER 4

Oliver set the lamp down on a bench, and gazed timidly about him. An unfinished coffin stood in the middle of the shop, looking so gloomy that a cold tremble came over him. Every time his eyes wandered in that direction he almost expected to see some frightful form slowly rear its head, to drive him mad with terror. Against the wall were ranged a long row of elm boards cut into the same shape. The shop was close and hot. The atmosphere seemed tainted with the smell of coffins. The recess beneath the counter in which his flock mattress was thrust resembled a grave.

Olive was alone in a strange place. He had no friends to care for, or to care for him. He wished, as he crept into his narrow bed, that it was his coffin, and that he could be laid in a calm and lasting sleep in the churchyard ground.

Oliver was awakened in the morning, by a loud kicking at the shop door. When he began to undo the chain, a voice began.

"Open the door, will yer?"

"I will, directly, sir," replied Oliver, turning the key.

"I suppose yer the new boy, ain't yer?" said the voice through the keyhole.

"Yes, sir," replied Oliver.

"How old are yer?" inquired the voice.

"Ten, sir," replied Oliver.

"Then I'll whop yer when I get in," said the voice. "My work'us brat!" Having made this promise, the voice began to whistle.

Oliver drew back the bolts with a trembling hand, and opened the door. He glanced up and down the street and saw nobody but a big charity-boy, sitting on a post in front of the house.

"I beg your pardon, sir," said Oliver at length, seeing that no other visitor made his appearance. "Did you knock?"

"I kicked," replied the charity-boy.

"Did you want a coffin, sir?" inquired Oliver, innocently.

"Yer don't know who I am, I suppose, Work'us?" said the charity-boy, descending from the post.

"No, sir," rejoined Oliver.

"I'm Mister Noah Claypole," said the charity-boy, "and you're under me. Take down the shutters, yer idle young ruffian!" With this, he administered a kick to Oliver, and entered the shop.

Oliver taking down the shutters, broke a pane of glass in his efforts. Noah consoled him with the assurance that "he'd catch it," then condescended to help him. Mr Sowerberry came down soon after. Then Mrs Sowerberry appeared. Oliver having "caught it," in fulfilment of Noah's prediction, went downstairs to breakfast.

"Come near the fire, Noah," said Charlotte, the scruffy maid. "I saved a nice bit of bacon from master's breakfast. Oliver, shut that door and take them bits on the cover of the bread-pan. There's your tea. Quick, for they'll want you to mind the shop. D'ye hear?"

Oliver sat shivering on the box in the coldest corner of the room, and ate the stale pieces saved for him.

Noah was a charity-boy, but not a workhouse orphan. He knew his mother was a washerwoman, and his father a drunken soldier. Fortune had now cast in his way an orphan, at whom he could point the finger of scorn.

Oliver had been at the undertaker's some three weeks when Mr and Mrs Sowerberry – the shop being shut – were taking their supper in the little back parlour. Mr Sowerberry, after several glances, said, "My dear – "

Mrs Sowerberry looked up shortly, so he stopped.

"Well," she said, sharply.

"My dear," said Sowerberry, "I want to ask your advice. It's about young Twist, my dear. A very-good-looking boy, that, my dear."

"He need be, for he eats enough," observed the lady.

"There's an expression of melancholy in his face, my dear," resumed Mr Sowerberry, "which is very interesting. He would make a delightful mute, my love."

Mrs Sowerberry looked up with an expression of amazement.

"I mean for children's funerals. It would have a superb effect."

Mrs Sowerberry was much struck by the novelty of this idea; but, as it would have compromised her dignity to say so, she merely inquired, sharply, why such an obvious suggestion had not presented itself to her husband's mind before?

Mr Sowerberry rightly construed this as approval, and it was speedily determined that Oliver should be at once initiated into the mysteries of the trade. He would therefore accompany his master on the very next occasion his services were required.

CHAPTER 5

The month's trial over, Oliver was formally apprenticed. It was a nice sickly season just at this time. Coffins were looking up; and, in the course of a few weeks, Oliver acquired a great deal of experience. The success of Mr Sowerberry's ingenious idea exceeded even his most sanguine hopes. The oldest inhabitants recollected no period at which measles had been so prevalent, or so fatal to infant life; and many were the mournful processions which little Oliver headed, in a hat-band reaching down to his knees, to the indescribable emotion of all the mothers in the town.

For many months he suffered the ill-treatment of Noah Claypole who used him far worse than before, now that his jealousy was roused by seeing the new boy promoted to the black stick and hat-band, while he remained stationary in the muffin-cap and leathers. Charlotte treated him ill, because Noah did. And Mrs Sowerberry was his decided enemy, because Mr Sowerberry was disposed to be his friend.

13

One day, Oliver and Noah were in the kitchen at the usual dinner-hour, to banquet upon a small joint of mutton. Charlotte was called out of the way, so there followed some moments that Noah, being hungry and vicious, considered he could not possibly devote to a worthier purpose than aggravating young Oliver Twist.

Noah put his feet on the tablecloth and pulled Oliver's hair. He declared him a "sneak;" and furthermore announced his intention of coming to see him hanged, whenever that desirable event should take place. But, as no taunt produced the desired effect of making Oliver cry, Noah got rather personal.

"Work'us," said Noah, "how's your mother?"

"She's dead," replied Oliver, "don't say anything about her!"

Oliver's colour rose as he said this and Noah returned to the charge.

"What did she die of, Work'us?" said Noah.

"Of a broken heart, the old nurses told me," replied Oliver, more to himself, than answering Noah. "I think I know how that feels."

"Tol de rol, right fol lairy, Work'us," said Noah, as a tear rolled down Oliver's cheek. "What's set you a snivelling now?"

"Not *you*," replied Oliver, hastily brushing the tear away.

"Oh, not me, eh!" sneered Noah.

"No, not you," replied Oliver, sharply. "That's enough. Don't say anything more to me about her!"

"Yer know, Work'us," continued Noah. "It can't be helped now and I'm very sorry for it. But yer must know, Work'us, yer mother was a regular right-down bad 'un."

"What did you say?" inquired Oliver, looking up very quickly.

"A regular right-down bad 'un, Work'us," replied Noah, coolly. "And it's better, Work'us, that she died when she did, or else she'd have been hard labouring in Bridewell, or transported, or hung; which is more likely than either, isn't it?"

Crimson with fury, Oliver started up; overthrew the chair and table; seized Noah by the throat, and shook him till his teeth chattered in his head. Then collecting his whole force into one heavy blow he felled him to the ground.

A minute ago, the boy had looked the mild, dejected creature that harsh treatment had made him. But the cruel insult to his dead mother had set his blood on fire. His whole person changed, as he stood glaring over the

14

cowardly tormentor who now lay crouching at his feet; as Oliver defied him with an energy he had never known before.

"He'll murder me!" blubbered Noah. "Charlotte! missis! He's a murdering of me! Help! Oliver's gone mad! Charlotte!"

Noah's shouts were responded to, by a loud scream from Charlotte and a louder one from Mrs Sowerberry. Charlotte rushed into the kitchen while Mrs Sowerberry paused on the stairs till she was quite certain that it was safe to come in.

"Oh, you little wretch!" screamed Charlotte, seizing Oliver, "Oh, you little un-grate-ful, mur-de-rous, hor-rid vil-lain!" Between every syllable, she gave Oliver a blow with all her might.

Mrs Sowerberry rushed in and held him with one hand, while scratching his face with the other. In this favourable position of affairs, Noah rose from the ground, and pommelled him behind.

When they could tear and beat no longer, they dragged Oliver, struggling and shouting, into the dust-cellar, and locked him up. Mrs Sowerberry then sank into a chair, and burst into tears.

"Bless her, she's going off!" said Charlotte. "A glass of water, Noah, dear. Make haste!"

"Oh! Charlotte," said Mrs Sowerberry; speaking as well as she could, through lack of breath, and the cold water, which Noah had poured over her head. "What a mercy we have not all been murdered in our beds!"

"Ah! Mercy indeed, ma'am," was the reply. "I only hope this'll teach master not to have any more of these dreadful creeturs, that are born to be murderers and robbers from their very cradle. Poor Noah! He was all but killed, ma'am, when I come in."

"Poor fellow!" said Mrs Sowerberry, looking piteously on the charity-boy.

Noah, whose top waistcoat-button might have been somewhere on a level with the crown of Oliver's head, rubbed his eyes with the inside of his wrists, and performed some affecting tears and sniffs.

"What's to be done!" exclaimed Mrs Sowerberry. "Your master's not at home, and he'll kick that door down in ten minutes." Oliver's vigorous kicks against the bit of timber in question rendered this occurrence highly probable.

"Dear, dear! I don't know, ma'am," said Charlotte, "unless we send for the police-officers."

"Or the millingtary," suggested Mr Claypole.

"No, no," said Mrs Sowerberry, thinking of Oliver's old friend. "Run to Mr Bumble, Noah, and tell him to come here directly, and not to lose a minute; never mind your cap! Make haste!"

Noah started off at his fullest speed; and it very much astonished the people who were out walking, to see a charity-boy tearing through the streets with no cap on his head.

CHAPTER 6

Noah Claypole did not pause for breath until he reached the workhouse-gate. Having rested here, for a minute or so, to collect a good burst of sobs and an imposing show of tears, he knocked at the wicket. The aged pauper who opened it, started back.

"Why, what's the matter!" he cried.

"Mr Bumble! Mr Bumble!" cried Noah, in tones so loud and agitated, that they caught the ear of Mr Bumble himself, and he rushed into the yard without his cocked hat.

"Oh, Mr Bumble, sir!" said Noah. "Oliver – Oliver has – "

"What? What?" interposed Mr Bumble: with a gleam of pleasure in his metallic eyes. "Not run away; he hasn't run away, has he?"

"No sir. Not run away, sir, but he's turned wicious," replied Noah. "He tried to murder me, sir, and then tried to murder Charlotte, and then missis. Oh! what dreadful pain it is! Such agony, please, sir!" And here, Noah writhed, giving Mr Bumble to understand that, he had sustained severe internal injury.

When Noah saw that Mr Bumble was all but paralysed by the news, he wailed ten times louder than before. When he saw a gentleman in a white waistcoat crossing the yard, he grew even louder, believing it important to attract the notice of the gentleman.

The gentleman turned angrily round, and inquired what that young cur was howling for.

"It's a poor boy from the free-school, sir," replied Mr Bumble, "who has been nearly murdered, sir – by young Twist."

"By Jove!" exclaimed the gentleman, stopping short. "I knew from the very first, that that young savage would be hung!"

"He has likewise attempted, sir, to murder the female servant," said Mr Bumble, his face ashen.

"And his missis," interposed Mr Claypole.

"And his master, too, I think you said, Noah?" added Mr Bumble.

"No! He's out, or he would have murdered him," replied Noah. "He said he wanted to."

"Ah! Said he wanted to, did he, my boy?" inquired the gentleman.

"Yes, sir," replied Noah. "And please, sir, missis wants to know whether Mr Bumble can spare time to come directly, and flog him: 'cause master's out."

"Certainly, my boy," said the gentleman in the white waistcoat: smiling, and patting Noah's head. "you're a very good boy. Here's a penny for you. Bumble, just step up to Sowerberry's with your cane, and see what's best to be done. Don't spare him, Bumble."

"No, I will not, sir," replied the beadle, adjusting the wax-end that was twisted round the bottom of his cane, for purposes of parochial flagellation.

"Tell Sowerberry not to spare him either. They'll never do anything with him, without stripes and bruises," said the gentleman in the white waistcoat.

Mr Bumble and Noah Claypole betook themselves with all speed to the undertaker's shop.

Sowerberry had not yet returned, and Oliver continued to kick, with undiminished vigour, at the cellar-door. The accounts of his ferocity, as related by Mrs Sowerberry and Charlotte, were of so startling a nature, that Mr Bumble judged it prudent to parley, before opening the door. With this view he gave a kick at the outside, and, then, applying his mouth to the keyhole, said, in a deep and impressive tone:

"Oliver!"

"You let me out!" replied Oliver, from the inside.

"Do you know this here voice, Oliver?" said Mr Bumble.

"Yes," replied Oliver.

"Ain't you afraid of it? Ain't you a-trembling while I speak?"

"No!" replied Oliver, boldly.

Mr Bumble stepped back from the keyhole, drew himself up to his full height and looked at each of the three bystanders.

"Oh, Mr Bumble, he must be mad," said Mrs Sowerberry. "No boy in half his senses could venture to speak so to you."

"It's not Madness, ma'am," replied Mr Bumble, after a few moments of deep meditation. "It's Meat."

"What?" exclaimed Mrs Sowerberry.

"Meat, ma'am, meat," replied Bumble, with stern emphasis. "You've over-fed him, ma'am. If you had kept the boy on gruel, ma'am, this would never have happened."

"Dear, dear!" ejaculated Mrs Sowerberry, piously raising her eyes to the kitchen ceiling. "This comes of being liberal!"

The liberality of Mrs Sowerberry to Oliver had consisted in giving him all the dirty scraps that nobody else would eat. To do her justice, she was innocent, in thought, word, and deed.

"Ah!" said Mr Bumble, when the lady brought her eyes down to earth again; "the only thing that can be done now is to leave him in the cellar for a day or so, till he's a little starved down; and then keep him on gruel all through his apprenticeship. He comes of a bad family. Both the nurse and doctor said that his mother made her way here, against difficulties and pain that would have killed any well-disposed woman weeks before."

Oliver, just hearing enough to know that there was some new mention of his mother, recommenced kicking, with a violence that rendered every other sound inaudible. Sowerberry returned at this juncture. Oliver's offence was explained, with such exaggerations that he unlocked the cellar-door in a twinkling, and dragged his rebellious apprentice out.

Oliver's clothes had been torn in the beating he had received; his face was bruised and scratched. The angry flush had not disappeared, however; and when he was pulled out of his prison, he scowled boldly on Noah, looking quite undismayed.

"Now, you are a nice young fellow, ain't you?" said Sowerberry; shaking Oliver.

"He called my mother names," replied Oliver.

"Well, and what if he did, you little ungrateful wretch?" said Mrs Sowerberry. "She deserved what he said, and worse."

"She didn't," said Oliver.

"She did," said Mrs Sowerberry.

"It's a lie," said Oliver.

18

Mrs Sowerberry burst into a flood of tears.

This flood of tears left Mr Sowerberry no alternative. He at once gave him a drubbing, which satisfied even Mrs Sowerberry herself, and rendered Mr Bumble's subsequent application of the parochial cane, rather unnecessary. For the rest of the day, he was shut up in the back kitchen, with a slice of bread. That night, Mrs Sowerberry, after making remarks about the memory of his mother, looked in the room and ordered him up to his dismal bed.

It was not until he was left alone in the silence and stillness of the gloomy workshop of the undertaker, that Oliver gave way to the feelings of the day's treatment. He had listened to their taunts with a look of contempt; he had borne the lash without a cry. But now, when there were none to see him, he fell upon his knees on the floor and wept such tears.

For a long time, Oliver remained motionless. The candle had burned low when he stood. He gazed cautiously round, and listening intently, gently undid the door, and looked out.

It was a cold, dark night. The stars seemed, to the boy's eyes, farther from the earth than he had ever seen them before. There was no wind. He softly closed the door. By the dying light of the candle he tied up in a handkerchief the few articles of clothing he had, sat down upon a bench, and waited for morning.

With the first ray of light Oliver arose, and again unbarred the door. One timid look around – one moment's pause of hesitation – he had closed it behind him, and was in the open street.

He looked to the right and to the left, uncertain where to fly. He remembered seeing the carts, as they left, toiling up the hill. He took the same route, arriving at a footpath across the fields that he knew led out again into the road, and walked quickly on.

CHAPTER 7

Oliver was nearly five miles away from the town, by eight o'clock but he ran, and hid behind the hedges, by turns, till noon, fearing that he might be pursued and overtaken. Then he sat down to rest by the side of the milestone, and began to think, for the first time, where he had better go and try to live.

The stone by which he sat bore, in large characters, the information that it was barely seventy miles to London. The name awakened a new train of ideas in the boy's mind. That great large place! Not even Mr Bumble could ever find him there! It was the very place for a homeless boy, who must die in the streets unless someone helped him. As these things passed through his thoughts, he jumped upon his feet, and again walked forward.

He was a full four miles closer to London, before he realised how much he must undergo ere he would reach his place of destination. He meditated upon his means of getting there. He had a crust of bread, a coarse shirt, and two pairs of stockings, in his bundle. He had a penny too – a gift after some funeral in which he had acquitted himself very well.

"A clean shirt," thought Oliver, "is a very comfortable thing. As are two pairs of darned stockings and a penny, but they are small help in a sixty-five mile walk in winter time." But Oliver could think of no feasible way of surmounting his difficulties, so, after a good deal of thinking to no particular purpose, he changed his little bundle to the other shoulder, and trudged on.

Oliver walked twenty miles that day, tasting nothing but the crust of dry bread, and a few draughts of water, which he begged at the cottage doors by the roadside. When night came, he turned into a meadow; and, creeping close under a hay-rick, determined to lie there, till morning. Being very tired with his walk, he soon fell asleep and forgot his troubles.

He felt cold and stiff, when he got up next morning, and so hungry that he was obliged to exchange the penny for a small loaf in the very first village he came to. He walked no more than twelve miles that day. His feet were sore, and his legs so weak that they trembled beneath him. Another night passed in the bleak damp air, and when he set forth on his journey next morning, he could hardly crawl along.

In some villages he passed through, large painted boards were fixed up, warning all beggars that they would be sent to jail. This frightened Oliver and made him leave those villages with all possible speed. In others, he stood about the inn-yards, looking mournfully at every one who passed. This generally terminated in the landlady's ordering one of the post-boys to drive that strange boy out of the place. If he begged at a farmer's house, ten to one they threatened to set the dog on him.

In fact, if it had not been for a good-hearted turnpike-man, and a benevolent old lady, Oliver's troubles would have been shortened by the very same process that had put an end to his mother's. He would most assuredly have fallen dead upon the king's highway.

Early on the seventh morning, Oliver limped slowly into the little town of Barnet. The shutters were closed, the street was empty, not a soul was awake. The sun was rising in all its splendid beauty to show the boy as he sat, with bleeding feet and covered with dust, upon a doorstep.

By degrees, the shutters were opened. The window-blinds were drawn up and people began passing to and fro. Some few stopped to gaze at Oliver but none relieved him, or troubled to inquire how he came there. He had no heart to beg. And there he sat.

He had been crouching on the step for some time when he suddenly realised that a boy, who had passed him carelessly some minutes before, had returned, and was now watching him from the opposite side of the way. He took little notice at first; but the boy remained there so long, that Oliver raised his head, and returned his steady look. Upon this, the boy crossed over and, walking close up to Oliver, said, "Hullo, my covey! What's the row?"

The boy was about his own age, but one of the queerest-looking boys that Oliver had ever seen. He was snub-nosed, common-faced enough and as dirty a juvenile as one would wish to see; but he had about him all the airs and manners of a man. He was short with rather bow legs, and little, sharp, ugly eyes. He wore a man's coat, which reached nearly to his heels, with the cuffs turned back halfway up his arm, to get his hands out of the sleeves, to thrust them into the pockets of his corduroy trousers. He was, altogether, as roystering and swaggering a young gentleman as ever stood four feet six, or something less, in his bluchers.

"I am very hungry and tired," replied Oliver, the tears standing in his eyes as he spoke. "I have been walking these seven days."

"Walking for sivin days!" said the young gentleman. "Oh, I see. Beak's order, eh? But," he added, noticing Oliver's look of surprise, "I suppose you don't know what a beak is, my flash com-pan-i-on?"

Oliver merely wondered what it had to do with a bird.

"My eyes, how green!" exclaimed the young gentleman. "Why, a beak's a madgst'rate. But come, you want grub, and you shall have it. I'm at low-water-mark myself – only one bob and a magpie; but, as far as it

21

goes, I'll fork out and stump. Up with you on your pins. There! Now then! Morrice!"

Assisting Oliver to rise, the young gentleman took him to an adjacent chandler's shop, where he purchased ham and a half-quartern loaf. The ham was kept clean from dust by the ingenious method of making a hole in the loaf by pulling out a portion and stuffing it therein. Taking the bread under his arm, the young gentleman turned into a small public house, and led the way to a tap-room. Here, a pot of beer was brought in, by direction of the mysterious youth. Oliver fell to, at his new friend's bidding, making a long and hearty meal. The strange boy eyed him from time to time with great attention.

"Going to London?" said the strange boy, when Oliver had at length concluded.

"Yes."

"Got any lodgings? Money?"

"No."

The strange boy whistled; and put his arms into his pockets, as far as the big coat sleeves would let them go.

"Do you live in London?" inquired Oliver.

"Yes. I do, when I'm at home," replied the boy. "I suppose you want some place to sleep in tonight, don't you?"

"I do, indeed," answered Oliver. "I have not slept under a roof since I left the country."

"Don't fret your eyelids on that score," said the young gentleman. "I've got to be in London tonight; and I know a 'spectable old genelman as lives there, wot'll give you lodgings for nothink."

This unexpected offer of shelter was too tempting to be resisted. This led to a more friendly dialogue from which Oliver discovered that his new friend's name was Jack Dawkins, and that he was a peculiar pet and protégé of the said elderly gentleman.

Mr Dawkins avowed that among his intimate friends he was better known as "The Artful Dodger". Oliver secretly resolved to cultivate the good opinion of the old gentleman as quickly as possible.

As John Dawkins objected to entering London before nightfall, it was nearly eleven o'clock when they reached the turnpike at Islington. They crossed from the Angel into St John's Road, struck down the small street that terminates at Sadler's Wells Theatre, through Exmouth Street and Coppice Row and down the little court by the side of the workhouse.

Although Oliver was busy keeping sight of his leader, he glanced either side of the way, as he passed along. A dirtier or more wretched place he had never seen. The sole places that seemed to prosper amid the general blight of the place, were the public houses. Covered ways and yards disclosed little knots of houses, where drunken men and women were positively wallowing in filth. From several of the doorways, great ill-looking fellows were cautiously emerging bound, on no harmless errands.

Oliver was just considering whether he hadn't better run away, when they reached the bottom of the hill. His conductor, catching him by the arm, pushed open the door of a house near Field Lane; and, drawing him into the passage closed it behind them.

"Now, then!" cried a voice from below, in reply to a whistle from the Dodger.

"Plummy and slam!" was the reply.

This seemed to be some watchword or signal that all was right; for the light of a feeble candle gleamed on the wall at the remote end of the passage; and a man's face peeped out.

"There's two on you," said the man, thrusting the candle farther out, and shading his eyes with his hand. "Who's the t'other one?"

"A new pal," replied Jack Dawkins, pulling Oliver forward.

"Where did he come from?"

"Greenland. Is Fagin up stairs?"

"Yes, he's a sortin' the wipes. Up with you!" The candle was drawn back, and the face disappeared.

Oliver, groping his way with one hand, and having the other firmly grasped by his companion, ascended the dark and broken stairs. His conductor mounted them with ease and speed, showing he was well acquainted with them. He threw open the door of a back room, pulling Oliver in after him.

The walls and ceiling of the room were perfectly black with age and dirt. There was a deal table before the fire upon which were a candle, stuck in a ginger-beer bottle, two or three pewter pots, a loaf and butter, and a plate. In a frying pan on the fire, some sausages were cooking. Standing over them, with a toasting fork in his hand, was a very old shrivelled Jew, whose villainous-looking face was obscured by a quantity of matted red hair. He was dressed in a greasy flannel gown, and seemed to be dividing his attention between the frying-pan and a clothes-horse, over which a great number of silk handkerchiefs were hanging. Several rough beds made of old sacks were huddled side by side on the floor. Seated round the table were four or five boys, none older than the Dodger, smoking long clay pipes, and drinking spirits with the air of middle-aged men. These all crowded about their associate as he whispered a few words to the Jew; and then turned round and grinned at Oliver. So did the Jew himself, toasting fork in hand.

"This is him, Fagin," said Jack Dawkins. "my friend Oliver Twist."

The Jew grinned; and, making a low bow to Oliver, took him by the hand, and hoped he should have the honour of his intimate acquaintance. The young gentlemen with the pipes then came round him, shaking both his hands very hard – especially the one in which he held his little bundle. One young gentleman was very anxious to hang up his cap for him; and another was pleased to empty his pockets, as he may well be too tired when he went to bed. These civilities would probably have been extended much farther, but for a tapping of the Jew's toasting fork on the heads and shoulders of the affectionate youths who offered them.

"We are very glad to see you, Oliver, very," said the Jew. "Dodger, take off the sausages; and draw a tub near the fire for Oliver. Ah, you're a-staring at the pocket-handkerchiefs! Eh, my dear! There are a good many of 'em, ain't there? They're ready for the wash; that's all, Oliver; that's all. Ha! Ha!"

The latter part of this speech was hailed by a boisterous shout from all the pupils of the merry old gentleman. In the midst of which, they went to supper.

Oliver ate his share, and the Jew then mixed him a glass of hot gin and water; telling him he must drink it off directly. Oliver did as desired. Immediately afterwards he felt himself gently lifted on to one of the sacks where he sunk into a deep sleep.

CHAPTER 8

It was late when Oliver awoke, from a sound, long sleep. There was no one in the room but the old Jew, who was boiling some coffee in a saucepan for breakfast, and whistling softly as he stirred it round and round, with an iron spoon. He stopped every now and then to listen when there was the least noise below. When he had satisfied himself, he would go on, whistling and stirring, as before.

Although Oliver had roused himself from sleep, he was not thoroughly awake. He saw the Jew with his half-closed eyes; heard his low whistling; and recognised the sound of the spoon grating.

When the coffee was done, the Jew drew the saucepan to the hob. Standing, then, in an undecided way, he turned and looked at Oliver, and called him by his name. He did not answer, and was to all appearance asleep.

The Jew stepped gently to lock the door. He then drew forth, as it seemed to Oliver, from some trap in the floor, a small box, which he placed carefully on the table. His eyes glistened as he raised the lid. Dragging an old chair to the table, he sat down and took from it a magnificent gold watch, sparkling with jewels.

"Aha!" said the Jew, shrugging his shoulders, and giving a hideous grin. "Clever dogs! Staunch to the last! Never told the old parson where they were. Never told on old Fagin! And why should they? It wouldn't have loosened the knot, or delayed the drop. No!"

With these muttered reflections, the Jew once more deposited the watch in its place of safety. At least half a dozen more were in turn drawn from the same box, and surveyed with equal pleasure. Besides rings, brooches, bracelets, were other articles of jewellery, of such magnificent materials, and costly workmanship.

The Jew turned and his bright dark eyes fell on Oliver's face – the boy's eyes were fixed on his in mute curiosity. The recognition was very brief, but he knew that he had been observed. He closed the lid of the box with a loud crash, and, laying his hand on a bread knife that was on the table, stood over Oliver.

"What do you watch me for?" said the Jew. "Why are you awake? What have you seen? Speak out, boy! Quick – for your life!"

"I wasn't able to sleep any longer, sir," replied Oliver, meekly. "I am very sorry if I have disturbed you, sir."

"You were not awake an hour ago?" said the Jew, scowling.

"No! No, indeed!" replied Oliver.

"Are you sure?" cried the Jew, looking still fiercer.

"Upon my word I was not, sir," replied Oliver, earnestly.

"Tush, tush, my dear!" said the Jew, resuming his old manner, and playing with the knife a little, before he laid it down. "Of course I know that, my dear. I only tried to frighten you. You're a brave boy, Oliver!" The Jew glanced uneasily at the box.

"Did you see any of these pretty things, my dear?" said the Jew, laying his hand upon it after a short pause.

"Yes, sir," replied Oliver.

"Ah!" said the Jew, turning rather pale. "They – they're mine. All I have to live on, in my old age. But people call me a miser!"

Oliver thought he must indeed be a miser to live in such a dirty place, with so many watches, but then again looking after the Dodger and the other boys, maybe cost him a good deal of money. Oliver asked if he might get up.

"Certainly, my dear," replied the old gentleman. "Stay. There's a pitcher of water in the corner by the door. Bring it here and I'll give you a basin to wash in, my dear."

Oliver walked across the room and stooped for an instant to raise the pitcher. When he turned his head, the box was gone.

He had scarcely washed himself, and made everything tidy by emptying the basin out of the window, when the Dodger returned, accompanied by a sprightly young friend, Charley Bates. The four sat down to breakfast, on the coffee, and hot rolls and ham that the Dodger had brought home.

"Well," said the Jew, glancing slyly at Oliver, and addressing himself to the Dodger, "I hope you've been at work this morning?"

"Hard," replied the Dodger.

"As Nails," added Charley Bates.

"Good boys!" said the Jew. "What have you got, Dodger?"

"A couple of pocket-books," replied that young gentleman.

"Lined?" inquired the Jew, with eagerness.

"Pretty well," replied the Dodger, producing two pocket-books – one green, and the other red.

"Not so heavy as they might be," said the Jew, after looking at the insides carefully, "but very neat and nicely made. Ingenious workman, ain't he, Oliver?"

"Very, indeed, sir," said Oliver. At which Mr Charles Bates laughed uproariously, very much to the amazement of Oliver, who saw nothing to laugh at.

"And what have you got, my dear?" said Fagin to Charley Bates.

"Wipes," replied Master Bates, at the same time producing four pocket-handkerchiefs.

"Well," said the Jew, inspecting them closely, "they're very good ones, very. You haven't marked them well, though, Charley. So the marks shall be picked out with a needle, and we'll teach Oliver how to do it. Shall us, Oliver, eh? Ha! Ha! You'd like to be able to make pocket-handkerchiefs as easy as Charley Bates, wouldn't you, my dear?"

"Very much, indeed, if you'll teach me, sir," replied Oliver.

Master Bates burst into another laugh; which laugh, meeting the coffee he was drinking, and carrying it down some wrong channel, very nearly terminated in his premature suffocation.

"He is so jolly green!" said Charley when he recovered, as an apology.

When the breakfast was cleared away, the merry old gentleman and the two boys played at a very curious game. The merry old gentleman, placing a snuffbox in one pocket of his trousers, a note case in the other, and a watch in his waistcoat pocket. With a mock diamond pin in his shirt, he buttoned his coat tight round him, and put his spectacle-case and handkerchief in his pockets. He then trotted up and down the room with a stick, in the way old gentlemen walk about the streets. Sometimes he stopped at the fireplace, and sometimes at the door, making believe that he was staring into shop-windows. At such times he looked round him, for fear of thieves, and would keep slapping all his pockets, to see that he hadn't lost anything. All this time, the two boys followed him closely about, getting out of his sight, so nimbly, every time he turned round, that it was impossible to follow their motions. At last, the Dodger trod upon his toes, or ran upon his boot accidentally, while Charley Bates stumbled up against him behind and in that one moment they took from him, with the most extraordinary rapidity, snuff-box, note-case, watch-guard, shirt-pin, pocket-handkerchief, even the spectacle-case. If the old gentleman felt a hand in any one of his pockets, he cried out where it was; and then the game began all over again.

When this game had been played a great many times, a couple of young ladies called to see the young gentlemen. One was named Bet, and the other Nancy. They wore a good deal of hair, not very neatly turned up behind, and were rather untidy about the shoes and stockings. They were not exactly pretty, perhaps; but they were remarkably free and agreeable in their manners, Oliver thought them very nice girls indeed.

These visitors stopped a long time. At length, Charley Bates expressed his opinion that it was time to pad the hoof. This, it occurred to Oliver, must be French for going out for, directly afterwards, the Dodger, and Charley, and the two young ladies, went away together, having been kindly furnished by the amiable old Jew with money to spend.

"There, my dear," said Fagin. "That's a pleasant life, isn't it? They have gone out for the day."

"Have they done work, sir?" inquired Oliver.

"Yes," said the Jew; "that is, unless they should unexpectedly come across any, when they are out. Make 'em your models, my dear." He tapped the fire-shovel on the hearth to add force to his words. "Do everything they bid you, and take their advice in all matters – especially the Dodger's, my dear. Is my handkerchief hanging out of my pocket, my dear?" said the Jew, stopping short.

"Yes, sir," said Oliver.

"See if you can take it out, without my feeling it: as you saw them do, when we were at play this morning."

Oliver held up the bottom of the pocket with one hand, as he had seen the Dodger hold it, and drew the handkerchief lightly out of it with the other.

"Is it gone?" cried the Jew.

"Here it is, sir," said Oliver, showing it in his hand.

"You're a clever boy, my dear," said the playful old gentleman, patting Oliver on the head approvingly. "I never saw a sharper lad. Here's a shilling. If you go on in this way, you'll be the greatest man of the time. And now come here, and I'll show you how to take the marks out of the handkerchiefs."

Oliver wondered what picking the old gentleman's pocket in play, had to do with his chances of being a great man. But, thinking that Fagin, being so much his senior, must know best, he followed him quietly to the table, and was soon involved in his new study.

CHAPTER 9

For many days, Oliver remained in the Jew's room, picking the marks out of handkerchiefs, and sometimes playing the game the two boys and the Jew played. At length, he began to long for fresh air, and repeatedly asked the old gentleman to allow him to go out to work, with his two companions.

Oliver was even more anxious to be actively employed, when he saw the stern morality of the old gentleman's character. Whenever the Dodger or Charley Bates came home empty-handed, he would lecture them on the misery of idle and lazy habits; and would send them supperless to bed. On one occasion, indeed, he even knocked them both down a flight of stairs.

Finally, one morning, Oliver was told he might go out, under the joint guardianship of Charley Bates, and his friend the Dodger.

The three boys sallied out – the Dodger with his coat-sleeves tucked up; Master Bates sauntering along with his hands in his pockets; and Oliver between them. He wondered where they were going, and what branch of manufacture he would be instructed in.

Oliver soon began to think his companions were going to deceive the old gentleman, by not going to work at all. But there was suddenly a very mysterious change of behaviour by the Dodger.

They were just emerging from a narrow court in Clerkenwell, when the Dodger suddenly stopped and, laying his finger on his lip, drew his companions back again, with the greatest caution.

"What's the matter?" demanded Oliver.

"Hush!" replied the Dodger. "Do you see that old cove at the book-stall?"

"The old gentleman over the way?" said Oliver. "Yes, I see him."

"He'll do," said the Dodger.

"A prime plant," observed Master Charley Bates.

Oliver looked from one to the other, with the greatest surprise; but he was not permitted to make any inquiries, for the two boys walked stealthily across the road. They slunk close behind the old gentleman. Oliver walked a few paces after them and then looked on in silent amazement.

The old gentleman was very respectable-looking, with a powdered head and gold spectacles. He was dressed in a bottle-green coat with a black velvet collar; wore white trousers; and carried a smart bamboo cane under his arm. He had taken up a book from the stall, and was reading away as if in his own study. It was plain, from his abstraction, that he saw nothing but the book itself.

Imagine Oliver's horror as he stood a few paces off, to see the Dodger plunge his hand into the old gentleman's pocket, and draw from thence a handkerchief! To see him hand the same to Charley Bates and finally to behold them both, running away at full speed.

In an instant the whole mystery of the handkerchiefs, and the watches, and the jewels, and the Jew, rushed upon the boy's mind. He stood, for a moment, with the blood so tingling through all his veins from terror, that he felt as if he were in a burning fire. Then, confused and frightened, he took to his heels.

This was all done in a minute's space. In the very instant that Oliver began to run, the old gentleman, putting his hand to his pocket, and missing his handkerchief, turned round. Seeing the boy scudding away at such speed, he very naturally concluded him to be the culprit and shouting, "Stop thief" with all his might, made off after him, book in hand.

But the old gentleman was not the only person to raise a hue-and-cry. The Dodger and Master Bates, unwilling to attract public attention by running down the open street, no sooner heard the cry, and saw Oliver running, than, guessing what had happened, issued forth, shouting "Stop thief!"

One wretched breathless child, panting with exhaustion, terror on his face, large drops of perspiration streaming down his face; strained every nerve to make head upon his pursuers.

Stopped at last! He is down upon the pavement; and the crowd eagerly gather around him. "Stand aside!" "Give him a little air!" "Nonsense! He don't deserve it." "Where's the gentleman?" "Here he is, coming down the street." "Make room for the gentleman!" "Is this the boy, sir!" "Yes."

Oliver lay, covered with mud and dust, and bleeding from the mouth, looking wildly round upon the faces that surrounded him, when the old gentleman was pushed into the circle.

"Yes," said the gentleman, "I am afraid it is the boy."

"Afraid!" murmured the crowd. "That's a good 'un!"

"Poor fellow!" said the gentleman. "He has hurt himself."

"I did that, sir," said a great lubberly fellow, stepping forward.

The fellow touched his hat with a grin, expecting something for his pains. But, the old gentleman, eyeing him with an expression of dislike, looked anxiously round. A police officer (generally the last person to arrive in such cases) at that moment made his way through the crowd, and seized Oliver by the collar.

"Come, get up," said the man, roughly.

"It wasn't me indeed, sir. Indeed, it was two other boys," said Oliver, looking round. "They are here somewhere."

"Oh no, they ain't," said the officer. And it was true, for the Dodger and Charley Bates had turned down the first convenient court they came to. "Come, get up!"

"Don't hurt him," said the old gentleman, compassionately.

"Oh no, I won't hurt him," replied the officer, tearing his jacket half off his back, in proof thereof. "Come. Stand upon your legs, you young devil!"

Oliver, who could hardly stand, was at once lugged along the streets by the jacket-collar, at a rapid pace. The gentleman walked on with them by the officer's side, and as many of the crowd as could achieve the feat, got a little ahead, and stared back at Oliver.

CHAPTER 10

The crowd had only the satisfaction of accompanying Oliver through two or three streets, when he was led beneath a low archway, into this dispensary of summary justice. It was a small paved yard into which they turned where they met a stout man with a bunch of keys in his hand.

"What's the matter now?" said the man carelessly.

"A young fogle-hunter," replied the man holding Oliver.

"Are you the party that's been robbed, sir?" inquired the man with the keys.

"Yes, I am," replied the old gentleman; "but I am not sure that this boy actually took the handkerchief. I would rather not press the case."

"Must go before the magistrate now, sir," replied the man.

Oliver was led into a stone cell. Here he was searched; and nothing being found upon him, locked up.

The old gentleman looked almost as rueful as Oliver when the key grated in the lock. He turned with a sigh to the book, which had been the innocent cause of the disturbance.

"There is something in that boy's face," muttered the old gentleman as he walked slowly away, tapping his chin with the cover of the book, "something that touches. Can he be innocent? He looked like – " exclaimed the old gentleman, halting abruptly, and staring up into the sky, "Bless my soul! Where have I seen that look before?"

After musing for some minutes, the old gentleman walked into a back ante-room opening from the yard. There, retiring into a corner, he called up before his mind's eye a vast amphitheatre of faces over which a dusky curtain had hung for many years. "No," he said at last, shaking his head; "it must be imagination."

He wandered over them again.

But the old gentleman could recall no one countenance of which Oliver's features bore a trace. So, he heaved a sigh over the recollections he had awakened; and being an absent old gentleman, buried them again in the pages of the musty book.

He was roused by a touch on the shoulder, and a request to follow him into the office. He closed his book hastily and was ushered into the imposing presence of the renowned Mr Fang.

The office was a front parlour. Mr Fang sat behind a bar, and on one side of the door was a sort of wooden pen in which poor little Oliver was trembling at the awfulness of the scene.

Mr Fang was a lean, long-backed, stiff-necked, middle-sized man. His face was stern.

The old gentleman bowed respectfully; and advancing to the magistrate's desk, said, "That is my name and address, sir." He then withdrew a pace or two. With another gentlemanly inclination of the head, he waited to be questioned.

"Who are you?" said Mr Fang.

The old gentleman pointed, with some surprise, to his card.

"Officer!" said Mr Fang, tossing the card contemptuously away. "Who is this fellow?"

"My name, sir, is Brownlow," said the old gentleman, speaking like a gentleman.

"Officer!" said Mr Fang. "What's this fellow charged with?"

"He's not charged at all, your worship," replied the officer. "He appears against the boy."

His worship knew this perfectly well, but it was a good annoyance, and a safe one.

"Appears against the boy, does he?" said Fang, surveying Mr Brownlow contemptuously from head to foot. "Swear him!"

"Before I am sworn, I must beg to say one word," said Mr Brownlow. "And that is, that I really never, without actual experience, could have believed – "

"Hold your tongue, sir!" said Mr Fang, peremptorily.

"I will not, sir!" replied the old gentleman.

"Hold your tongue this instant, or I'll have you turned out of the office!" said Mr Fang. "You're an insolent, impertinent fellow. How dare you bully a magistrate!"

"What!" exclaimed the old gentleman, reddening.

"Swear this person!" said Fang to the clerk. "I'll not hear another word. Swear him."

Mr Brownlow's indignation was greatly roused, but reflecting perhaps, that he might only injure the boy by giving vent to it, he suppressed his feelings and submitted to be sworn at once.

"Now," said Fang. "What's the charge against this boy? What have you got to say, sir?"

"I was standing at a book-stall – " Mr Brownlow began.

With many interruptions, and repeated insults, Mr Brownlow contrived to state his case, saying that, in the surprise of the moment, he had run after the boy because he saw him running away. He expressed his hope that he would deal as leniently with him as justice would allow.

"He has been hurt already," said the old gentleman in conclusion. "And I really fear that he is ill."

"Oh! Yes, I dare say!" said Mr Fang, with a sneer. "Come, none of your tricks here, you young vagabond, they won't do. What's your name?"

Oliver tried to reply, but his tongue failed him. He was deadly pale.

"What's your name, you scoundrel?" demanded Mr Fang. "Officer, what's his name?"

This was addressed to a bluff old fellow, in a striped waistcoat, who stood by the bar. He bent over Oliver, and repeated the inquiry, but finding him incapable of understanding the question, and knowing that his not replying would only infuriate the magistrate, he hazarded a guess.

"He says his name's Tom White, your worship," said this kind-hearted thief-taker.

"Oh, he won't speak out, won't he?" said Fang. "Very well. Where does he live?"

"Where he can, your worship," replied the officer; again pretending to receive Oliver's answer.

"Has he any parents?" inquired Mr Fang.

"He says they died in his infancy, your worship," replied the officer, hazarding the usual reply.

At this point of the inquiry, Oliver raised his head and murmured a feeble prayer for a draught of water.

"Stuff and nonsense!" said Mr Fang. "Don't make a fool of me."

"I think he really is ill, your worship," remonstrated the officer.

"I know better," said Mr Fang.

"Take care of him, officer," said the old gentleman, raising his hands instinctively; "he'll fall down."

"Stand away, officer," cried Fang. "Let him."

Oliver fell to the floor in a fainting fit. The men in the office looked at each other, but no one stirred.

"I knew he was shamming," said Fang, as if this were proof of the fact. "Let him lie there; he'll soon tire of that."

"How do you propose to deal with the case, sir?" inquired the clerk in a low voice.

"Three months," replied Mr Fang, "hard labour. Clear the office."

The door opened, and a couple of men prepared to carry the insensible boy to his cell. Then an elderly man of decent appearance, clad in an old suit of black, rushed in and advanced towards the bench.

"Stop, stop! Don't take him away! For Heaven's sake stop a moment!" cried the newcomer, breathless with haste.

"Who is this? Turn him out. Clear the office!" cried Mr Fang.

"I will speak," cried the man; "I will not be turned out. I saw it all. I keep the bookstall. I demand to be sworn. Mr Fang, you must hear me." His manner was determined.

"Swear the man," growled Mr Fang. "Now, what have you to say?"

"This," said the man. "I saw three boys, two others and the prisoner here, loitering on the opposite side of the way, when this gentleman was reading. The theft was committed by a different boy. I saw it done, and this boy was perfectly amazed by it." Having by this time recovered breath, the worthy bookseller then told the exact circumstances of the robbery.

"Why didn't you come here before?" said Fang, after a pause.

"I hadn't a soul to mind the shop," replied the man. "Everybody had joined in the pursuit. I only got someone five minutes ago. I've run all the way."

"The prosecutor was reading, eh?" inquired Fang, after another pause.

"Yes," replied the man. "The very book he has in his hand."

"Oh, that book, eh?" said Fang. "Is it paid for?"

"No, it is not," replied the man, with a smile.

"I forgot all about it!" exclaimed the old gentleman, innocently.

"A nice person to prefer a charge against a poor boy!" said Fang, with a comical effort to look humane. "I consider, sir, that you obtained possession of that book, under very suspicious circumstances. You may think yourself fortunate that the owner of the property declines to prosecute. Let this be a lesson to you, my man. The boy is discharged. Clear the office."

"Damn me!" cried the old gentleman, bursting out with the rage he had kept down so long.

"Clear the office!" said the magistrate. "Clear the office!"

The indignant Mr Brownlow was ushered out, with the book in one hand, and the bamboo cane in the other, in a frenzy of rage and defiance. He reached the yard and his passion vanished in a moment. Little Oliver Twist lay on his back on the pavement, with his shirt unbuttoned, his face deathly white, trembling.

"Poor boy!" said Mr Brownlow. "Call a coach!"

A coach was obtained, and Oliver was carefully laid on one seat, while the old gentleman got in and sat on the other.

"May I accompany you?" said the bookseller, looking in.

"Bless me, yes, my dear sir," said Mr Brownlow. "I forgot you. I have this unhappy book still! Jump in. There's no time to lose."

The bookseller got in and away they drove.

CHAPTER 11

The coach rattled away, stopping at length before a neat house, in a quiet shady street near Pentonville. Here, a bed was swiftly prepared, in which Mr Brownlow saw his young charge carefully deposited. Here, he was tended with a kindness that knew no bounds.

But for many days, Oliver remained insensible to all the goodness of his new friends. He lay stretched on his sickbed for many days; dwindling away beneath the dry and wasting heat of fever.

Weak, and thin, and pallid, he awoke at last from what seemed to have been a long and troubled dream. Feebly raising himself in the bed, he looked anxiously around.

"What room is this? Where have I been brought to?" said Oliver.

He uttered these words in a feeble voice, but they were overheard at once. The curtain at the bed's head was hastily drawn back, and a motherly old lady, very neatly and precisely dressed, rose from an armchair close by.

"Hush, my dear," said the old lady softly. "You must be very quiet, or you will be ill again. Lie down again, there's a dear!" The old lady gently placed Oliver's head on the pillow, smoothed back his hair from his forehead. Oliver held out his hand and laid it on hers.

"Save us!" said the old lady, with tears in her eyes, "What a grateful little dear it is. Pretty creetur! What would his mother feel if she had sat by him as I have, and could see him now!"

"Perhaps she does see me," whispered Oliver, folding his hands together. "Perhaps she has sat by me. I almost feel as if she had."

"That was the fever, my dear," said the old lady mildly.

She brought some cool stuff for Oliver to drink. Then, patting him on the cheek, told him he must lie very quiet, or be ill again.

So Oliver kept very still, partly because he was anxious to obey the kind old lady in all things, and partly, to tell the truth, because he was exhausted. He soon fell into a gentle doze, from which he was awakened by the light of a candle. It showed a gentleman with a very large and loud-ticking gold watch in his hand, who felt his pulse, and said he was a great deal better.

"You are a great deal better, are you not, my dear?" he said.

36

"Yes, thank you, sir," replied Oliver.

"Thirsty. Are you?"

"Yes, sir, rather thirsty," answered Oliver.

"Just as I expected, Mrs Bedwin," said the doctor. "It's very natural that he should be thirsty. Give him a little tea, ma'am, and some dry toast without any butter. Don't keep him too warm, ma'am, but be careful that you don't let him be too cold."

The old lady dropped a curtsey. The doctor, after tasting the cool stuff, and expressing a qualified approval of it, hurried away.

Oliver dozed off again.

The night crept on. Oliver woke and lay counting the little circles of light which the rushlight-shade threw upon the ceiling.

Gradually, he fell into that deep tranquil sleep, that calm and peaceful rest that it is pain to wake from. It had been bright day, for hours, when Oliver opened his eyes; he felt cheerful and happy. The crisis of the illness was safely past. He belonged to the world again.

In three days' time he was able to sit in an easy chair propped up with pillows. As he was still too weak to walk, Mrs Bedwin had him carried down stairs.

"You're very, very kind to me, ma'am," said Oliver.

"Well, never you mind that, my dear," said the old lady. "The doctor says Mr Brownlow may come in to see you this morning and the better we look, the more he'll be pleased." And with this, the old lady applied herself to warming up a saucepan of broth.

"Are you fond of pictures, dear?" inquired the old lady, seeing Oliver staring most intently on a portrait which hung against the wall just opposite his chair.

"I don't quite know, ma'am," said Oliver, without taking his eyes from the canvas; "I have seen so few, that I hardly know. What a beautiful, mild face that lady's is!"

"Ah!" said the old lady, "painters always make ladies out prettier than they are, or they wouldn't get any custom, child."

"Is that a likeness, ma'am?" said Oliver.

"Yes," said the old lady, looking up for a moment from the broth. "That's a portrait."

"Whose, ma'am?" asked Oliver.

"Why, really, my dear, I don't know," answered the old lady in a good-humoured manner. "It's not a likeness of anybody that you or I know, I expect. It seems to strike your fancy, dear."

"It is so very pretty," replied Oliver.

"Why, sure you're not afraid of it?" said the old lady in surprise, seeing the look of awe with which Oliver regarded the painting.

"Oh no, no," returned Oliver quickly; "but the eyes look so sorrowful, and where I sit, they seem fixed upon me. It makes my heart beat, as if it was alive, and wanted to speak to me, but couldn't."

"Lord save us!" exclaimed the old lady, starting. "Don't talk that way, child. You're weak after your illness. Let me wheel your chair round to the other side; and then you won't see it. There!" said the old lady, suiting the action to the word. "You don't see it now."

Oliver did see it in his mind's eye as distinctly as if he had not been moved. He thought it better not to worry the kind old lady, so he smiled gently when she looked at him. Mrs Bedwin, satisfied that he felt more comfortable, broke bits of toasted bread into the broth. Oliver had scarcely swallowed the last spoonful, when there came a soft rap at the door. "Come in," said the old lady, and in walked Mr Brownlow.

Now, the old gentleman came in briskly but he had no sooner raised his spectacles on his forehead to take a good long look at Oliver, than his countenance underwent a variety of odd contortions. Oliver looked very worn from the sickness, and made an ineffectual attempt to stand up, out of respect to his benefactor. He ended up sinking back into the chair again and the fact is that Mr Brownlow's heart, being large enough for six old gentlemen of humane disposition, forced a supply of tears into his eyes.

"Poor boy!" said Mr Brownlow, clearing his throat. "I'm rather hoarse this morning, Mrs Bedwin. How do you feel, my dear?"

"Very happy, sir," replied Oliver. "And very grateful indeed, sir, for your goodness to me."

"Good boy," said Mr Brownlow, stoutly. "Have you given him any nourishment, Bedwin? Any slops, eh?"

"He has just had a basin of beautiful strong broth, sir," replied Mrs Bedwin. She drew herself up slightly, laying strong emphasis on the last word, to intimate that between slops and well-made broth there existed no similarity whatsoever.

"Ugh!" said Mr Brownlow, with a slight shudder, "a couple of glasses of port wine would have done a great deal more good. Wouldn't they, Tom White, eh?"

"My name is Oliver, sir," replied the little invalid with a look of great astonishment.

"Oliver," said Mr Brownlow; "Oliver what? Oliver White, eh?"

"No, sir, Twist, Oliver Twist."

"Queer name!" said the old gentleman. "What made you tell the magistrate your name was White?"

"I never told him so, sir," returned Oliver in amazement.

This sounded so like a lie that the old gentleman looked sternly on Oliver. But it was impossible to doubt him. There was truth in every one of its thin features.

"Some mistake," said Mr Brownlow. But, as he looked, the old idea of the resemblance between his features and some familiar face came upon him so strongly.

"I hope you are not angry with me, sir?" said Oliver.

"No, no," replied the old gentleman. "Why! What's this? Bedwin, look there!"

As he spoke, he pointed hastily to the picture above Oliver's head, and then to the boy's face. There was its living copy. The eyes, head, mouth – every feature was the same! The expression was, at that moment, so precisely alike, that the minutest line seemed copied with startling accuracy!

Oliver knew not the cause of this sudden exclamation, and not being strong enough to bear the start it gave him, he fainted away.

Meanwhile the two young gentlemen, Bates and Hawkins, after the hue and cry of chasing after young Oliver, had made immediately for their home by the shortest possible cut.

"What'll Fagin say?" inquired the Dodger.

"What?" repeated Charley Bates.

"Ah, what?" said the Dodger.

The noise of footsteps on the creaking stairs, a few minutes after this conversation, roused the merry old gentleman as he sat over the fire with a saveloy and a small loaf in his left hand, a pocket-knife in his right and a pewter pot on the trivet. There was a rascally smile on his face as he turned, and, looking sharply out from under his thick red eyebrows, listened.

"Why, how's this?" muttered the Jew. "Only two of 'em? Where's the third? They can't have got into trouble. Hark!"

The footsteps approached nearer, reaching the landing. The door was slowly opened, and the Dodger and Charley Bates entered, closing it behind them.

CHAPTER 12

"Where's Oliver?" said the Jew, rising with a menacing look. "Where's the boy?"

The young thieves eyed Fagin and looked uneasily at each other. But they made no reply.

"What's become of the boy?" asked the Jew, seizing the Dodger tightly by the collar. "Speak out, or I'll throttle you!"

Charley Bates dropped to his knees, and raised a loud, well-sustained, and continuous roar.

"Will you speak?" thundered the Jew, shaking the Dodger so much that his staying in the big coat at all seemed miraculous.

"Why, the traps have got him," said the Dodger, sullenly. "Let go o' me, will you!" And, he swung himself, at one jerk, clean out of the big coat, leaving it in the Jew's hands. He armed himself with the fork.

The Jew stepped back, with more agility than expected, and, seizing up the pot, prepared to hurl it at the Dodger. But Charley Bates calling his attention by a perfectly terrific howl, he suddenly altered its destination, and flung it full at that young gentleman.

"Why, what the blazes is in the wind now!" growled a deep voice. "Who pitched that 'ere at me? It's well it's the beer, and not the pot, as hit me or I'd have settled somebody. Wot's it all about, Fagin? Come in, you sneaking warmint; wot are you stopping outside for, as if you was ashamed of your master! Come in!"

The man who growled out these words was a stoutly built fellow of about thirty-five, in a black velveteen coat, very soiled drab breeches, lace-up half boots, and grey cotton stockings, which enclosed a bulky pair of legs, with large swelling calves. He had a brown hat on his head, and a dirty handkerchief around his neck. He used the long frayed ends to wipe the beer from his face as he spoke. He had a broad heavy face with a beard of three days' growth, and two scowling eyes.

"Come in, d'ye hear?" growled this engaging ruffian.

A white shaggy dog, with his face scratched and torn in twenty different places, skulked into the room.

"Why didn't you come in afore?" said the man. "You're getting too proud to own me afore company, are you? Lie down!"

This command was accompanied with a kick, which sent the animal to the other end of the room. He appeared well used to it, however, for he coiled himself up in a corner very quietly.

"What are you up to? Ill-treating the boys, you avaricious old fence?" said the man, seating himself deliberately. "I wonder they don't murder you! If I was yer 'prentice, I'd have done it ages ago."

"Hush! Mr Sikes," said the Jew, trembling.

"None of your mistering," replied the ruffian. "You always mean mischief when you use that. You know my name. I shan't disgrace it when the time comes."

Mr Sikes noticed the young gentlemen. This led to a conversation concerning Oliver's capture with such alterations on the truth, as the Dodger deemed necessary.

"I'm afraid," said the Jew, "that he may say something to get us into trouble."

"That's very likely," returned Sikes with a malicious grin. "You're blowed upon, Fagin."

"And I'm afraid, you see," added the Jew, speaking as if he had not noticed the interruption; and regarding the other closely as he did so. "If the game was up with us, it might be up with a good many more."

The man started, and turned to the Jew. But his shoulders were shrugged up to his ears and he vacantly stared at the opposite wall.

There was a long pause. All appeared deep in his own reflections.

"Somebody must find out wot's happened," said Mr Sikes.

The Jew nodded assent.

"If he hasn't peached, and is committed, there's no fear till he comes out again," said Mr Sikes, "and then he must be taken care of. You must get hold of him."

Again the Jew nodded.

But, there was one very strong objection to its being adopted. Dodger, Charley Bates, Fagin, and Mr William Sikes each had a violent antipathy to going near a police-office for any reason whatsoever.

How long they might have sat and looked at each other is difficult to guess. However, the sudden entrance of the two young ladies whom Oliver had seen on a former occasion, caused the conversation to flow afresh.

"Nancy, my dear," said the Jew in a soothing manner, "will you go up the office?"

"It's no use a-trying it on, Fagin," replied Nancy.

"What do you mean by that?" said Mr Sikes, looking up.

"What I say, Bill," replied the lady collectedly.

"Why, you're just the very person for it," reasoned Mr Sikes. "Nobody about here knows anything of you."

"And I don't want 'em to, neither," replied Nancy in the same composed manner.

"She'll go, Fagin," said Sikes.

"No, she won't, Fagin," said Nancy.

"Yes, she will, Fagin," said Sikes.

And Mr Sikes was right. By dint of alternate threats, promises, and bribes, the lady in question was ultimately prevailed upon to undertake the commission.

Accordingly, with a clean white apron tied over her gown, and her curl-papers tucked up under a straw bonnet – provided from the Jew's inexhaustible stock – Miss Nancy prepared to issue forth.

"Stop a minute, my dear," said the Jew, producing a little covered basket. "Carry that. It looks more respectable, my dear."

"Give her a door-key to carry in her t'other one, Fagin," said Sikes.

"Yes, yes, my dear, so it does," said the Jew, hanging a large street-door key on the forefinger of the young lady's right hand. "There; very good! Very good indeed, my dear!" said the Jew, rubbing his hands.

Nancy made the best of her way to the police-office. Entering by the back way, she tapped softly with the key at one of the cell-doors, and listened. There was no sound within, so she spoke.

"Nolly, dear?" murmured Nancy, gently. "Nolly?"

There was nobody inside but a miserable shoeless criminal, so Nancy passed on to the next cell, and knocked there.

"Well!" cried a faint and feeble voice.

"Is there a little boy here?" inquired Nancy, with a preliminary sob.

"No," replied the voice; "God forbid."

Nancy made straight up to the desk.

"Oh, my brother! My poor, sweet, innocent little brother!" exclaimed Nancy, bursting into tears, and wringing the little basket and the street-door key. "What has become of him! Do have pity, and tell me what's been done with the dear boy!"

"I haven't got him, my dear," said the desk officer. "The gentleman's got him."

"Oh, gracious heavens! What gentleman?" exclaimed Nancy.

In reply, the officer informed her that Oliver had been taken ill in the office, and a witness had proved that another boy had committed the robbery. The prosecutor had carried him away, ill, to his own residence, somewhere at Pentonville.

The young woman staggered to the gate, and then swiftly ran, by the most devious route she could, back to the Jew.

Mr Bill Sikes no sooner heard her account, than he very hastily called up the white dog and left.

"The boy must be found, my dears," said the Jew, greatly excited. "Charley, skulk about, till you bring home some news of him! Nancy, my dear, I must have him found. I trust to you, my dear, and the Artful for everything!" Then the Jew unlocked a drawer with a shaking hand. "Here's money, my dears. I shall shut up this shop tonight. You'll know where to find me!"

With these words, he pushed them from the room. Carefully he double-locked and barred the door behind them, then drew from its hiding place the box he had inadvertently shown Oliver. He hastily hid the watches and jewellery in his clothing.

A rap at the door startled him. "Who's there?" he cried.

"Me!" replied the Dodger, through the keyhole.

"What now?" cried the Jew impatiently.

"Is he to be taken to the other ken?" inquired the Dodger.

"Yes," replied the Jew, "wherever she finds him. Just find him! I shall know what to do next; never fear. He has not peached so far," said the Jew as he pursued his occupation. "If he means to blab us among his new friends, we may stop his mouth yet."

43

CHAPTER 13

As Oliver recovered from the fainting fit into which Mr Brownlow's abrupt exclamation had thrown him into, the subject of the picture was carefully avoided.

He was still too weak to get up to breakfast but, when he came down into the housekeeper's room next day, he looked up at the wall, in the hope of again looking on the face of the beautiful lady. However, the picture had been removed.

"Ah!" said Mrs Bedwin. "It is gone, you see."

"I see it is, ma'am," replied Oliver. "Why is it taken down?"

"Mr Brownlow said that as it seemed to worry you, perhaps it might prevent your getting well, you know," rejoined the old lady.

"Oh. It didn't worry me, ma'am," said Oliver. "I liked to see it."

"Well, well!" said the housekeeper, good-humouredly, "you get well as fast as you can, dear, and it shall be hung up again. I promise you that! Now, let us talk about something else."

This was all the information Oliver could obtain about the picture at that time. Soon it was time for tea. After tea she began to teach Oliver cribbage: which he learnt as quickly as she could teach. They played until it was time for him to have some warm wine and water, with a slice of dry toast, and then to go easily to bed.

They were happy days. Everything was so quiet, and neat, and orderly; everybody was kind and gentle that it seemed like Heaven itself. He was no sooner strong enough to put his clothes on, properly, than Mr Brownlow had a complete new suit, and a new cap, and a new pair of shoes, made for him.

One evening, about a week after the affair of the picture, as he sat with Mrs Bedwin, a message came down from Mr Brownlow, that if Oliver Twist felt pretty well, he should like to see him in his study, and talk to him a little while.

"Bless us! Wash your hands, child," said Mrs Bedwin. "If we had known he was to ask for you, we would have put a clean collar on, and made you as smart as sixpence!"

Moments later Oliver tapped at the study door. On Mr Brownlow calling to him to come in, he found himself in a little back room, quite full of books, with a window, looking into some pleasant little gardens. There was a table drawn up before the window, at which Mr Brownlow was seated reading. When he saw Oliver, he pushed the book away from him, and told him to come near the table, and sit down.

"Now," said Mr Brownlow, speaking in a serious manner. "I want you to pay great attention, my boy, to what I am going to say. I shall talk to you without any reserve, because I am sure you are as able to understand me, as many older persons would be."

"Oh, don't tell me you are going to send me away, sir, pray!" exclaimed Oliver, alarmed at the serious tone. "Don't turn me out to wander in the streets again. Let me stay and be a servant. Don't send me back to the wretched place. Have mercy, sir!"

"My dear child," said the old gentleman, moved by the warmth of Oliver's appeal. "You need not be afraid of my deserting you, unless you give me cause."

"I never, never will, sir," interposed Oliver.

"I hope not," rejoined the old gentleman. "I do not think you ever will. I have been deceived before, but I feel strongly disposed to trust you and I am more interested in your behalf than I can well account for, even to myself. The people on whom I have bestowed my dearest love lie deep in their graves; but, although the delight of my life lies buried there too, I have not yet made a coffin of my heart. Deep affliction has but strengthened and refined it."

The old gentleman said this in a low voice, more to himself, and as he remained silent for a short time afterwards, Oliver sat quite still.

"Well!" said the old gentleman at length, in a more cheerful tone. "I only say this, because you have a young heart, and knowing that I have suffered great pain and sorrow, you will be careful, perhaps, not to wound me again. You say you are an orphan, without a friend in the world. All the inquiries I have made confirm this. Tell me your story; where you come from and how you got into the company in which I found you. Speak the truth, and you shall not be friendless while I live."

Oliver was on the point of relating how he had been brought up at the farm, and carried to the workhouse by Mr Bumble, when a servant ran upstairs, and announced Mr Grimwig.

"Is he coming up?" inquired Mr Brownlow.

"Yes, sir," replied the servant. "He asked if there were muffins in the house; and, when I told him yes, he said he had come to tea."

Mr Brownlow smiled, and turning to Oliver, said that Mr Grimwig was an old friend of his, and he must not mind his being a little rough in his manners.

"Shall I go down stairs, sir?" inquired Oliver.

"No," replied Mr Brownlow. "I would rather you remained here."

At this moment, there walked into the room, supporting himself by a thick stick, a stout old gentleman, rather lame in one leg, who was dressed in a blue coat, striped waistcoat, nankeen breeches and gaiters and, a broad-brimmed white hat, with the sides turned up. He had a manner of screwing his head on one side when he spoke; and of looking out of the corners of his eyes at the same time.

"Hallo! What's that?" he said, looking at Oliver.

"This is Oliver Twist, whom we spoke about," said Mr Brownlow.

Oliver bowed.

"You mean the boy who had the fever," said Mr Grimwig, recoiling a little more. He then sat down.

"That's the boy, is it?" said Mr Grimwig, at length.

"That is the boy," replied Mr Brownlow.

"How are you, boy?" said Mr Grimwig.

"A great deal better, thank you, sir," replied Oliver.

Mr Brownlow, fearing that his singular friend was about to say something disagreeable, asked Oliver to step down stairs and tell Mrs Bedwin they were ready for tea. This he was happy to do.

"He is a nice-looking boy, is he not?" inquired Mr Brownlow.

"I don't know," replied Mr Grimwig, pettishly. "Where does he come from? Who is he?"

In the inmost recesses of his heart, Mr Grimwig was inclined to agree that Oliver's appearance and manner were unusually prepossessing, but he had a strong appetite for contradiction.

Oliver made one of the party for muffins, and began to feel more at his ease in the fierce old gentleman's presence.

"And when are you going to hear a full, true, and particular account of the life and adventures of Oliver Twist?" asked Grimwig of Mr Brownlow, at the conclusion of the meal.

"Tomorrow morning," replied Mr Brownlow. "I would rather he was alone with me at the time. Come to me tomorrow morning at ten o'clock, my dear."

"Yes, sir," replied Oliver.

Mrs Bedwin chose that particular moment to bring in a parcel of books, which Mr Brownlow had purchased. Having laid them on the table, she prepared to leave the room.

"Stop the boy, Mrs Bedwin!" said Mr Brownlow. "There is something to go back."

"He has gone, sir," replied Mrs Bedwin.

"Call after him," said Mr Brownlow. "It's important. He is a poor man, and they are not paid for. There are some to go back, too."

The street door was opened. Oliver ran one way; and the girl ran another. Mrs Bedwin stood on the step and screamed for the boy, but there was no boy in sight. Oliver and the girl returned, in a breathless state, to report that there were no tidings of him.

"Dear me, I am very sorry for that," exclaimed Mr Brownlow. "I particularly wished those books to be returned tonight."

"Send Oliver with them," said Mr Grimwig, with an ironical smile. "He will be sure to deliver them safely, you know."

"Yes, do let me take them, sir," said Oliver. "I'll run all the way."

The old gentleman was about to say that Oliver should not go out, when a malicious cough from Mr Grimwig determined him that he should.

"You shall go, my dear," said the old gentleman. "The books are on a chair by my table. Fetch them down."

Oliver, delighted to be of use, brought down the books and waited, cap in hand, to hear what message he was to take.

"You are to say," said Mr Brownlow, glancing steadily at Grimwig, "that you have brought those books back; and that you have come to pay the four pound ten I owe him. This is a five-pound note, so you will have to bring back ten shillings change."

"I won't be ten minutes, sir," replied Oliver, eagerly. Having buttoned up the bank note in his jacket pocket, and placed the books carefully under his arm, he made a respectful bow, and left the room. Mrs Bedwin followed him to the street door, giving him directions and the name of the bookseller, and the name of the street, all of which Oliver said, he clearly understood. The old lady at length permitted him to depart.

"Bless his sweet face!" said the old lady, looking after him. "I can't bear, somehow, to let him go out of my sight."

47

At this moment, Oliver looked gaily round, and nodded before he turned the corner. The old lady smilingly returned his salutation, and, closing the door went back to her own room.

"Let me see – he'll be back in twenty minutes, at the longest," said Mr Brownlow, pulling out his watch, and placing it on the table. "It will be dark by then."

"You really expect him to return, do you?" asked Mr Grimwig.

"Don't you?" asked Mr Brownlow, smiling.

The spirit of contradiction was strong in Mr Grimwig and rendered stronger by his friend's confident smile.

"No," he said, smiting the table with his fist. "I do not. The boy has a new suit of clothes on his back, a set of valuable books under his arm and a five-pound note in his pocket. He'll join his old friends the thieves, and laugh at you. If ever that boy returns to this house, sir, I'll eat my head."

With these words he drew his chair closer to the table; and there the two friends sat with the watch between them.

It grew so dark, that the figures on the dial-plate were scarcely discernible; but there the two old gentlemen continued to sit, in silence, with the watch between them.

CHAPTER 14

When he got into Clerkenwell, Oliver accidentally went the wrong way, but not discovering his mistake until he had got halfway down it, and knowing it must lead in the right direction, he marched on, as quickly as he could, with the books under his arm.

He was walking along, when he was startled by a young woman screaming out very loud, "Oh, my dear brother!" And he had hardly looked up to see what the matter was, when two arms were thrown tight round his neck.

"Don't," cried Oliver, struggling. "Let go of me. Who is it? What are you stopping me for?"

The only reply to this was great sobbing from the young woman who embraced him. She had a little basket in her hand.

48

"Oh my gracious!" said the young woman. "I've found him! Oh! Oliver! You naughty boy, to make me suffer sich distress on your account! Come home, dear. Thank gracious heavins, I've found him!"

"What's the matter, ma'am?" inquired a woman bystander.

"Oh, ma'am," replied the young woman. "He ran away, near a month ago, from his parents, who are respectable people, and joined a set of thieves and almost broke his mother's heart."

"Young wretch!" said another woman.

"I don't know her," replied Oliver, greatly alarmed. "I haven't a sister, or father and mother. I'm an orphan. I live at Pentonville."

"Only hear him, how he braves it out!" cried the young woman.

"Why, it's Nancy!" exclaimed Oliver who now saw her face for the first time, and started back, in astonishment.

"You see – he knows me!" cried Nancy, appealing to the bystanders.

"What the devil's this?" said a man, bursting out of a beer-shop, a white dog at his heels. "Oliver! Come home to your poor mother."

"I don't belong to them. I don't know them. Help!" cried Oliver, struggling in the man's powerful grasp.

"Help!" repeated the man. "Yes; I'll help you, you young rascal! What books are these? You've been a stealing 'em, have you? Give 'em here." With these words, the man tore the volumes from his grasp, and struck him on the head.

"That's the only way of bringing him to his senses!" said the two women.

The man seized Oliver by the collar. "Come on, young villain! Here, Bull's-eye, mind him!"

Weak with recent illness, stunned by the blows and the suddenness of the attack, terrified by the fierce growling of the dog, and the brutality of the man, what could one poor child do? Darkness had set in. Resistance was useless. A moment later he was dragged into a labyrinth of dark narrow courts.

The gas-lamps were lighted, Mrs Bedwin was waiting anxiously at the open door, the servant had run up the street twenty times to see if there were any traces of Oliver, and still the two old gentlemen sat in the dark parlour, with the watch between them.

CHAPTER 15

The narrow streets and courts finally ended in a large open space. Sikes slowed down, the girl unable to maintain the speed. Turning to Oliver, he roughly ordered him to take hold of Nancy's hand.

"Do you hear?" growled Sikes. Oliver hesitated, looking round.

Oliver saw that resistance would be of no avail. He held out his hand, which Nancy clasped in hers.

"Give me the other," said Sikes.

It was Smithfield that they were crossing, although it might have been Grosvenor Square, for all Oliver knew. The night was foggy.

They walked on, by dirty ways, for a full half-hour, meeting very few people. At length they turned into a very filthy narrow street and stopped before the door of a closed shop.

"All right," cried Sikes, glancing cautiously about.

Nancy stooped below the shutters, and Oliver heard the sound of a bell. They crossed to the opposite side of the street, and stood for a few moments under a lamp. A noise, as if a sash window were gently raised, was heard. Then the door softly opened. Mr Sikes seized the terrified boy by the collar and all three were quickly inside the house.

The passage was perfectly dark. They waited, while the person who had let them in, chained and barred the door.

"Anybody here?" inquired Sikes.

"No," replied a voice, which Oliver thought he had heard before.

"Is the old 'un here?" asked the robber.

"Yes," replied the voice. "And down in the mouth he has been. Won't he be glad to see you? Oh, no!"

The style of this reply seemed familiar to Oliver.

"Let's have a glim," said Sikes, "or we shall go breaking our necks, or treading on the dog. Look after your legs if you do!"

"Stand still a moment, and I'll get you one," replied the voice. A moment later the form of Mr John Dawkins, otherwise the Artful Dodger, appeared. He bore in his right hand a tallow candle stuck in the end of a cleft stick.

The young gentleman did not stop to bestow any other mark of recognition upon Oliver than a humorous grin. Turning away, he beckoned the visitors down a flight of stairs. They opened the door of a low earthy-smelling room, which seemed to have been built in a small backyard, and were received with a shout of laughter.

"Oh, my wig!" cried Master Charles Bates. "Here he is! Oh, Fagin, look at him! Hold me, somebody, while I laugh it out."

With this irrepressible outburst, Master Bates laid himself flat on the floor. Then jumping to his feet, he snatched the cleft stick from the Dodger and, advancing to Oliver, viewed him round and round. The Jew made a great number of low bows to the bewildered boy. The Artful, meantime, rifled Oliver's pockets with steady assiduity.

"Look at his togs, Fagin!" said Charley, putting the light close to his new jacket. "Superfine cloth! And books, too! Nothing but a gentleman, Fagin!"

"Delighted to see you looking so well, my dear," said the Jew, bowing with mock humility. "The Artful shall give you another suit, my dear, for fear you spoil that Sunday one. Why didn't you write, my dear, and say you were coming? We'd have got something for supper."

At this, Master Bates roared again. The Artful drew forth the five-pound note at that instant.

"Hallo! What's that?" inquired Sikes, stepping forward as the Jew seized the note. "That's mine, Fagin."

"No, my dear," said the Jew. "Mine, Bill. You shall have the books."

"If that ain't mine!" said Bill Sikes, putting on his hat. "Mine and Nancy's that is, I'll take the boy back."

The Jew started. Oliver started too, hoping that the dispute might really end in his being taken back.

"Come! Hand over, will you?" said Sikes.

"This is hardly fair, Bill. Nancy?" inquired the Jew.

"Fair, or not fair," retorted Sikes. "Hand over, I tell you! Do you think Nancy and me has got nothing else to do with our precious time but to spend it in scouting arter and kidnapping every young boy as gets grabbed through you? Give it here!"

Mr Sikes plucked the note from between the Jew's finger and thumb, and looking the old man coolly in the face, folded it and tied it in his neckerchief.

"That's for our share of the trouble," said Sikes. "You may keep the books, if you're fond of reading. If you a'n't, sell 'em."

"They're very pretty," said Charley Bates. "Beautiful writing, isn't it, Oliver?" At sight of the dismayed look with which Oliver regarded his tormentors, Master Bates fell into another fit of laughing.

"They belong to the old gentleman," said Oliver, wringing his hands. "He took me into his house, and had me nursed, when I was near dying of the fever. Oh, pray send them back. Keep me here all my life long; but pray send them back. He'll think I stole them. All of them, who were so kind to me, will think I stole them. Oh, do have mercy upon me, and send them back!"

With those words Oliver fell upon his knees at the Jew's feet, and beat his hands together, in perfect desperation.

"The boy's right," remarked Fagin, looking round, and knitting his shaggy eyebrows into a hard knot. "Oliver, you're right. They will think you have stolen 'em. Ha! ha!" chuckled the Jew, rubbing his hands. "It couldn't have happened better!"

"Of course it couldn't," replied Sikes. "I know'd that, directly I see him coming through Clerkenwell, with the books under his arm. It's all right enough. They'll ask no questions after him, fear they should be obliged to prosecute, and so get him lagged."

Oliver had looked from one to the other, while these words were being spoken, as if he could scarcely understand what passed. But when Bill Sikes concluded, he jumped suddenly to his feet, and tore wildly from the room, screaming for help.

"Keep back the dog, Bill!" cried Nancy, springing before the door, and closing it, as the Jew and his two pupils darted out in pursuit. "Keep back the dog, he'll tear the boy to pieces."

"Serve him right!" cried Sikes, struggling to disengage himself from the girl. "Stand off, or I'll split your head against the wall."

"I don't care for that, Bill," screamed the girl, struggling violently with the man. "The child shan't be torn down by the dog, unless you kill me first."

"Shan't he!" said Sikes. "I'll soon do that, if you don't keep off."

The housebreaker flung the girl from him to the far end of the room, just as the Jew and the two boys returned, dragging Oliver.

"What's the matter here!" said Fagin, looking round.

"The girl's gone mad, I think," replied Sikes, savagely.

"No," said Nancy, pale and breathless from the scuffle. "She hasn't, Fagin. Don't think it."

"Then keep quiet, will you?" said the Jew, with a threatening look.

"I won't do that, neither," replied Nancy, speaking very loud. "Come! What do you think of that?"

Mr Fagin was fairly certain that it would be rather unsafe to prolong any conversation with her at present. So with the view of diverting the attention of the company, he turned to Oliver.

"So you wanted to get away, my dear, did you?" he said, taking up a jagged and knotted club which lay in a corner of the fireplace.

Oliver made no reply. But he watched the Jew's motions.

"Wanted to get assistance, called for the police, did you?" sneered the Jew, catching the boy by the arm. "We'll cure you of that."

The Jew inflicted a smart blow on Oliver's shoulders with the club, and was raising it for a second, when the girl, rushing forward, wrested it from his hand. She flung it into the fire with a force that brought some of the glowing coals whirling out into the room.

"I won't see it done, Fagin," cried the girl. "You've got the boy. What more would you have? Let him be or I shall put that mark on some of you, that will bring me to the gallows before my time."

The girl stamped her foot violently on the floor as she vented this threat, and with her lips compressed, and her hands clenched, looked alternately at the Jew and the other robber.

"Why, Nancy!" said the Jew, in a soothing tone. He and Mr Sikes had stared at one another in a disconcerted manner for a moment. "You – you're more clever than ever to-night. Ha! My dear, you are acting beautifully."

"Am I?" said the girl. "Take care I don't overdo it. You will be the worse for it, Fagin, if I do, and so I tell you to keep clear of me."

Shrinking involuntarily back a few paces, the Jew cast a glance, half imploring and half cowardly at Sikes as if to hint that he was the fittest person to pursue the dialogue.

Mr Sikes, thus mutely appealed to, gave utterance to about a couple of score of curses and threats. As they produced no visible effect he resorted to more tangible arguments.

"What do you mean by this?" said Sikes. "Burn my body! Do you know who you are, and what you are?"

"Oh, yes, I know all about it," replied the girl, laughing hysterically and shaking her head from side to side.

53

"Well, then, keep quiet," rejoined Sikes, with a growl that he was accustomed to use when addressing his dog, "or I'll quiet you for a good long time to come."

The girl laughed again, even less composedly than before and, darting a hasty look at Sikes, turned her face aside, and bit her lip till blood came.

"You're a nice one," added Sikes, as he surveyed her with a contemptuous air. "To take up the humane and genteel side! A pretty subject for the child, as you call him, to make a friend of!"

"God Almighty help me, I am!" cried the girl passionately. "And I wish I had been struck dead in the street, or had changed places with them we passed so near tonight, before I had lent a hand in bringing him here. He's a thief, a liar, a devil, all that's bad, from this night forth. Isn't that enough for the old wretch, without blows?"

"Come, come, Sikes," said the Jew, appealing to him and motioning towards the boys, who were eagerly attentive to all that passed. "We must have civil words; civil words, Bill."

"Civil words!" cried the girl, whose passion was frightful to see. "Civil words, you villain! Yes, you deserve 'em from me. I thieved for you when I was a child not half his age. I have been in the same trade, and in the same service, for twelve years since!"

"Well," replied the Jew, with an attempt at pacification, "and, if you have, it's your living!"

"Aye, it is!" returned the girl, not speaking, but pouring out the words in one continuous and vehement scream. "It is my living; and the cold, wet, dirty streets are my home, and you're the wretch that drove me there so long ago, and that'll keep me there, day and night till I die!"

"I shall do you a mischief!" interposed the Jew, goaded by these reproaches, "a mischief worse than that, if you say much more!"

The girl said nothing more, but, tearing her hair and dress, made such a rush at the Jew as would probably have left signal marks of her revenge upon him, had not her wrists been seized by Sikes. Then she made a few ineffectual struggles and fainted.

"She's all right now," said Sikes, laying her down in a corner. "She's uncommon strong in the arms when she's up in this way."

The Jew wiped his forehead: and smiled, as if it were a relief to have the disturbance over, but neither he, nor Sikes, nor the dog, seemed to consider it anything other than a common occurrence.

54

"It's the worst of having to do with women," said the Jew, replacing his club. "They're clever, and we can't get on, in our line, without 'em. Charley, show Oliver to bed."

"I suppose he'd better not wear his best clothes tomorrow, Fagin, had he?" inquired Charley Bates.

"Certainly not," replied the Jew.

Master Bates took the cleft stick and led Oliver into an adjacent kitchen. Here, he produced the identical old suit of clothes that Oliver had got rid of at Mr Brownlow's. The accidental display of them to Fagin, by the Jew who purchased them, had been the very first clue received of his whereabouts.

"Pull off the smart ones," said Charley, "and I'll give 'em to Fagin to take care of."

Poor Oliver unwillingly complied. Master Bates rolling up the new clothes under his arm departed from the room, leaving Oliver in the dark.

The noise of Charley's laughter might have kept many people awake under more happy circumstances, but Oliver was sick and weary, and he soon fell sound asleep.

CHAPTER 16

At six o'clock one morning, Mr Bumble encasing his person in a blue great-coat, took his place on the outside of a coach, accompanied by two pauper orphans whose settlement was to be disputed in London. The two paupers persisted in shivering, and complaining of the cold, in a manner which, Mr Bumble declared made him feel uncomfortable; although he had a great-coat on.

Having disposed of the paupers for the night, Mr Bumble sat himself down in the house where the coach stopped and took a dinner of steaks, oyster sauce, and porter. Putting a glass of hot gin-and-water on the chimney place, he drew his chair to the fire and composed himself to read the paper.

The very first words upon which Mr Bumble's eye rested, was the following advertisement:

"FIVE GUINEAS REWARD.

"Whereas a young boy, named Oliver Twist, absconded, or was enticed, on Thursday evening last, from his home, at Pentonville and has not since been heard of. The above reward will be paid to any person who will give such information as will lead to the discovery of the said Oliver Twist, or tend to throw any light upon his previous history, in which the advertiser is, for many reasons, warmly interested."

There followed a full description of Oliver's dress, person, appearance, and disappearance, with the name and address of Mr Brownlow at full length.

Mr Bumble read the advertisement, slowly and carefully, three times and five minutes later was on his way to Pentonville.

"Is Mr Brownlow at home?" inquired Mr Bumble of the girl who opened the door.

To this inquiry the girl returned the not uncommon, but rather evasive reply of, "I don't know, where do you come from?"

Mr Bumble no sooner uttered Oliver's name, in explanation of his errand, than Mrs Bedwin, who had been listening at the parlour door, hastened into the passage in a breathless state.

"Come in, come in," said the old lady. "I knew we should hear of him. Poor dear! I was certain of it. Bless his heart! I said so, all along."

Having said this, the worthy old lady hurried back into the parlour, and seating herself on a sofa, burst into tears. The girl had run up stairs meanwhile, and now returned with a request that Mr Bumble follow her immediately, which he did.

He was shown into the little back study, where sat Mr Brownlow and his friend Mr Grimwig, with decanters and glasses before them. The latter gentleman at once burst into the exclamation: "A beadle! A parish beadle, or I'll eat my head."

"Pray don't interrupt just now," said Mr Brownlow. "Take a seat, will you?"

Mr Bumble sat himself down. Mr Brownlow moved the lamp, so as to obtain an uninterrupted view of the beadle's countenance, and said, "Now, sir, you come having seen the advertisement?"

"Yes, sir," said Mr Bumble.

"Do you know where this poor boy is now?"

"No more than nobody," replied Mr Bumble.

"Well, what do you know of him?" inquired the old gentleman. "Speak out, my friend, if you have anything to say."

"You don't happen to know any good of him, do you?" said Mr Grimwig, caustically.

Mr Bumble, catching at the inquiry very quickly, shook his head.

"You see?" said Mr Grimwig, looking triumphantly at Mr Brownlow.

Mr Brownlow looked apprehensively at Mr Bumble and requested him to communicate what he knew regarding Oliver, in as few words as possible.

Mr Bumble put down his hat, unbuttoned his coat, folded his arms, inclined his head in a retrospective manner, and, after a few moments' reflection, commenced his story.

The sum and substance of the tale was that Oliver was a foundling, born of low and vicious parents. That he had, from his birth, displayed no better qualities than treachery, ingratitude, and malice. That he had terminated his brief career in the place of his birth, by making a cowardly attack and running away in the night-time from his master's house. In proof of his really being the person he represented himself, Mr Bumble laid upon the table the papers he had brought to town. Folding his arms again, he awaited Mr Brownlow's observations.

"I fear it is all too true," said the old gentleman sorrowfully, after looking over the papers. "I would gladly have given you treble the money, if it had been favourable to the boy."

It is not improbable that if Mr Bumble had known this earlier in the interview, he might have given a very different colouring to his little history. It was too late to do it now, however; so he shook his head gravely, and, pocketing the five guineas, withdrew.

Mr Brownlow paced the room for some minutes, so disturbed by the beadle's tale, that even Mr Grimwig forbore to vex him further.

At length he stopped, and rang the bell violently.

"Mrs Bedwin," said Mr Brownlow, when the housekeeper appeared. "That boy, Oliver, is an impostor."

"It can't be, sir. It cannot be," said the old lady, energetically.

"I tell you he is," retorted the old gentleman. "What do you mean by can't be? We have just heard a full account of him from his birth and he has been a thorough little villain, all his life."

"I never will believe it, sir," replied the old lady, firmly. "Never!"

"You old women never believe anything but quack-doctors, and lying story-books," growled Mr Grimwig. "I knew it all along."

"He was a dear, grateful, gentle child, sir," retorted Mrs Bedwin, indignantly. "I know what children are, sir; and have done these forty years. People who can't say the same, shouldn't say anything about them. That's my opinion!"

This was a hard hit at Mr Grimwig, who was a bachelor. As it extorted nothing from that gentleman but a smile, the old lady tossed her head, and smoothed down her apron ready to speak again, when she was prevented by Mr Brownlow.

"Silence!" said the old gentleman, feigning an anger he was far from feeling. "Never let me hear the boy's name again. You may leave the room, Mrs Bedwin. Remember! I am in earnest."

There were sad hearts at Mr Brownlow's that night.

Oliver's heart sank within him, when he thought of his good kind friends; it was well for him that he could not know what they had heard, or it might have broken outright.

CHAPTER 17

About noon next day, the Dodger and Master Bates left to pursue their customary vocations. Mr Fagin took the opportunity of lecturing Oliver on the crying sin of ingratitude. He had wilfully absented himself from the society of his anxious friends, and, still more had tried to escape from them after so much trouble and expense had been incurred in his recovery. Mr Fagin stressed how he had taken Oliver in, and cherished him, when, without his timely aid, he might have perished with hunger.

The Jew, smiling hideously, patted Oliver on the head, and said that if he kept himself quiet, and applied himself to business, he saw they would be very good friends yet. Then, taking his hat and an old patched great-coat, he went out, locking the door behind him.

And so Oliver remained all that day, and for the greater part of many subsequent days, seeing nobody, between early morning and midnight, left to commune with his own thoughts. Which, never failing to revert to his kind friends, and the opinion they must long ago have formed of him, were sad indeed.

After the lapse of a week or so, the Jew left the door unlocked; and he was at liberty to wander about the house.

It was a very dirty place. The rooms upstairs had great high wooden chimney-pieces and large doors, with panelled walls and cornices to the ceilings; which, although they were black with neglect and dust, were ornamented in various ways. From all of this Oliver concluded that a long time ago, before the old Jew was born, it had belonged to better people, and had perhaps been quite handsome.

One afternoon, as the Dodger and Master Bates were going out that evening, the first-named young gentleman commanded Oliver to assist him in his toilet, straightway.

Oliver was but too glad to make himself useful. So he at once expressed his readiness; and, kneeling on the floor, while the Dodger sat upon the table so that he could take his foot in his lap, he applied himself to a process which Mr Dawkins designated as "japanning his trotter-cases." The phrase, rendered into plain English, meant cleaning his boots.

He looked down on Oliver, with a thoughtful look, for a moment and then, raising his head, and sighing, said, half in abstraction, and half to Master Bates, "What a pity it is he isn't a prig."

"Why not put yourself under Fagin, Oliver?" asked Charley.

"And make your fortun'?" added the Dodger, with a grin.

"I don't like it," rejoined Oliver, timidly. "I – I – would rather go."

"And Fagin would rather not!" rejoined Charley.

Oliver knew this too well; but thinking it might be dangerous to express his feelings more openly, he only sighed, and went on with his boot cleaning.

"Go!" exclaimed the Dodger. "Why, where's your spirit? Would you go and be dependent on your friends?"

"Oh, blow that!" said Master Bates. "That's too mean, that is."

"I couldn't do it," said the Dodger, with an air of haughty disgust.

"You can leave your friends, though," said Oliver with a half smile. "And let them be punished for what you did."

"That," rejoined the Dodger, with a wave of his pipe, "was all out of consideration for Fagin, 'cause the traps know that we work together, and he might have got into trouble if we hadn't."

"Look here!" said the Dodger, drawing forth a handful of coins. "Here's a jolly life! What's the odds where it comes from? Here, catch hold; there's plenty more where they were took from. You won't, won't you?"

"It's naughty, ain't it, Oliver?" inquired Charley Bates. "He'll come to be scragged, won't he?"

"I don't know what that means," replied Oliver.

"Something in this way, old feller," said Charley. Master Bates caught up an end of his neckerchief, and, holding it erect in the air, dropped his head on his shoulder, thereby indicating that scragging and hanging were one and the same thing.

"That's what it means," said Charley. "Look how he stares, Jack! I never did see such prime company as that 'ere boy; he'll be the death of me, I know he will."

"You've been brought up bad," said the Dodger, surveying his boots with much satisfaction when Oliver had polished them. "Fagin will make something of you, though, or you'll be the first turned out unprofitable. You're only losing time, Oliver."

"And always put this in your pipe, Nolly," said the Dodger, as the Jew was heard unlocking the door above. "If you don't take pocket handkechers and watches," he said, reducing his conversation to the level of Oliver's understanding, "some other cove will."

"To be sure, to be sure!" said the Jew, who had entered, unseen by Oliver. "Take the Dodger's word for it. Ha! He understands the catechism of his trade."

The old man had returned home. Chairs were pulled up to the fire and the Jew, telling Oliver to come and sit by him, led the conversation to the topics most calculated to interest his hearers. These were the great advantages of the trade, the proficiency of the Dodger, the amiability of Charley Bates, and the liberality of the Jew himself.

From this day, Oliver was seldom left alone; but was with the two boys, who played the old game with the Jew every day – whether for their own improvement or Oliver's, Mr Fagin best knew. At other times the old man would tell them stories of robberies he had committed in his younger days: mixed up with so much that was droll and curious, that Oliver could not help laughing heartily, and showing that he was amused in spite of all his better feelings.

In short, the wily old Jew had the boy in his toils. Having prepared his mind, by solitude and gloom, to prefer any society to the companionship of his own sad thoughts, he was now slowly instilling into his soul the poison which he hoped would blacken it, and change it forever.

CHAPTER 18

It was a damp, windy night, when the Jew, buttoning his great-coat tight round his shrivelled body, emerged from his den. He paused on the step as the door was locked and chained behind him and then slunk down the street as quickly as he could.

The house to which Oliver had been taken, was in Whitechapel. The Jew stopped for an instant at the corner of the street and, glancing suspiciously round, crossed the road, and struck off in the direction of Spitalfields.

The mud lay thick upon the stones, and a black mist hung over the streets; the rain fell sluggishly down, and everything felt cold and clammy to the touch.

He kept on his course, through many winding and narrow ways, until he reached a maze of the mean and dirty streets. He hurried through several alleys, and at length turned into one. At the door of a house in this street, he knocked. Having exchanged a few muttered words with the person who opened it, he walked upstairs.

A dog growled as he touched the handle of a room-door, and a man's voice demanded who was there.

"Only me, Bill, my dear," said the Jew, looking in.

"Bring in your body then," said Sikes. "Lie down, you stupid brute! Don't you know the devil when he's got a great-coat on?"

The dog retired to the corner from which he had risen, wagging his tail as he went.

"Well!" said Sikes.

"Well, my dear," replied the Jew. "Ah! Nancy."

Mr Fagin and his young friend had not met, since she had interfered on behalf of Oliver. All doubts he may have had, however, were speedily removed by the young lady's behaviour. She took her feet off the fender, pushed back her chair, and bade Fagin draw up his, without saying more about it.

"It is cold, Nancy dear," said the Jew, as he warmed his skinny hands over the fire. "It seems to go right through one," he added.

"It must be a piercer, if it finds its way through your heart," said Mr Sikes.

The Jew glanced round the room, as his companion tossed down a glassful of brandy, in a restless and suspicious manner habitual to him. It was meanly furnished, with two or three heavy bludgeons standing in a corner.

"There," said Sikes, smacking his lips. "Now I'm ready."

"For business?" inquired the Jew.

"For business," replied Sikes. "So say what you've got to say."

"About the crib at Chertsey, Bill?" said the Jew, drawing his chair forward, and speaking in a very low voice.

"Yes. Wot about it?" inquired Sikes. "Speak out, and call things by their right names. Don't sit there talking in hints. Wot d'ye mean?"

"Hush, Bill, hush!" said the Jew, who had in vain attempted to stop this burst of indignation. "Somebody will hear us, my dear."

"Let 'em hear!" said Sikes. "I don't care." But as he did care, he dropped his voice, and grew calmer.

"There, there," said the Jew coaxingly. "About that crib at Chertsey – when is it to be done, Bill, eh? Such plate, my dear!" said the Jew, rubbing his hands, and raising his eyebrows in a rapture of anticipation.

"Not at all," replied Sikes coldly.

"Not at all!" echoed the Jew, leaning back in his chair.

"No, not at all," rejoined Sikes. "Toby Crackit has been hanging about there for a fortnight, and he can't get one of the servants into a line."

"Do you mean to say, Bill," said the Jew, "that neither of the two men in the house can be got over?"

"Yes, I do mean to tell you so," replied Sikes. "The old lady has had 'em these twenty year; and if you were to give 'em five hundred pound, they wouldn't be in it."

"It's a sad thing," said the old man, dropping his hands on his knees, "to lose so much when we had set our hearts upon it."

"So it is," said Mr Sikes. "Worse luck!"

A long silence ensued during which the Jew was plunged into deep thought. Sikes eyed him furtively from time to time. Nancy, apparently fearful of irritating the housebreaker, sat with her eyes fixed upon the fire, as though deaf to all that passed.

"Fagin," said Sikes, abruptly breaking the stillness, "is it worth fifty shiners extra, if it's safely done from the outside?"

"Yes," said the Jew, as suddenly rousing himself.

"Is it a bargain?" inquired Sikes.

"Yes, my dear, yes," rejoined the Jew, eyes glistening.

"Then," said Sikes, "let it come off as soon as you like. Toby and me were over the garden wall the night afore last, sounding the panels of the door and shutters. The crib's barred up at night like a jail, but there's one part we can crack, safe and softly."

"Which is that, Bill?" asked the Jew eagerly.

"Why," whispered Sikes, "as you cross the lawn – "

"Yes?" said the Jew, bending his head forward.

"Umph!" muttered Sikes, stopping short, as the girl, scarcely moving her head, pointed for an instant to the Jew's face. "Never mind which part it is. You can't do it without me."

"As you like," replied the Jew. "Is there no help wanted?"

"None," said Sikes. "'Cept a boy. You can find us the boy."

"A boy!" exclaimed the Jew. "Oh! Then it's a panel, eh?"

"Never mind wot it is!" replied Sikes. "I want a boy, and he mustn't be a big un."

The Jew nodded his head towards Nancy, who still gazed at the fire, and intimated, by a sign, that she should leave the room. Sikes shrugged his shoulders, then requested that Nancy fetch beer.

"You don't want any beer," said Nancy, folding her arms.

"I tell you I do!" replied Sikes.

"Nonsense," rejoined the girl coolly. "Go on, Fagin. I know what he's going to say, Bill. He needn't mind me."

The Jew still hesitated. Sikes looked from one to the other in some surprise.

"Tell Bill at once, about Oliver!" said Nancy.

"Ha! you're a clever one, my dear!" said the Jew, patting her on the neck. "It was about Oliver I was going to speak."

"What about him?" demanded Sikes.

"He's the boy for you, my dear," replied the Jew in a hoarse whisper, and grinning.

"He!" exclaimed Sikes.

"Have him, Bill!" said Nancy. "I would, if I was you. He's only to open a door for you. Depend upon it he's a safe one, Bill."

"I know he is," rejoined Fagin. "He's been in good training these last few weeks, and it's time he began to work for his bread. Besides, the others are all too big."

"Well, he is just the size I want," said Mr Sikes, ruminating.

"And will do everything you want, Bill, my dear," interposed the Jew, "he can't help himself. That is, if you frighten him enough."

"Frighten him!" echoed Sikes. "It'll be no sham frightening, mind you. If there's anything queer about him, you won't see him alive again, Fagin. Think of that, before you send him. Mark my words!"

"I've thought of it all," said the Jew with energy. "I've had my eye upon him, my dears, close. Once fill his mind with the idea that he has been a thief; and he's ours! For life. Oho! It couldn't have come about better!" The old man crossed his arms, literally hugging himself for joy.

"Ours!" said Sikes. "Yours, you mean."

"Perhaps I do, my dear," said the Jew, with a shrill chuckle.

"And wot," said Sikes, scowling fiercely, "wot makes you take so much pains about one chalk-faced kid, when you know there are fifty boys you might pick from?"

"Because they're of no use to me, my dear," replied the Jew, with some confusion, "not worth the taking. Their looks convict 'em when they get into trouble. With this boy, properly managed, my dears, I could do what I couldn't with twenty of them. Besides," said the Jew, recovering his self-possession, "he must be in the same boat with us. Never mind how he came there; it's quite enough for my power over him that he was in a robbery. That's all I want."

"When is it to be done?" asked Nancy.

"Ah, to be sure," said the Jew, "when is it to be done, Bill?"

"I planned with Toby, the night arter tomorrow," rejoined Sikes in a surly voice, "if he heerd nothing from me to the contrairy."

"Good," said the Jew. "There's no moon."

"No," rejoined Sikes. "You'd better bring the boy here tomorrow night. I shall get off the stones an hour arter daybreak. Then you hold your tongue and keep the melting-pot ready, and that's all you'll have to do."

After some discussion, it was decided that Nancy should go to the Jew's next evening, and bring Oliver away with her. Fagin felt he would be more willing to accompany the girl who had so recently interfered in his behalf, than anybody else. Poor Oliver should, for the purposes of the contemplated expedition, be unreservedly consigned to the care and custody of Mr William Sikes. Sikes should deal with him as he thought fit, and should not be held responsible by the Jew for any mischance that might befall him, or any punishment that might be necessary.

Mr Sikes proceeded to drink brandy at a furious rate. At length, in a fit of professional enthusiasm, he insisted upon producing his box of housebreaking tools. He explained the nature and properties of the various implements, and the peculiar beauties of each; then he fell over the box upon the floor, and went to sleep where he fell.

"Good night, Nancy," said the Jew, muffling himself up as before.

Their eyes met, and the Jew scrutinised her, narrowly. He bestowed a sly kick upon the prostrate form of Mr Sikes while her back was turned, then groped down stairs.

The Dodger was sitting up, impatiently awaiting his return.

"Is Oliver a-bed? I want to speak to him," was Fagin's first remark as they descended the stairs.

"Hours ago," replied the Dodger, throwing open a door. "Here he is!"

The boy was lying, fast asleep, so pale with anxiety, and the closeness of his prison, that he looked like death.

"Not now," said the Jew, turning softly away. "Tomorrow. Tomorrow."

CHAPTER 19

When Oliver awoke in the morning, he was surprised to find a new pair of shoes, with strong thick soles, at his bedside. His old shoes had been removed. He hoped that it might be the forerunner of his release; but such thoughts were quickly dispelled, on his sitting down to breakfast along with the Jew. He told him that he was to be taken to Bill Sikes that night.

"To – to – stop there, sir?" asked Oliver, anxiously.

"No, no, my dear. Not to stop there," replied the Jew. "We shouldn't like to lose you."

"I suppose," said the Jew, fixing his eyes on Oliver, "you want to know what you're going to Bill's for – eh, my dear?"

Oliver blushed to find that the old thief had been reading his thoughts, but boldly said, Yes, he did want to know.

"Why, do you think?" inquired Fagin, parrying the question.

"Indeed I don't know, sir," replied Oliver.

"Bah!" said the Jew in disappointment, turning away from a close perusal of the boy's face. "Wait till Bill tells you, then."

The Jew remained very surly and silent till night, when he prepared to go abroad.

"You may burn a candle," said the Jew, putting one upon the table. "And here's a book till they come for you. Good night!"

"Good night!" replied Oliver, softly.

The Jew walked to the door looking over his shoulder at the boy as he went. Suddenly stopping, he called him by his name.

"Take heed, Oliver!" said the old man, shaking his hand before him. "He's a rough man, and thinks nothing of blood when his own is up. Do what he bids you."

Oliver leaned his head upon his hand when the old man disappeared, and pondered on the words he had just heard. He concluded that he would be doing something menial for the housebreaker, until another boy, better suited for his purpose, could be engaged. He was too well accustomed to suffering, and had suffered too much where he was, to bewail the prospect of change very severely. He remained lost in thought for some minutes and then, with a heavy sigh, began to read.

He turned over the leaves. Carelessly at first, but, the pages soon attracted his attention, he became intent upon the volume. It was a history of the lives and trials of great criminals; and the pages were soiled with use. Here, he read of dreadful crimes that made the blood run cold, of secret murders that had been committed by the lonely wayside and of bodies hidden from the eye of man in deep pits and wells. The terrible descriptions were so real and vivid, that the sallow pages seemed to turn red with gore.

In total fear, the boy closed the book, and thrust it from him. Then, falling upon his knees, he prayed Heaven to spare him from such deeds.

He slowly grew more calm, and begged, in a broken voice, that he might be rescued from his present dangers. He had concluded his prayer, with his head buried in his hands, when a rustling noise aroused him.

"What's that!" he cried, starting up, and catching sight of a figure standing by the door. "Who's there?"

"Only me," replied a tremulous voice.

Oliver raised the candle above his head: it was Nancy.

"Put down the light," said the girl, turning. "It hurts my eyes."

Oliver saw that she was very pale, and gently inquired if she were ill. The girl threw herself into a chair, with her back towards him and wrung her hands; but made no reply.

"God forgive me!" she cried after a while. "I never thought of this."

"Has anything happened?" asked Oliver. "Can I help you?"

She rocked herself and, uttering a gurgling sound, gasped for breath.

"Nancy!" cried Oliver. "What is it?"

The girl beat her hands upon her knees, and her feet upon the ground and, suddenly stopping, drew her shawl close round her, and shivered with cold. Oliver stirred the fire. Drawing her chair close to it, she sat there, for a little time, without speaking. At length she raised her head, and looked round.

"I don't know what comes over me sometimes," said she, busying herself in arranging her dress. "It's this damp dirty room, I think. Now, Nolly, dear, are you ready?"

"Am I to go with you?" asked Oliver.

"Yes. I have come from Bill," replied the girl. "You are to go with me."

"What for?" asked Oliver, recoiling.

"What for?" echoed the girl, raising her eyes, and averting them again, when they encountered the boy's face. "Oh! For no harm."

"I don't believe it," said Oliver who had watched her closely.

"Have it your own way," rejoined the girl, affecting to laugh. "For no good, then."

Oliver could see that he had some power over the girl's better feelings, and, for an instant, thought of appealing to her. But, then, he realised that it was barely eleven o'clock; and that there would still be many people on the streets. Surely some might be found who would believe him. As the thought occurred to him, he stepped forward: and said, somewhat hastily, that he was ready.

Nancy eyed him narrowly, while he spoke and looked at him in a way that showed she guessed what his thoughts had been.

"Hush!" said the girl, stooping over him, and pointing to the door as she looked cautiously round. "You can't help yourself. I have tried hard for you, but all to no purpose. If ever you are to be free this is not the time."

Struck by her words, Oliver looked up in her face with surprise. She seemed to speak the truth – she trembled with very earnestness.

"I have saved you from being ill-used once, and I will again, and I do now," continued the girl aloud. "For those who would have fetched you, if I had not, would have been far more rough than me. I have promised you will be quiet, if not, you will only do harm to yourself and me too, and perhaps be my death. See here! I have borne all this for you already, as true as God sees me show it."

She pointed, hastily, to some livid bruises on her neck and arms, and continued swiftly: "Remember this! Don't let me suffer more for you. If I could help you, I would, but I have not the power. They don't mean to harm you. Whatever they make you do is no fault of yours. Hush! Every word from you is a blow for me. Give me your hand. Make haste!"

She caught the hand that Oliver instinctively placed in hers, and, blowing out the light drew him after her up the stairs. The door was opened, quickly, by someone hidden in the darkness, and was as quickly closed. A hackney-cabriolet was waiting. The girl pulled him in with her, and closed the curtains. The driver wanted no directions, but lashed his horse into full speed, without a moment's delay.

The girl still held Oliver by the hand, and continued to pour into his ear the warnings she had already imparted. All was so quick that he had scarcely time to know where he was when the carriage stopped at the house the Jew had visited the previous evening.

For one brief moment, Oliver cast a hurried glance along the empty street, and a cry for help hung upon his lips. But the girl's voice was in his ear, beseeching him in agonised tones to remember her, that he could not utter it. He hesitated and the moment was gone. He was in the house, and the door was shut.

"This way," said the girl, releasing him for the first time. "Bill!"

"Hallo!" replied Sikes, from the head of the stairs. "Come on! Bull's-eye's gone home with Tom. He'd have been in the way."

"That's right," rejoined Nancy.

"So you've got the kid," said Sikes, when they had all reached the room. He closed the door as he spoke.

"Yes, here he is," replied Nancy.

"Did he come quiet?" inquired Sikes.

"Like a lamb," rejoined Nancy.

"I'm glad to hear it," said Sikes, looking grimly at Oliver, "for the sake of his young carcass. Come here, young un and let me read you a lectur', which is as well got over at once."

Mr Sikes pulled off Oliver's cap and threw it into a corner; and then, taking him by the shoulder, sat down by the table, and stood the boy in front of him.

"Now, first, do you know wot this is?" inquired Sikes, taking up a pocket-pistol that lay on the table.

Oliver nodded.

"Well, then, look here," continued Sikes. "This is powder, that 'ere's a bullet and this is a little bit of a old hat for waddin'." He then proceeded to load the pistol, with great nicety and deliberation.

"Now it's loaded," said Mr Sikes, when he had finished.

"Yes, I see it is, sir," replied Oliver.

"Well," said the robber, grasping Oliver's wrist, touching the barrel to his temple, "if you speak a word when you're out o' doors with me, except when I speak to you, that loading will be in your head without notice. So, if you do decide to speak without leave, say your prayers first."

"What you mean," said Nancy slightly frowning at Oliver as if to have his full attention to her words. "Is that if you're crossed by him in this job you'll prevent his ever telling tales afterwards, by shooting him through the head."

"That's it!" observed Mr Sikes, approvingly. "Now, let's have some supper, and get a snooze before starting."

Nancy quickly laid the cloth and added a pot of porter and a dish of sheep's heads. Mr Sikes was in great spirits and good humour and humorously drank all the beer at a draught.

Supper over, Mr Sikes disposed of a couple of glasses of spirits and water, and threw himself on the bed, ordering Nancy to call him at five precisely. Oliver stretched himself on a mattress upon the floor and the girl sat before the fire, ready to rouse them.

For a long time Oliver lay awake, thinking that Nancy might whisper further advice, but the girl sat brooding over the fire, without moving, save now and then to trim the light. Weary with watching and anxiety, he at length slept.

When he awoke, the table was covered with tea-things, and Sikes was thrusting various articles into the pockets of his great-coat, which hung over the back of a chair. Nancy was busily preparing breakfast. It was not yet daylight; for the candle was still burning. A sharp rain, too, was beating against the windows, and the sky looked black and cloudy.

"Now, then!" growled Sikes, as Oliver started up. "Half-past five! Look sharp, or you'll get no breakfast, for it's late as it is."

Oliver had some breakfast, and was then quite ready.

Nancy, scarcely looking at the boy, threw him a handkerchief to tie round his throat. Sikes gave him a large rough cape to go over his shoulders. Then he gave his hand to the robber, who, pausing to show him that he had the pistol in a side pocket, clasped it firmly in his, and, exchanging a farewell with Nancy, led him off.

Oliver turned at the door, hoping for a look from the girl. But she was in her old seat before the fire, sitting perfectly motionless.

CHAPTER 20

It was a cheerless morning when they got into the street; blowing and raining hard; and the clouds looking dull and stormy. The night had been wet – large pools of water lay in the road and the kennels were overflowing. There was a faint glimmering of the coming day in the sky. The windows of the houses were all closely shut, and the streets they passed through were empty.

By the time they had turned into the Bethnal Green Road, the day had fairly begun to break. Many of the lamps were already extinguished. The public houses, with gas-lights burning inside, were already open. Other shops began to open, and a few scattered people were met with. Then, came straggling groups of labourers – people with fish-baskets on their heads, carts laden with vegetables, live-stock or whole carcasses of meat, milk-women with pails. As they approached the City, the noise and traffic increased. When they threaded the streets between Shoreditch and Smithfield, it had swelled into a roar of sound and bustle. It was as light as it was likely to be, till night came on again.

Mr Sikes, dragging Oliver after him, elbowed his way through the thickest of the crowd, and bestowed very little attention on the numerous sights and sounds, which so astonished the boy. He nodded, twice or thrice, to a passing friend, and, resisting as many invitations to take a morning dram, pressed steadily onward, until they were clear of the turmoil, and into Holborn.

"Now, young un!" said Sikes, looking up at the clock of St Andrew's Church. "Hard upon seven! You must step out. Don't lag behind already, Lazylegs!"

Mr Sikes accompanied this speech with a jerk at his little companion's wrist. Oliver quickened to a kind of trot, keeping up with the rapid strides of the housebreaker as well as he could.

They held their course at this rate, until they had passed Hyde Park corner, and were on their way to Kensington.

An empty cart came up. Seeing "Hounslow" written on it, Mr Sikes asked the driver with as much civility as he could assume, for a lift as far as Isleworth.

"Jump up," said the man. "Is that your boy?"

"Yes; he's my boy," replied Sikes, looking hard at Oliver, and putting his hand on the pocket where the pistol was.

"Your father walks rather too quick for you, don't he, my man?" inquired the driver, seeing that Oliver was out of breath.

"Not a bit of it," interposed Sikes. "He's used to it. Here, take my hand, Ned. In with you!"

Thus addressing Oliver, he helped him into the cart. The driver, pointing to a heap of sacks, told him to rest.

As they passed the different milestones, Oliver wondered, more and more, where his companion meant to take him. Kensington, Hammersmith, Chiswick, Kew Bridge, Brentford, were all passed. At length, they came to a public house called the Coach and Horses, a little way beyond which another road turned off. Here, the cart stopped.

Sikes dismounted swiftly, holding Oliver's hand all the while. He rapped his side pocket with his fist.

"Good-bye, boy," said the man.

"He's sulky," replied Sikes, giving him a shake. "Don't mind him."

"Not I!" rejoined the other, getting into his cart. "It's a fine day, after all." And he drove away.

They then turned round to the left, a short way past the public house. Taking a right-hand road, they passed many large gardens and gentlemen's houses on both sides of the way until they reached a town. Here, Oliver saw written up in pretty large letters, "Hampton." They lingered in the fields for some hours. At length, they went into an old public house to have some cold meat for dinner, and sat so long after it, while Sikes indulged himself with several pipes, that Oliver began to feel quite certain they were not going any further. Being tired with the walk and getting up so early, he dozed a little at first then, quite overpowered by fatigue and the fumes of the tobacco, fell asleep.

It was quite dark when he was awakened by a push from Sikes. Rousing himself, he found him in close conversation with a labouring man, over a pint of ale.

"So, you're going on to Lower Halliford, are you?" inquired Sikes. "Could you give my boy and me a lift as far as there?"

"If you're going directly, I can," replied the man. "Going to Halliford?"

"On to Shepperton," replied Sikes.

"I'm your man, as far as I go," replied the other.

The night was very dark. A damp mist rose from the river. It was piercing cold, too. Not a word was spoken. The driver had grown sleepy and Sikes was in no mood for conversation. Oliver sat huddled, in a corner of the cart, totally bewildered.

As they passed Sunbury Church, the clock struck seven. Two or three miles later the cart stopped. Sikes alighted, took Oliver by the hand, and they once again walked on.

They turned into no house at Shepperton, as the weary boy had expected, but kept walking on, in mud and darkness, through gloomy lanes, until they came within sight of the lights of a town. Oliver could see that they were coming to the foot of a bridge.

Sikes kept straight on, until they were close upon the bridge, then turned suddenly down a bank upon the left.

"The water!" thought Oliver, sick with fear. "He has brought me to this lonely place to murder me!"

He was about to throw himself on the ground, when he saw they stood before a solitary house. There was a window on each side of the dilapidated entrance and one storey above. No light was visible. The house was dark, and uninhabited.

Sikes, with Oliver's hand still in his, softly approached the low porch, and raised the latch. The door opened and they passed in.

CHAPTER 21

"Hallo!" cried a loud, hoarse voice, as they set foot in the passage.

"Don't make such a row," said Sikes, bolting the door. "Show a glim, Toby. Here! You get on first." He put Oliver in front of him. "Quicker, or I shall tread upon your heels."

They entered a low dark room with a smoky fire, two or three broken chairs, a table, and a very old couch. A man was reposing at full length on the couch, smoking a long clay pipe. He was dressed in a snuff-coloured coat, with large brass buttons and drab breeches. Mr Crackit (for he it was) had no great quantity of hair, either upon his head or face, but what he had, was of a reddish dye, and tortured into long corkscrew curls.

"Bill, my boy!" said Toby, turning towards the door, "I'm glad to see you. I was almost afraid you'd given up. Hallo!" Uttering this exclamation in a tone of surprise, as his eye rested on Oliver, Mr Toby Crackit sat up, and demanded who that was.

"Only the boy!" replied Sikes, drawing a chair towards the fire.

"One of Fagin's lads," exclaimed Toby. "Wot an inwalable boy, for the old ladies' pockets in chapels! His mug is a fortun' to him."

"There's enough of that," interposed Sikes, and he whispered a few words in his ear. Mr Crackit laughed immensely, and honoured Oliver with a long stare of astonishment.

"Now," said Sikes, as he took a seat, "give us something to eat and drink while we're waiting. Sit down by the fire, younker, and rest; for you're out with us again tonight, though not far."

Oliver pulled a stool to the fire, and sat with his aching head upon his hands, scarcely knowing where he was.

73

"Here," said Toby. "Success to the crack!" He advanced to the table, filled a glass with spirits, and drank off its contents. Mr Sikes did the same.

"A drain for the boy," said Toby, half-filling a wine glass. "Down with it, innocence."

"Indeed, I – " said Oliver, looking piteously up into the man's face.

"Down with it!" echoed Toby. "Tell him to drink it, Bill."

"He had better!" said Sikes, clapping his hand upon his pocket.

Frightened by the two men, Oliver hastily swallowed the contents, and immediately fell into a fit of coughing, which delighted Toby Crackit.

Sikes ate (Oliver could eat nothing but a small crust of bread that they made him swallow), and the two men laid themselves down on chairs for a short nap. Oliver kept his stool by the fire.

Oliver fell into a heavy doze, imagining himself straying along the gloomy lanes, or wandering about the dark churchyard. He was roused by Toby jumping up and declaring it was half-past one.

In an instant, Sikes and his companion had enveloped their necks and chins in large dark shawls, and drew on their great-coats.

"Barkers for me," declared Toby. "The persuaders?"

"I've got 'em," replied Sikes.

"Crape, keys, centre-bits, darkies – nothing forgotten?" inquired Toby, fastening a small crowbar to a loop inside his coat.

"Now then!" said Sikes, holding out his hand.

Oliver who was completely stupefied by the unwonted exercise, and the air, and the drink that had been forced upon him, put his hand mechanically into that of Sikes.

"Take his other hand, Toby," said Sikes.

They went to the door, to see that all was quiet. The two robbers issued forth with Oliver between them.

It was now intensely dark. The fog was much heavier than it had been in the early part of the night. They crossed the bridge, and kept on towards the lights he had seen before. They were at no great distance off and, as they walked pretty briskly, they soon reached Chertsey.

"Straight through the town," whispered Sikes.

They hurried through the main street, which at that late hour was wholly deserted. Occasionally a dim light shone from a bedroom window and the barking of dogs occasionally broke the silence. They had cleared the town, as the church bell struck two.

Quickening their pace, they turned up a road. After walking about a quarter of a mile, they stopped by a detached house surrounded by a wall. Toby Crackit climbed to the top of this in a twinkling.

"The boy next," said Toby. "Hoist him up. I'll catch hold of him."

Before Oliver had time to look round, Sikes had caught him under the arms. Three or four seconds later he and Toby were lying on the grass on the other side. Sikes followed directly. And they stole cautiously towards the house.

For the first time, Oliver, almost mad with grief and terror, saw that housebreaking and robbery, if not murder, were the objects of the expedition. He clasped his hands together, and involuntarily uttered a subdued exclamation of horror. A mist came before his eyes, cold sweat stood upon his ashy face. He sank to his knees.

"Get up!" murmured Sikes, trembling with rage, and drawing the pistol from his pocket. "Or I'll strew your brains upon the grass."

"Oh! For God's sake let me go!" cried Oliver; "Let me run away and die in the fields. I will never come near London! Oh! Pray do not make me steal. For the love of all the Angels, have mercy!"

Sikes swore and had cocked the pistol, when Toby, striking it from his grasp, placed his hand upon the boy's mouth, and dragged him to the house.

"Hush!" cried the man. "Say another word, and I'll do it myself with a crack on the head. That makes no noise, and is just as effective. Here Bill, pull at the shutter. He's game now. I've seen older hands his age do the same, for a moment, on a cold night."

Sikes, muttering threats upon Fagin's head, plied the crowbar vigorously, but with little noise. After some delay, and some assistance from Toby, the shutter swung open on its hinges.

It was a little lattice window, about five feet above the ground, at the back of the house. It belonged to a scullery at the end of the passage. The aperture was so small, that the residents had probably not thought it worth defending more securely. However it was large enough to admit a boy of Oliver's size. Moments later the lattice stood wide open also.

"Now listen," whispered Sikes, drawing a dark lantern from his pocket, and throwing the glare full on Oliver's face. "I'm a going to put you through there. Take this light, go softly up the steps straight afore you, and along the hall, to the main door. Unfasten it, and let us in."

"There's a bolt at the top, you won't be able to reach," interposed Toby. "Stand upon one of the hall chairs."

Although Mr Crackit spoke in a scarcely audible whisper, Sikes commanded him to be silent, and to get to work. Toby complied, by first producing his lantern, then by planting himself firmly with his head against the wall beneath the window, so as to make a step of his back. Sikes, mounting upon him, put Oliver gently through the window with his feet first. Without releasing his collar, he planted him safely on the floor inside.

"Take this lantern," said Sikes, looking into the room. "You see the stairs?"

Oliver, more dead than alive, gasped out: "Yes." Sikes, pointing to the street-door with the pistol-barrel, advised him that he was within shot all the way and that if he faltered, he would fall dead.

"It's done in a minute," said Sikes, in the same low whisper. "Directly I leave go of you, do your work. Hark!"

"What's that?" whispered the other man.

They listened intently.

"Nothing," said Sikes, releasing his hold of Oliver. "Now!"

At that moment, the boy had firmly resolved that, whether he died in the attempt or not, he would try to dart up stairs from the hall, and alarm the family. He advanced at once, but stealthily.

"Come back!" cried Sikes aloud suddenly. "Back!"

Scared by the sudden breaking of the dead stillness, Oliver let his lantern fall, and knew not whether to advance or fly.

The cry was repeated – a light appeared – a vision of two terrified half-dressed men at the top of the stairs. A flash! A loud noise! Smoke. A crash somewhere and he staggered back.

Sikes had disappeared for an instant but he was up again, and had him by the collar before the smoke had cleared away. He fired his own pistol after the men, who were already retreating, and dragged the boy up.

"Clasp your arm tighter," said Sikes, drawing him through the window. "Give me a shawl. They've hit him. How the boy bleeds!"

Then the loud ringing of a bell mingled with the noise of guns, and the shouts of men, and the sensation of being swiftly carried over uneven ground. The noises grew confused in the distance. A cold feeling crept over the boy and he saw or heard no more.

CHAPTER 22

The night was bitter cold. The snow lay on the ground, frozen into a hard thick crust. Bleak, dark, and piercing cold, it was a night for the well-housed and fed to draw round the bright fire and thank God they were at home – and for the homeless, starving wretch to lay down and die.

And so Mrs Corney, the matron of the workhouse, the birthplace of Oliver Twist, sat herself down before a cheerful fire. She was about to have a cup of tea.

"Well!" said the matron, leaning her elbow on the table, and looking reflectively at the fire. "I'm sure we all have a great deal to be grateful for! A great deal, if we did but know it. Ah!"

Mrs Corney shook her head mournfully, as if deploring the mental blindness of those paupers who did not know it. She then thrust a silver spoon (private property) into the inmost recesses of a two-ounce tin tea-caddy, and proceeded to make the tea.

The black teapot, being very small and easily filled, ran over while Mrs Corney was moralising. The water slightly scalded Mrs Corney's hand.

"Drat the pot!" said the worthy matron, setting it down. "A little stupid thing, that only holds a couple of cups! What use is it of, to anybody! Except," said Mrs Corney, pausing, "except to a poor desolate creature like me. Oh dear!"

With these words, she dropped into her chair, and, once more resting her elbow on the table, thought of her solitary fate. The small teapot and the single cup had awakened in her mind sad recollections of Mr Corney, five-and-twenty years dead.

"I shall never get another!" said Mrs Corney. "Not like him."

Whether this remark concerned the husband, or the teapot, is uncertain. It might have been the latter for Mrs Corney looked at it as she spoke. She had just tasted her first cup, when there was a soft tap at the door.

"Oh, come in with you!" said Mrs Corney, sharply. "Some of the old women dying, I suppose. They always die when I'm at meals. Don't stand there, letting the cold air in. What's amiss now, eh?"

"Nothing, ma'am, nothing," replied a man's voice.

"Dear me!" exclaimed the matron, in a much sweeter tone, "is that Mr Bumble?"

"At your service, ma'am," said Mr Bumble, who had stopped outside to rub his shoes clean, and to shake the snow off his coat. He now appeared, bearing the cocked hat in one hand and a bundle in the other. "Shall I shut the door, ma'am?"

The lady modestly hesitated to reply, lest there should be any impropriety in holding an interview with Mr Bumble, with closed doors. Mr Bumble taking advantage of the hesitation, shut it.

"Hard weather, Mr Bumble," said the matron.

"Hard, indeed, ma'am," replied the beadle. "We have given away a matter of twenty quartern loaves and a cheese and a half, this very blessed afternoon and still them paupers are not contented."

"When would they be, Mr Bumble?" said the matron, sipping tea.

"When, indeed, ma'am," rejoined Mr Bumble. "Why here's one man with a large family, received a quartern loaf and a good pound of cheese. Is he grateful, ma'am? Not a farthing's worth! What does he do but ask for a few coals – if it's only a pocket handkerchief full, he says! What would he do with coals? Toast his cheese with 'em, and then come back for more. That's the way with these people, give 'em a apron full of coals today, and they'll come back for more, tomorrow."

The matron smiled in agreement

The beadle paused to unpack his bundle. "These are official secrets, ma'am, not to be spoken of. This is the port wine, ma'am, ordered for the infirmary. Real, fresh, genuine port wine, out of the cask this forenoon!"

Mr Bumble placed both bottles on the top of a chest of drawers. He then folded the handkerchief in which they had been wrapped, put it in his pocket; and took up his hat, as if to go.

"You'll have a very cold walk, Mr Bumble," said the matron.

"It blows, ma'am," replied Mr Bumble, turning up his coat-collar, "enough to cut one's ears off."

The matron looked, from the little kettle, to the beadle, who was moving towards the door. As the beadle coughed, preparatory to bidding her good night, she bashfully inquired whether he wouldn't take a cup of tea?

Mr Bumble instantly turned back his collar again, laid his hat and cane upon a chair; and drew another chair up to the table. As he slowly seated himself, he looked at the lady. She fixed her eyes upon the little teapot. Mr Bumble coughed again, and smiled.

Mrs Corney rose to get another cup and saucer from the closet.

"Sugar? Mr Bumble?" inquired the matron, taking up the sugar.

"Indeed, ma'am," replied Mr Bumble. He fixed his eyes on Mrs Corney as he said this, and if ever a beadle looked tender, Mr Bumble was that beadle at that moment.

The tea was made, and handed in silence.

The beadle drank his tea to the last drop, finished his toast, wiped his lips, and deliberately kissed the matron.

"Mr Bumble!" cried the lady in a whisper, for the fright was so great, she quite lost her voice, "Mr Bumble, I shall scream!" Mr Bumble made no reply; but slowly put his arm round her waist.

There was a hasty knocking at the door which was no sooner heard, than Mr Bumble darted, with much agility, to the wine bottles, and began dusting them with great violence. The matron sharply demanded who was there. It is worthy of remark, that her voice had quite recovered all its official asperity.

"If you please, mistress," said a withered old female pauper. "Old Sally is a-going fast."

"Well, what's that to me?" demanded the matron. "I can't keep her alive, can I?"

"No, no, mistress," replied the old woman, "nobody can, she's far beyond the reach of help. But she's troubled and she says she has got something to tell, which you must hear. She'll never die quiet till you come, mistress."

At this intelligence, the worthy Mrs Corney, muttering about old women who would not die quietly, muffled herself in a thick shawl, and requested Mr Bumble to stay till she came back, lest anything particular should occur. Bidding the messenger walk fast, and not be all night hobbling up the stairs, she followed her.

Mr Bumble's conduct was then rather inexplicable. He opened the closet, counted teaspoons, weighed sugar-tongs, inspected a silver milk-pot to be sure that it was genuine. He then stood before the fire and seemed to be mentally taking an inventory of the furniture.

CHAPTER 23

The messenger of death who had disturbed the quiet of the matron's room was bent by age, her limbs trembling with palsy. She tottered along the passages, and up the stairs. Pausing for breath, she put the light into her companion's hand, and followed as she might, while the more nimble superior made her way to the room where the sick woman lay.

It was a bare garret-room, with a dim light burning at the far end. Another old woman watched the bed. There was a moan from the bed.

The mistress, with an expression of impatience, wrapped herself in her shawl, and sat at the foot of the bed. The old crone finally joined them.

"You, Martha, tell me," demanded the mistress. "Has she been in this way before?"

"Often," answered the first woman.

"Well, it's not my duty to see all the old women in the house die."

She turned away, when a cry from the two women, who had turned towards the bed, caused her to look round. The patient had raised herself upright, and was stretching her arms towards them.

"Who's that?" she cried, in a hollow voice.

"Hush, hush!" said one of the women, going to her. "Lie down!"

"I'll never lie down again alive!" said the woman, struggling. "I will tell her! Come nearer! Let me whisper in your ear."

She clutched the matron by the arm, forcing her into a chair by the bedside. She caught sight of the two old women.

"Turn them away," said the old woman, drowsily. "Make haste!"

The superior pushed them from the room, closed the door, and returned to the bedside.

"Now listen to me," said the dying woman. "In this very room – in this very bed – I once nursed a pretty young creetur, that was brought into the house with her feet cut and bruised with walking. She gave birth to a boy, and died. What was the year again?"

"Never mind the year," said Mrs Corney, "what about her?"

"I robbed her, so I did! She wasn't cold, when I stole it!"

"Stole what, for God's sake?" cried the matron.

"It!" replied the woman, laying her hand over the other's mouth. "The

80

only thing she had. She needed clothes and food but she had kept it safe. It was gold, that might have saved her life!"

"Gold!" echoed the matron, bending over the woman as she fell back. "Go on – what of it? Who was the mother? When was it?"

"She charged me to keep it safe," groaned the woman, "and trusted me as the only woman near her. I stole it in my heart when she first showed it me, and the child's death, perhaps, is on me too! They would have treated him better, if they had known it all!"

"Known what?" asked the other. "Speak!"

"The boy grew so like his mother," said the woman, rambling on, "that I could never forget it when I saw his face. Poor girl! She was so young, too! Wait, I have not told you all."

"Be quick, or it may be too late!" replied the matron, inclining her head to catch the words.

"The mother," said the woman, making a more violent effort than before, "the mother, feeling that death was close, whispered in my ear that if her baby lived, the day might come when it would not feel disgraced to hear its poor young mother named. 'And oh, kind Heaven!' she said, folding her thin hands together, 'whether it be boy or girl, find some friends for it in this troubled world, and take pity upon a lonely child.'"

"The boy's name?" demanded the matron.

"They called him Oliver," replied the woman, feebly. "The gold I stole was – "

"Yes, yes – what?" cried the other.

She once again rose slowly into a sitting position, then clutched the cover with both hands, muttered some indistinct sounds and fell lifeless on the bed.

"Stone dead!" said one of the old women, hurrying in as soon as the door was opened.

"And nothing to tell, after all," rejoined the matron, walking away.

CHAPTER 24

While these things were passing in the country workhouse, Mr Fagin sat in the den – brooding over a dull, smoky fire.

At a table behind him sat the Artful Dodger and Master Charles Bates, intent upon a game of cards. It being a cold night, the Dodger wore his hat, as, indeed, was often his custom within doors.

"Hark!" cried the Dodger suddenly. "I heard the tinkler." Catching up the light, he crept softly up stairs.

The bell was rung again, with some impatience, while the party were in darkness. After a short pause, the Dodger reappeared, and whispered to Fagin.

"What!" cried the Jew, "alone?"

The Dodger nodded in the affirmative, and, shading the flame of the candle with his hand gave Charley Bates a private intimation, in dumb show, that he had better not be funny just then. He then awaited his directions.

The old man bit his yellow fingers, meditating for some seconds. At length he raised his head.

"Where is he?" he asked.

The Dodger pointed to the floor above.

"Bring him down," said the Jew, answering the mute inquiry. "Hush! Quiet, Charley! Scarce!"

This brief direction to Charley Bates was immediately obeyed. The Dodger descended the stairs, bearing the light in his hand, followed by a man in a coarse smock frock. After a hurried glance round the room, he pulled off a large wrapper to reveal the haggard, unwashed and unshaved features of Toby Crackit.

"How are you, Faguey?" he said, nodding to the Jew. "Pop that shawl away in my castor, Dodger."

With these words he pulled up the smock frock and, winding it round his middle, drew a chair to the fire.

"See there, Faguey," he said, pointing disconsolately to his top-boots. "Not a bubble of blacking, by Jove! But don't look at me like that, man. All in good time. I can't talk business till I've eat and drank; so let's have something for the first time in three days!"

The Jew motioned to the Dodger to place what eatables there were upon the table, and, seating himself opposite Toby, waited.

Toby was by no means in a hurry. At first, the Jew patiently watched his countenance, as if to gain some clue to the intelligence he brought; but in vain. The Jew then paced up and down the room in irrepressible excitement. It was all of no use. Toby continued to eat with the utmost outward indifference, until he could eat no more. Then, ordering the Dodger out, he closed the door, mixed a glass of spirits and water, and composed himself for talking.

"First and foremost, Faguey," said Toby, "how's Bill?"

"What!" screamed the Jew, starting from his seat.

"Why, you don't mean to say – " began Toby, turning pale.

"Mean!" cried the Jew, stamping furiously on the ground. "Where are they? Sikes and the boy! Why have they not been here?"

"The crack failed," said Toby, faintly.

"I know it," replied the Jew, tearing a newspaper from his pocket. "What more?"

"They fired and hit the boy. We cut over the field, with him between us – through hedge and ditch. They gave chase. The whole country was awake, and the dogs upon us."

"The boy!"

"Bill had him on his back, and scudded like the wind. We stopped to take him between us – his head hung down, and he was cold. They were close on our heels, every man for himself! We parted and left the youngster lying in a ditch. Alive or dead, that's all I know about him."

The Jew stopped to hear no more; but uttering a loud yell, and tearing his hair, rushed from the room, and from the house.

CHAPTER 25

The old man had gained the street corner, before he began to recover the effect of Toby Crackit's news. He had relaxed nothing of his unusual speed but skulking only through the byways and alleys, he at length emerged on Snow Hill. Here he walked even faster until he had again turned into a court.

Near to the spot on which Snow Hill and Holborn Hill meet, there opens a dismal alley leading to Saffron Hill. Hundreds of second-hand handkerchiefs hang dangling from pegs outside the windows, and the shelves within are piled with them.

It was into this place that the Jew turned. He was well known there and was nodded to, familiarly, as he passed along. He replied to their salutations in the same way.

The Three Cripples, known as the Cripples, was the public house in which Mr Sikes and his dog have already figured. Making a sign to a man at the bar, Fagin walked straight upstairs, and opening the door of a room, he looked anxiously about, as if in search of someone.

The room was illuminated by two gas-lights. Barred shutters, and closely-drawn curtains prevented the light from being visible outside. The ceiling was blackened, and the place was so full of dense tobacco smoke, that at first it was scarcely possible to discern anything more. By degrees, however, some of it cleared away through the open door.

Fagin stepped softly in, to see a numerous company, male and female crowded round a long table. A professional gentleman, with a bluish nose, and his face tied up for the benefit of a toothache, presided at a jingling piano in a remote corner.

The professional gentleman, running over the keys by way of prelude, occasioned a general cry of order for a song. A young lady proceeded to entertain the company with a ballad in four verses.

Near him the singers received the compliments of the company, and applied themselves, in turn, to a dozen proffered glasses of spirits and water, tendered by their more boisterous admirers. Women – some with the last lingering tinge of their early freshness fading as you looked. Others with every stamp of their sex utterly beaten out, and presenting but one loathsome blank of crime. Some mere girls, others but young women, and none past the prime of life – all formed the dark and sad portion of this dreary picture.

Fagin looked eagerly from face to face, but apparently without seeing that of which he was in search. Succeeding, at length, in catching the eye of the man who occupied the chair, he beckoned to him slightly, and left the room, as quietly as he had entered it.

"What can I do for you, Mr Fagin?" inquired the landlord, as he followed him out to the landing. "Won't you join us?"

The Jew shook his head, and said in a whisper, "Is he here?"

"No," replied the landlord. "He won't stir till it's all safe. Depend on it."

"Will Monks be here tonight?" asked the Jew.

"Certain," replied the man, drawing out a gold watch. "I expected him here before now. If you wait ten minutes, he'll be – "

"No, no," said the Jew, hastily; as though, however much he might wish to see the person in question, he was nevertheless relieved by his absence. "Tell him I came here to see him and that he must come to me tonight. No, say tomorrow. Tomorrow will be time enough."

"Good!" said the man. "Nothing more?"

"Not a word now," said the Jew, descending the stairs.

The landlord returned to his guests. The Jew was no sooner alone, than his countenance resumed its former expression of anxiety and thought. After a moment, he called a hack cabriolet, was taken to within a quarter of a mile of Mr Sikes's residence, and walked the remainder of the distance.

"Now," muttered the Jew, as he knocked at the door, "if there is any deep play here, I shall have it out of you, my girl."

She was in her room, the woman said. Fagin crept softly upstairs, and entered to find the girl alone. She sat at the table, head resting on the board.

"She has been drinking," thought the Jew, "or perhaps she is only miserable."

The old man turned to close the door, and the noise roused the girl. She eyed his crafty face narrowly, as she inquired whether there was any news, and as she listened to his recital of Toby Crackit's story. When it was concluded, she sank into her former attitude. She pushed the candle impatiently away and once or twice changed her position.

During the silence, the Jew looked restlessly about the room, as if to check that there were no signs of Sikes having secretly returned. Apparently satisfied with his inspection, he tried to open a conversation but the girl took no notice of him. At length he made another attempt, "and where do you think Bill is now, my dear?"

The girl moaned out a half intelligible reply, that she could not tell and seemed, from the noise that escaped her, to be crying.

"And the boy, too," said the Jew, straining to catch a glimpse of her face. "Left in a ditch, Nance, only think!"

"The child," said the girl, suddenly looking up, "is better where he is, than among us. As long as no harm comes to Bill from it, I hope he lies dead in the ditch, and may his bones rot there."

"What!" cried the Jew, in amazement.

"Ay, I do," returned the girl, meeting his gaze. "I shall be glad to know that the worst is over. I can't bear to have him about me. The sight of him turns me against myself, and all of you."

"Pooh!" said the Jew, scornfully. "you're drunk."

"Am I?" cried the girl, bitterly. "It's no fault of yours, if I am not! You'd never have me anything else, if you had your will, except now. The humour doesn't suit you, does it?"

"No!" rejoined the Jew, furiously. "It does not."

"Change it, then!" responded the girl, with a laugh.

"Change it!" exclaimed the Jew, exasperated beyond all bounds. "I *will* change it! Listen to me, you drab. Listen to me, who with six words, can strangle Sikes as surely as if I had his bull's throat between my fingers now. If he comes back, and leaves the boy behind him – murder him yourself if you would have him escape Jack Ketch. And do it the moment he sets foot in this room, or mind me, it will be too late!"

"What is all this?" cried the girl involuntarily.

"What is it?" pursued Fagin, mad with rage. "When the boy's worth hundreds of pounds to me, am I to lose what chance has thrown me in the way of getting safely through the whims of a drunken gang that I could whistle away the lives of! And me bound, too, to a born devil that only wants the will, and has the power to, to – "

Panting for breath, the old man stammered for a word and in that instant checked the torrent of his wrath, and changed his whole demeanour. Now he shrunk into a chair, and trembled with fear that he had revealed some hidden villainy. After a short silence, he ventured to look round at his companion. She was still in the same listless attitude from which he had first roused her.

"Nancy, dear!" croaked the Jew, in his usual voice. "Did you mind me, dear?"

"Don't worry me now, Fagin!" replied the girl, raising her head languidly. "If Bill has not done it this time, he will another, and will do many more."

"Regarding this boy, my dear?" said the Jew, rubbing the palms of his hands nervously together.

"The boy must take his chance with the rest," interrupted Nancy, hastily. "And I say again, I hope he is dead, and out of harm's way and out of yours – that is, if Bill comes to no harm. And if Toby got clear, Bill's sure to be safe; for Bill's worth two of Toby any time."

"And about what I was saying, my dear?" observed the Jew, keeping his glistening eye steadily upon her.

"You must say it again, if it's something you want me to do," rejoined Nancy. "And if it is, wait till tomorrow."

Fagin asked several other questions to see if the girl had heard his unguarded hints, but, she answered them so readily, and was so utterly unmoved by his searching looks, that his original impression of her being more than a trifle in liquor, was confirmed.

Having accomplished his twofold object of telling the girl what he had heard that night, and of ascertaining, with his own eyes, that Sikes had not returned, Mr Fagin again turned his face homeward, leaving his young friend asleep, with her head upon the table. It was within an hour of midnight. The weather being piercing cold he had no great temptation to loiter.

He had reached the corner of his own street, and was already fumbling in his pocket for the door key, when a dark figure emerged from shadowed gateway, and, crossing the road, glided up to him unperceived.

"Fagin!" whispered a voice close to his car.

"Ah!" said the Jew, turning quickly round. "Is that – "

"Yes!" interrupted the stranger. "I have been lingering here these two hours. Where the devil have you been?"

"On your business, my dear," replied the Jew, glancing uneasily at his companion. "And nothing good comes of it."

"Nothing bad, I hope?" said the stranger stopping short, and turning a startled look on his companion.

The Jew shook his head, and was about to reply. The stranger, interrupting him, motioned to the house, remarking that he had better say what he had got to say, under cover, for his blood was chilled with standing about so long.

Fagin muttered something about having no fire, but his companion repeated his request; so he unlocked the door, and requested him to close it softly, while he got a light.

"It's as dark as the grave," said the man, groping forward a few steps. "Make haste!"

"Shut the door," whispered Fagin from the end of the passage. As he spoke, it closed with a loud noise.

"The wind blew it," said the other man. "Or it shut of its own accord, one or the other. Be quick with the light, or I shall knock my brains out against something in this confounded hole."

Fagin descended the kitchen stairs. A moment later he returned with a lighted candle, saying that Toby Crackit was asleep in the back room below, and that the boys were in the front one. Beckoning the man to follow him, he led the way up stairs.

"We can say what we've got to say in here, my dear Monks," said the Jew, throwing open a door on the first floor. "As there are holes in the shutters, and we never show lights, we'll set the candle on the stairs."

The Jew stooped and placed the candle on an upper flight of stairs, exactly opposite to the room door. Then he led the way into the apartment, empty of furniture save a broken armchair, and an old sofa, which stood behind the door. The stranger wearily sat and the Jew drew up the armchair so they sat face to face. The candle threw a feeble shadow on the opposite wall.

They conversed for some time in whispers.

"I tell you again, it was badly planned. Why not have kept him here, and made a sneaking, snivelling pickpocket of him?"

"Only hear him!" exclaimed the Jew, shrugging his shoulders.

"Why, do you mean to say you couldn't have done it if you had chosen?" demanded Monks, sternly. "Haven't you done it with other boys, scores of times? If you had had patience for a twelvemonth, couldn't you have got him convicted and sent safely out of the kingdom – perhaps for life?"

"Whose turn would that have served, my dear?" inquired the Jew.

"Mine," replied Monks.

"But not mine," said the Jew, submissively. "He might have become of use to me. It is only fair that the interests of both parties should be consulted, my friend?"

"What then?" demanded Monks.

"It was not easy to train him to the business," replied the Jew. "He was not like other boys in the same circumstances."

"Curse him, no!" muttered the man, "or he would have been a thief, long ago.

"I had no way of making him worse," pursued the Jew. "His hand was not in. I had nothing to frighten him with. We always must have something in the beginning, or we labour in vain. What could I do? Send him out with the Dodger and Charley? We had enough of that, the first time, my dear. I trembled for us all."

"That was not my doing," observed Monks.

"No, my dear!" renewed the Jew. "But if it had never happened, you might never have clapped eyes upon the boy, and so led to the discovery that it was him you were looking for. I got him back for you by means of the girl and then she begins to favour him."

"Throttle the girl!" said Monks, impatiently.

"Why, we can't afford to do that just now, my dear," replied the Jew, smiling. "Besides, that sort of thing is not in our way. I know what these girls are, Monks. As soon as the boy begins to harden, she'll care no more for him. You want him made a thief. If he is alive, I can make him one from this time; and if –if – " said the Jew, drawing nearer. "It's not likely, mind – but if the worst comes to the worst, and he is dead – "

"It's no fault of mine if he is!" interposed the other man, with a look of terror, and clasping the Jew. "Mind that, Fagin! I had no hand in it. Anything but his death, I told you. I won't shed blood – it's always found out and haunts a man. If they shot him dead, I was not the cause; do you hear? This infernal den! What's that?"

"What!" cried the Jew, grasping the coward round the body, with both arms, as he sprung to his feet. "Where?"

"Yonder!" replied the man, glaring at the opposite wall. "I saw the shadow of a woman pass along the wainscot!"

The Jew released him, and they rushed from the room. The candle was standing where it had been placed. It showed only the empty staircase, and their own white faces. They listened intently.

"It's your fancy," said the Jew, taking up the light and turning to his companion.

"I swear I saw it!" replied Monks, trembling. "It was bending forward when I saw it first, and when I spoke, it darted away."

The Jew glanced contemptuously at the pale face of his associate, and telling him to follow, if he pleased, ascended the stairs. They looked into all the cold and empty rooms. All was still as death.

"What do you think now?" said the Jew, when they had regained the passage. "Besides ourselves, there's not a creature in the house except Toby and the boys, and they're safe enough. See here!"

As a proof of the fact, the Jew drew forth two keys from his pocket and explained that he had locked them in, to prevent any intrusion on the conference.

Mr Monks' protestations gradually lessened as they proceeded in their search without making any discovery. He gave several grim laughs, and confessed it must have been his imagination. There was no more conversation that night – it was past one o'clock. The amiable couple parted.

CHAPTER 26

Mr Bumble had re-counted the teaspoons, re-weighed the sugar-tongs, made a closer inspection of the milk-pot, and ascertained the exact condition of the furniture. He had repeated each process half a dozen times before he began to think that it was time for Mrs Corney to return. As there were no sounds of her approach, it occurred to Mr Bumble that it would be an innocent and virtuous way of spending the time, to have a cursory glance at the interior of Mrs Corney's chest of drawers.

Having listened at the keyhole to assure himself that nobody was approaching the chamber, Mr Bumble, beginning at the bottom, proceeded to check the contents of the three long drawers. These were filled with various garments of good fashion and texture, carefully preserved between two layers of old newspapers, speckled with dried lavender, and seemed to yield him exceeding satisfaction. Arriving in due course at the right-hand corner drawer (in which was the key), and beholding therein a small padlocked box, which, being shaken, gave forth a pleasant sound, as of the chinking of coin, Mr Bumble returned with a stately walk to the fireplace. He resumed his old attitude, and said, with a grave air, "I'll do it!"

Ten minutes later, Mrs Corney hurried into the room, threw herself, in a breathless state, on a chair by the fireside, and covering her eyes with one hand, placed the other over her heart, and gasped for breath.

"Mrs Corney," said Mr Bumble, stooping over the matron, "what is this, ma'am? Has anything happened, ma'am? Pray answer me. I'm on – on – " Mr Bumble could not immediately think of the word "tenterhooks" so he said, "broken bottles."

"Mr Bumble!" cried the lady, "I have been so put out!"

"Put out, ma'am!" exclaimed Mr Bumble. "Who has dared to – ? this is them wicious paupers!"

"It's dreadful to think of!" said the lady, shuddering.

"Then don't think of it, ma'am," rejoined Mr Bumble.

"I can't help it," whimpered the lady.

"Then take something, ma'am," said Mr Bumble soothingly.

"Not for the world!" replied Mrs Corney. "I couldn't – oh! The top shelf in the right-hand corner – oh!" Uttering these words, the good lady pointed, distractedly, to the cupboard. Mr Bumble rushed to the closet and, snatching a pint green-glass bottle, filled a teacup, and held it to the lady's lips.

"I'm better now," said Mrs Corney, after drinking half of it.

Mr Bumble lifted the cup to his nose.

"Peppermint," exclaimed Mrs Corney, in a faint voice, smiling gently on the beadle. "Try it! There's a little – something else in it."

Mr Bumble tasted the medicine with a doubtful look, smacked his lips, took another taste; and put the cup down empty.

"It's very comforting," said Mrs Corney.

"Very much so, ma'am," said the beadle. As he spoke, he tenderly inquired what had happened to distress her.

"Nothing," replied Mrs Corney. "I am a foolish, weak creetur."

"Not weak, ma'am," retorted Mr Bumble, drawing his chair a little closer. "Are you a weak creetur, Mrs Corney?"

"We are all weak creeturs," said Mrs Corney, laying down a general principle.

"So we are," said the beadle.

Nothing was said for a minute or two afterwards. By then, Mr Bumble had illustrated the position by removing his left arm from the back of Mrs Corney's chair to Mrs Corney's apron-string, round which it gradually became entwined.

"We are all weak creeturs," said Mr Bumble.

Mrs Corney sighed.

"Don't sigh, Mrs Corney," said Mr Bumble.

"I can't help it," said Mrs Corney.

"This is a very comfortable room, ma'am," said Mr Bumble, looking round. "Another room, and this would be complete."

"It would be too much for one," murmured the lady.

"But not for two, ma'am," rejoined Mr Bumble, in soft accents. "Eh, Mrs Corney?"

Mrs Corney, with great propriety, turned her head away when the beadle said this, and released her hand to get at her pocket-handkerchief, but insensibly replaced it in that of Mr Bumble.

"The board allow you coals, don't they, Mrs Corney?" inquired the beadle, affectionately pressing her hand.

"And candles," replied Mrs Corney, slightly returning the pressure.

"Coals, candles, and house-rent free," said Mr Bumble. "Oh, Mrs Corney, what a Angel you are!"

The lady was not proof against this burst of feeling. She sank into Mr Bumble's arms; and that gentleman imprinted a passionate kiss upon her chaste nose.

"Such porochial perfection!" exclaimed Mr Bumble, rapturously. "You know that Mr Slout is worse tonight, my fascinator? His death will cause a wacancy that must be filled. Oh, Mrs Corney, what a prospect this opens! What a opportunity for a jining of hearts and housekeepings!"

Mrs Corney sobbed.

"The little word?" said Mr Bumble, bending over the bashful beauty. "The one little, little word, my blessed Corney?"

"Ye-ye-yes!" sighed out the matron.

"One more," pursued the beadle. "Compose your darling feelings for only one more. When is it to come off?"

Mrs Corney twice essayed to speak: and twice failed. At length she threw her arms round Mr Bumble's neck, and said, it might be as soon as ever he pleased, and that he was "a irresistible duck."

Matters being thus amicably arranged, the contract was solemnly ratified in another teacupful of the peppermint mixture. While it was being disposed of, she acquainted Mr Bumble with the old woman's decease.

"Very good," said that gentleman, sipping his peppermint. "I'll call at Sowerberry's as I go home, and tell him to send tomorrow morning. Was it that as frightened you, love?"

"It wasn't anything particular, dear," said the lady, evasively.

"It must have been something, love," urged Mr Bumble. "Won't you tell your own B.?"

"Not now," rejoined the lady. "After we're married, dear."

Mr Bumble left the building with a light heart, and bright visions of his future promotion: which served to occupy his mind until he reached the shop of the undertaker.

CHAPTER 27

"Wolves tear your throats!" muttered Sikes, grinding his teeth. "I wish I was among some of you, you'd howl the hoarser for it."

Sikes rested the body of the wounded boy across his bent knee and turned his head, for an instant, to look back at his pursuers.

"It's all up, Bill!" cried Toby; "drop the kid, and show 'em your heels." With this parting advice, Mr Crackit, preferring the chance of being shot by his friend, to the certainty of being taken by his enemies, darted off at full speed. Sikes took one look around and threw his cape over the prostrate form of Oliver. He then ran along the front of the hedge, as if to distract the attention of those behind from the spot where the boy lay, paused for a second before another hedge, then cleared it at a bound, and was gone.

"Ho, ho, there!" cried a voice in the rear. "Pincher! Neptune!"

The dogs, in common with their masters, seemed to have no particular relish for the sport in which they were engaged, readily answered to the command. Three men, who had by now advanced some distance into the field, stopped to take counsel together.

"My advice, or, I should say, my orders is," said the fattest man of the party, "that we 'mediately go home again."

"I am agreeable to anything that is agreeable to Mr Giles," said a shorter man, by no means slim, and who was very pale in the face.

"I shouldn't wish to appear ill-mannered, gentlemen," said the third, who had called the dogs back. "Mr Giles ought to know."

"But it's wonderful," said Mr Giles. "What a man will do, when his blood is up. I should have committed murder – I know I should – if we'd caught one of them rascals. It was the gate. You may depend upon it, that that gate stopped the flow of the excitement."

This dialogue was held between the two men who had surprised the burglars, and a travelling tinker who had been sleeping in an outhouse, and who had been roused, together with his two mongrel curs, to join in the pursuit. Mr Giles acted as both butler and steward to the old lady of the mansion. Brittles was a lad of all-work who, having entered her service a mere child, was treated as a promising young boy still, though he was something past thirty.

Encouraging each other but, keeping very close together, the three men hurried back to the tree where they had left their lantern, lest its light should inform the thieves in what direction to fire. They then made the best of their way home.

The air grew colder, as day came slowly on and the mist rolled along the ground. The grass was wet and the damp wind went languidly by, with a hollow moaning. Oliver lay motionless where Sikes had left him.

Morning drew on apace. The air became more sharp and piercing. The objects that had looked dim and terrible in the darkness grew more and more defined, and gradually resolved into their familiar shapes. The rain came down, thick and fast, and pattered among the leafless bushes. But Oliver felt it not for he still lay helpless and unconscious.

At length, a low cry of pain broke the stillness; and uttering it, the boy awoke. His left arm, rudely bandaged in a shawl, hung useless at his side, the bandage saturated with blood. He was so weak, that he could scarcely raise himself into a sitting posture. When he had done so, he looked feebly round for help, and groaned with pain. Trembling in every joint, from cold and exhaustion, he made an effort to stand upright but, shuddering from head to toe, fell to the ground.

After a few moments lying there, Oliver, pushed by a creeping sickness at his heart, warning him that if he lay there, he must surely die, got up on his feet, and tried to walk. His head was dizzy, and he staggered like a drunken man. But he kept going, his head drooping on his breast, he knew not where.

He staggered on, almost mechanically, between the bars of gates, or through hedge-gaps as they came in his way, until he reached a road. Here the rain began to fall so heavily, that it roused him.

He looked about, and saw at no great distance a house, which perhaps he could reach. Pitying his condition, they might have compassion on him. And if they did not, it would be better, he thought, to die near human beings, than in the lonely open fields. He summoned up all his strength for one last trial.

As he drew nearer to this house, he felt that he had seen it before. He remembered nothing of its details but the shape of the building seemed familiar.

On the grass inside the garden wall, he had fallen on his knees to beg for the two men's mercy. It was the house they had tried to rob.

Oliver felt such fear that for a moment, he forgot the agony of his wound, and thought only of flight. Flight! He could hardly stand! Besides, where could he fly? He pushed against the garden gate. It was unlocked, and swung open on its hinges. He tottered across the lawn, climbed the steps, knocked faintly at the door; and, strength failing, he sunk down against one of the pillars of the little portico.

About this time, Mr Giles, Brittles, and the tinker, after the fatigues and terrors of the night, were taking tea and sundries, in the kitchen. It was not Mr Giles's usual habit to admit to too great familiarity the humbler servants, but death, fires, and burglary make all men equals.

"It was about half-past two," said Mr Giles, "when I fancied I heerd a noise."

The cook turned pale, and asked the housemaid to shut the door.

" – Heerd a noise," continued Mr Giles. "I says, at first, 'This is illusion;' and was composing myself off to sleep, when I heerd the noise again, distinct."

"What sort of a noise?" asked the cook.

"A kind of a busting noise," replied Mr Giles, looking round.

"More like the noise of powdering a iron bar on a nutmeg-grater," suggested Brittles.

"It was, when you heerd it, sir," rejoined Mr Giles. "But, at this time, it had a busting sound. I sat up in bed; and listened."

The cook and housemaid simultaneously ejaculated "Lor!"

"I heerd it now, quite apparent," resumed Mr Giles.

"'Somebody,' I says, 'is forcing of a door or window. What's to be done? I'll call up that poor lad, Brittles.'"

Here, all eyes turned to Brittles.

"I tossed off the clothes," said Giles, looking very hard at the cook and housemaid, "got softly out of bed; drew on a pair of – "

"Ladies present, Mr Giles," murmured the tinker.

" – of *shoes,* sir," said Giles, turning upon him, and laying great emphasis on the word. "I seized the loaded pistol that always goes up stairs with the plate-basket and walked on tiptoes to his room. 'Brittles,' I says, when I had woke him, 'don't be frightened!'"

"So you did," observed Brittles, in a low voice.

"'We're dead men, I think, Brittles,' I says," continued Giles. "'But don't be frightened.'"

"Was he frightened?" asked the cook.

"He was pretty near as firm as I was," replied Mr Giles.

"I should have died at once, I'm sure, if it had been me," observed the housemaid.

"You're a woman," retorted Brittles, plucking up a little.

"Brittles is right," said Mr Giles, nodding his head, approvingly. "From a woman, nothing else would be expected. We, being men, took a dark lantern, and groped our way downstairs in the dark."

Mr Giles had risen from his seat, and taken two steps with his eyes shut, to describe the action, when he started violently, along with the rest of the company, and hurried back to his chair. The cook and housemaid screamed.

"It was a knock," said Mr Giles, assuming perfect serenity. "Open the door, somebody."

Nobody moved.

"It seems strange – a knock coming at this time in the morning," said Mr Giles, surveying the pale faces that surrounded him. "But the door must be opened."

Mr Giles, as he spoke, looked at Brittles. But that young man, being naturally modest, considered himself nobody, and therefore the inquiry could have nothing to do with him. Anyway he gave no reply. Mr Giles directed an appealing glance at the tinker, but he had suddenly fallen asleep. The women were out of the question.

"If Brittles would rather open the door, in the presence of witnesses," said Mr Giles, after a short silence, "I am ready to make one."

"So am I," said the tinker, waking, as suddenly as he had slept.

Brittles agreed on these terms and the party realising it was now broad day, went up stairs, with the dogs in front. The two women, afraid to stay below, brought up the rear.

Mr Giles held on fast to the tinker's arm (to prevent his running away), and gave the word of command to open the door. Brittles obeyed. The group peered over each other's shoulders to see no more formidable an object than poor little Oliver Twist, speechless and exhausted.

"A boy!" exclaimed Mr Giles, valiantly pushing the tinker into the background. "What's the matter with the – eh? Why – Brittles – look here – don't you know?"

Brittles no sooner saw Oliver, than he uttered a loud cry. Mr Giles, seizing the boy by one leg and one arm (fortunately not the broken limb) lugged him straight into the hall.

"Here he is!" bawled Giles, in great excitement up the staircase. "Here's one of the thieves, ma'am! Wounded, miss! I shot him, miss, and Brittles held the light."

The two women-servants ran up stairs to give the news that Mr Giles had captured a robber. In the midst of all this noise and commotion, there was heard a sweet female voice.

"Giles!" whispered the voice from the stair-head.

"I'm here, miss," replied Mr Giles. "Don't be frightened, miss. I ain't much injured. He didn't make a very desperate resistance, miss! I was too many for him."

"Hush!" replied the young lady. "You frighten my aunt as much as the thieves did. Is the poor creature much hurt?"

"Wounded desperate, miss," replied Giles.

"He looks as if he is a-going, miss," bawled Brittles. "Wouldn't you like to come and look at him, miss!"

"Hush, pray, there's a good man!" rejoined the lady. "Wait quietly while I speak to aunt."

With a footstep as soft and gentle as the voice, the speaker tripped away. She soon returned to say that the wounded person was to be carried, carefully, to Mr Giles's room. Brittles was to saddle the pony and ride to Chertsey for a constable and doctor.

"But won't you take a look at him, first, miss?" asked Mr Giles, as if Oliver were some bird of rare plumage, that he had skilfully brought down. "Not one little peep, miss?"

"Not now, for the world," replied the young lady. "Poor fellow! Treat him kindly, Giles, for my sake!"

The old servant looked up at the speaker, as she turned away, with a glance as proud and admiring as if she had been his own child. Then, bending over Oliver, he helped to carry him up stairs.

CHAPTER 28

In a handsome room, though its furniture had the air of old-fashioned comfort, there sat two ladies at a well-spread breakfast-table. Mr Giles, dressed with scrupulous care in a full suit of black, was in attendance upon them.

Of the two ladies, one was well advanced in years, but the high-backed oak chair where she sat, was no more upright than she. Dressed in a quaint mixture of by-gone costume, with some slight concessions to the prevailing taste, she sat, in a stately manner, with her hands folded on the table before her. Her eyes were attentively fixed upon her young companion.

The younger lady was in the lovely bloom and spring-time of womanhood. She was not past seventeen. Cast in a slight and exquisite mould, so mild and gentle, so pure and beautiful. The intelligence that shone in her deep blue eye, and was stamped upon her noble head, seemed scarcely of her age.

She was busy in the little offices of the table. Chancing to raise her eyes as the elder lady was regarding her, she playfully put back her hair, which was simply braided on her forehead and threw into her beaming look, such an expression of affection and artless loveliness, that blessed spirits might have smiled to look upon her.

"And Brittles has been gone upwards of an hour, has he?" asked the old lady, after a pause.

"An hour and twelve minutes, ma'am," replied Mr Giles, referring to a silver watch.

"He is always slow," remarked the old lady.

"Brittles always was a slow boy, ma'am," replied the attendant.

"He gets worse instead of better, I think," said the elder lady.

At that moment a gig drove up to the garden gate. A fat gentleman jumped out and ran straight up to the door. He got into the house quickly by some mysterious process, burst into the room, and nearly overturned Mr Giles and the breakfast-table together.

"I never heard of such a thing!" exclaimed the fat gentleman. "My dear Mrs Maylie – bless my soul – in the silence of night, too – I never heard of such a thing!"

With such expressions of condolence, the gentleman shook hands with both ladies, drew up a chair, and inquired how they were.

"You ought to be dead with the fright," said the fat gentleman. "Why didn't you send? And you, Miss Rose, I – "

"I'm well," said Rose, interrupting him. "But there is a poor creature upstairs, whom aunt wishes you to see."

"Ah! To be sure," replied the doctor, "so there is. That was your handiwork, Giles, I understand. Where is he? Show me the way. I'll look in again, as I come down, Mrs Maylie."

Talking all the way, he followed Mr Giles up stairs.

Mr Losberne was absent much longer than either he or the ladies had anticipated. A large flat box was fetched out of the gig and a bedroom bell was rung very often, and servants ran up and down stairs perpetually. At length he returned and in reply to an anxious inquiry after his patient, closed the door carefully.

"This is a very extraordinary thing, Mrs Maylie," said the doctor, standing with his back to the door. "Have you seen him?"

"No," rejoined the old lady. "He is not in danger, I hope?"

"I beg your pardon, ma'am," interposed Mr Giles. "But I was going to tell you about him when Doctor Losberne came in."

Mr Giles had not, at first, been able to face the fact that he had shot a boy. Such commendations had been bestowed upon his bravery, that he could not, for the life of him, help postponing the explanation for a few delicious minutes.

"Rose wished to see the man," said Mrs Maylie, "but I wouldn't hear of it."

"Humph!" rejoined the doctor. "There is nothing very alarming in his appearance. Have you an objection to see him in my presence?"

"If it's necessary," replied the old lady, "certainly not."

"I think it is necessary," said the doctor. "Besides, I am quite sure you would deeply regret not having done so. He is perfectly quiet now. Allow me – Miss Rose, will you permit me? Not the slightest fear, I pledge you my honour!"

CHAPTER 29

With many assurances that they would be agreeably surprised, the doctor led them, with much ceremony and stateliness, up stairs.

"Now," said the doctor, in a whisper, softly turning the handle of a bedroom door. "Let us hear what you think of him. He has not been shaved very recently, but he don't look at all ferocious."

Stepping before them, he looked into the room. Motioning them to advance, he closed the door when they had entered. He gently drew back the curtains of the bed. Upon it, in lieu of the dogged, black-faced ruffian they had expected to behold, there lay a mere child: worn with pain and exhaustion, and sunk into a deep sleep. His wounded arm, bound and splinted, was crossed upon his breast. His head reclined upon the other arm, which was half hidden by his long hair as it streamed over the pillow.

The honest gentleman held the curtain in his hand, and looked on for a minute or so, in silence. The younger lady glided softly past, and sat by the bedside gathering Oliver's hair from his face. As she stooped over him, her tears fell upon his forehead.

The boy stirred, and smiled in his sleep, as though these marks of pity and compassion had awakened some pleasant dream.

"What can this mean?" exclaimed the elder lady. "This poor child can never have been the pupil of robbers!"

"Vice," sighed the surgeon, replacing the curtain, "takes up her abode in many temples. Who can say that a fair outside shall not enshrine her?"

"But can you really believe that this delicate boy has been the voluntary associate of the worst outcasts of society?"

The surgeon shook his head, in a manner intimating that he feared it was possible. He then led the way into an adjoining apartment.

"But even if he has been wicked," pursued Rose, "think how young he is. He may never have known a mother's love, or the comfort of a home. Ill-usage and blows, or the want of bread may have driven him to be with men who have forced him to guilt. Dear aunt, for mercy's sake, think of this, before you let them drag this sick child to a prison."

"My dear love," said the elder lady, as she folded the weeping girl to her bosom, "do you think I would harm a hair of his head?"

"Oh, no!" replied Rose, eagerly.

"No, surely," said the old lady. "My days are drawing to their close and may mercy be shown to me as I show it to others! What can I do to save him, sir?"

"Let me think, ma'am," said the doctor.

Mr Losberne thrust his hands into his pockets, and took several turns up and down the room, frowning. After various exclamations of "I've got it now," and "no, I haven't," and as many renewals of the walking and frowning, he at length made a dead halt, and spoke as follows:

"I think if you give me a full commission to bully Giles, and that little boy, Brittles, I can manage it. You don't object to that?"

"Unless there is some other way of preserving the child," replied Mrs Maylie.

"There is no other," said the doctor. "Take my word for it."

"Then my aunt invests you with full power," said Rose, smiling through her tears. "But pray don't be harder upon them than is necessary."

"You seem to think," retorted the doctor, "that everybody is disposed to be hard-hearted today, except yourself, Miss Rose."

"You are as great a boy as Brittles himself," said Rose, blushing.

"Well," said the doctor, laughing heartily, "that is no very difficult matter. But back to this boy. He will wake in an hour or so. Although I have told that constable-fellow down stairs that he mustn't be moved, on peril of his life, I think we may talk with him without danger. But I make this condition – that I shall examine him in your presence. If, from what he says, we judge, that he is a real and thorough bad one, (which is more than possible), he shall be left to his fate."

"Oh no, aunt!" entreated Rose.

"Oh yes, aunt!" said the doctor. "Is it a bargain?"

"He cannot be hardened in vice," said Rose. "It is impossible."

"Then all the more reason for acceding to my proposition," retorted the doctor.

It was evening, indeed, before the kind-hearted doctor came to say that Oliver was sufficiently recovered to speak. The boy was very ill, he said, and weak from the loss of blood, but he was anxious to disclose something.

The conference was long. Oliver told them all his simple history, and was often compelled to stop, by pain and want of strength. It was a solemn thing, to hear, in the darkened room, the feeble voice of the sick child recounting a weary catalogue of evils that hard men had brought upon him.

Oliver's pillow was smoothed by gentle hands that night and loveliness and virtue watched him as he slept. He felt calm and happy, and could have died without a murmur.

The momentous interview was no sooner over, and Oliver resting again, than the doctor, after wiping his eyes, and condemning them for being weak, betook himself down stairs to speak to Mr Giles.

There were assembled in the kitchen the women servants, Mr Brittles, Mr Giles, the tinker and the constable.

The adventures of the previous night were still under discussion when the doctor entered.

"Sit still!" said the doctor, waving his hand.

"How is the patient to-night, sir?" asked Giles.

"So-so," returned the doctor. "I am afraid you have got yourself into a scrape, Mr Giles."

"I hope you don't mean to say, sir," said Mr Giles, trembling, "that he's going to die. If I thought it, I should never be happy again, sir."

"That's not the point," said the doctor, mysteriously. "Are you going to swear, that that boy up stairs is the same boy that was put through the little window last night?"

The doctor, who was universally considered one of the best-tempered creatures on earth, made this demand in such a dreadful tone, that Giles and Brittles stared at each other in amazement.

"Pay attention to the reply, constable, will you?" said the doctor. "Something may come of this before long."

The constable looking as wise as possible, took up his staff.

"It's a simple question of identity, you will observe," said the doctor.

"That's what it is, sir," replied the constable.

"Here's a house broken into," said the doctor, "and a couple of men catch one glimpse of a boy, in the midst of gunpowder smoke, in all the distraction of alarm and darkness. Here's a boy comes to that very same house, next morning, and because he happens to have his arm tied up, these men lay violent hands upon him – placing his life in great danger – and swear he is the thief. Now, the question is, whether these men are justified by the fact. If not, in what situation do they place themselves?"

The constable nodded profoundly.

"I ask you again," thundered the doctor, "are you, on your solemn oaths, able to identify that boy?"

Brittles looked doubtfully at Mr Giles. Mr Giles looked doubtfully back. The constable put his hand behind his ear, to catch the reply. The doctor glanced keenly round when a ring was heard at the gate, and at the same moment, the sound of wheels.

"It's the runners!" cried Brittles, to all appearance much relieved.

"The what?" exclaimed the doctor, aghast in his turn.

"The Bow Street officers, sir," replied Brittles, taking up a candle. "Me and Mr Giles sent for 'em this morning."

"You did, did you? Then confound your slow coaches down here; that's all," said the doctor, walking away.

CHAPTER 30

"Who's that?" inquired Brittles, opening the door a little and peeping out, shading the candle with his hand.

"Open the door," replied a man outside. "It's the officers from Bow Street, as was sent to, today."

Brittles opened the door to its full width, and confronted a portly man in a great-coat who walked in, without saying anything more.

He was a stout personage of middle height, aged about fifty: with shiny black hair, cropped pretty close; half-whiskers, a round face, and sharp eyes. The other was a red-headed, bony man, in top-boots, with a turned-up sinister-looking nose.

"Tell your governor that Blathers and Duff is here, will you?" said the stout man. "Oh! Good evening, master. Can I have a word or two with you in private, if you please?"

This was addressed to Mr Losberne, who now made his appearance. That gentleman, motioning Brittles to retire, brought in the two ladies, and shut the door.

"This is the lady of the house," said Mr Losberne, motioning towards Mrs Maylie.

Mr Blathers made a bow. Being desired to sit down, he put his hat on the floor, and taking a chair, motioned Duff to do the same.

"Now, with regard to this here robbery, master," said Blathers. "What are the circumstances?"

Mr Losberne recounted them at great length, and with much circumlocution. Messrs Blathers and Duff looked very knowing.

"Now, what is this, about this here boy that the servants are a-talking on?" said Blathers.

"Nothing at all," replied the doctor. "One of the frightened servants decided, that he had something to do with this attempt to break into the house, but it's nonsense."

"Who is the boy?" observed Blathers. "Where did he come from? He didn't drop out of the clouds, did he, master?"

"Of course not," replied the doctor, with a nervous glance at the two ladies. "I know his whole history, but we can talk about that presently. You would like to see the place where the thieves made their attempt, I suppose?"

"Certainly," rejoined Mr Blathers. "We had better inspect the premises first, and examine the servants arterwards. That's the usual way of doing business."

Lights were then procured; and Messrs Blathers and Duff, attended by the native constable, Brittles, Giles, and everybody else went into the little room at the end of the passage to investigate the scene of the crime. Mr Giles and Brittles then gave several melodramatic representations of the previous night's adventures, contradicting each other in not more than one important respect the first time, and in not more than a dozen the last. Blathers and Duff cleared the room, and held a long council together.

Meanwhile, the doctor walked up and down the next room in a very uneasy state. Mrs Maylie and Rose looked on anxiously.

"Upon my word," he said, stopping, after a great number of very rapid turns, "I hardly know what to do."

"Surely," said Rose, "the poor child's story, faithfully repeated to these men, will be sufficient to exonerate him."

"I doubt it, my dear young lady," said the doctor, shaking his head. "I don't think it would exonerate him, either with them, or with legal functionaries of a higher grade. He is, after all, a run-away. Judged by worldly considerations and probabilities, his story is very doubtful."

"You believe it, surely?" interrupted Rose.

"I believe it, strange as it is," rejoined the doctor. "But I don't think it is exactly the tale for a practised police-officer."

"Why not?" demanded Rose.

"Because, my pretty cross-examiner," replied the doctor, "viewed with their eyes, there are many ugly points about it. He can only prove the parts that look ill, and none of those that look well. Those fellows will take nothing for granted. He has been the companion of thieves for some time, and carried to a police-office on a charge of picking a gentleman's pocket. He has been taken away, forcibly, from that gentleman's house, to a place he cannot describe, or point out, and the whereabouts of which he has not the remotest idea. He is brought down to Chertsey and is put through a window to rob a house. Then, at the very moment he is going to alarm the inmates, and so set him all to rights, in rushes a blundering butler who shoots him!"

"But still I see nothing to incriminate the poor child," replied Rose, smiling at the doctor.

"No," replied the doctor. "Of course not! Bless your bright eyes!"

The doctor put his hands into his pockets, and walked up and down the room. "The more I think of it," he said, "the more I see endless trouble and difficulty if we tell them the boy's real story. I am certain it will not be believed."

"What is to be done?" cried Rose. "Why did they send for them?"

"Why, indeed!" exclaimed Mrs Maylie. "I would not have had them here, for the world."

"All I know is," said Mr Losberne, "that we must try and carry it off with a bold face. The boy is sick with fever, and in no condition to be talked to, that's one comfort. We must make the best of it; and if bad be the best, it is no fault of ours. Come in!"

105

"Well, master," said Blathers, entering the room followed Duff, and closing the door before he said anything. "This warn't a put-up thing. The servants warn't in it."

"Nobody suspected them," said Mrs Maylie.

"Wery likely not, ma'am," replied Blathers; "but they might have been. We find it was a town job for the style of work is first-rate."

"Wery pretty indeed it is," remarked Duff, in an undertone.

"There was two of 'em in it," continued Blathers. "And they had a boy with 'em, that's plain from the size of the window. So we'll see this lad at once, if you please."

"Perhaps they will take something to drink first, Mrs Maylie?" said the doctor, his face brightening, as if some new thought had occurred to him.

"To be sure!" exclaimed Rose, eagerly. "You shall have it immediately, if you will."

"Why, thank you, miss!" said Blathers, drawing his coat-sleeve across his mouth. "It's dry work, this sort of duty."

"What shall it be?" asked the doctor, following the young lady to the sideboard.

"A little drop of spirits, master, if it's all the same," replied Blathers. "It is a cold ride from London, ma'am."

The doctor slipped from the room for a few moments.

Blathers stood awkwardly, Duff by his side. And while they drank, Blathers and Duff entertained Rose with reminiscences of past cases.

The doctor returned. "Now, if you please, you can walk up stairs."

"If *you* please, sir," returned Mr Blathers. Closely following Mr Losberne, the two officers ascended to Oliver's bedroom. Mr Giles preceded the party, with a lighted candle.

Oliver had been dozing, but looked worse, and was more feverish than he had appeared yet. Being assisted by the doctor, he managed to sit up in bed for a minute or so, and looked at the strangers without at all understanding what was going on, in fact, without even remembering where he was, or what had happened.

"This," said Mr Losberne, speaking softly, "is the lad, who, being accidentally wounded by a spring-gun in some prank on Mr What-d'ye-call-him's grounds, at the back here, comes to the house this morning. He is immediately grabbed by that ingenious gentleman with the candle in

106

his hand, placing his life in considerable danger, as I can professionally certify."

Messrs Blathers and Duff looked at Mr Giles. The bewildered butler gazed from them towards Oliver, and from Oliver towards Mr Losberne.

"You don't mean to deny that, I suppose?" said the doctor, laying Oliver gently down again.

"It was all done for the – for the best, sir?" answered Giles. "I am sure I thought it was the boy, or I wouldn't have meddled with him. I am not of an inhuman disposition, sir."

"Thought it was what boy?" inquired the senior officer.

"The housebreaker's boy, sir!" replied Giles.

"Well? Do you think so now?" inquired Blathers. "That it's the same boy?"

"I really don't know," said Giles, ruefully. "I couldn't swear."

"Has this man been a-drinking, sir?" inquired Blathers, turning to the doctor.

"What a precious muddle-headed chap you are!" said Duff.

Mr Losberne had been feeling the patient's pulse during this short dialogue, but he now rose from the chair by the bedside, and remarked, that if the officers had any doubts, they would perhaps like to step into the next room, and have Brittles before them.

They adjourned to a neighbouring room, where Mr Brittles was called in. He then tied himself and his superior in a wonderful tangle of fresh contradictions and impossibilities, which threw no particular light on anything. But he declared that he shouldn't know the real boy, if he were put before him that instant. He had only thought Oliver was the boy, because Mr Giles had said he was.

Among other ingenious surmises, the question was then raised, whether Mr Giles had really hit anybody. Upon examination of the fellow-pistol to that which was fired, it turned out to have no more destructive loading than gunpowder and brown paper – this made a considerable impression on everybody but the doctor, who had removed the ball about ten minutes before. It made an even greater impression on Mr Giles who had laboured under the fear that he had wounded a fellow-creature; he much favoured this new idea. Finally, the officers, without troubling too much about Oliver, left, promising to return next morning.

After some more examination, and a great deal more conversation, a neighbouring magistrate agreed to take the joint bail of Mrs Maylie and Mr Losberne for Oliver's appearance if he should ever be called upon. Blathers and Duff, being rewarded with a couple of guineas, returned to town.

Meanwhile, Oliver gradually prospered under the united care of Mrs Maylie, Rose, and the kind-hearted Mr Losberne. If fervent prayers, gushing from hearts overcharged with gratitude, are heard in heaven, the blessings that the orphan child called down upon them, sunk into their souls, diffusing peace and happiness.

CHAPTER 31

In addition to the broken arm, Oliver's exposure to the wet and cold had brought on fever that hung about him for many weeks, and reduced him sadly. But, he began, by slow degrees, to get better, and to be able to say sometimes, in a few tearful words, how deeply he felt the goodness of the two sweet ladies. How he hoped that when he grew strong and well again, he could do something to show his gratitude. The poor boy whom their charity had rescued from misery, or death, was eager to serve them with his whole heart and soul.

"Poor fellow!" said Rose, "you shall have many opportunities. We are going into the country, and my aunt intends that you shall accompany us. The quiet, the pure air, and all the pleasures of spring will restore you in a few days. We will employ you in a hundred ways, when you can bear the trouble."

"The trouble!" cried Oliver. "Oh! Dear lady, if I could but work for you; if I could only give you pleasure by watering your flowers or running up and down the whole day long, to make you happy; what would I give to do it!"

"You shall give nothing at all," said Miss Maylie, smiling. "As I told you before, we shall employ you in a hundred ways; and if you only take half the trouble to please us, that you promise now, you will make me very happy indeed. Do you understand me?" she inquired, watching Oliver's thoughtful face.

"Oh yes, ma'am, yes!" replied Oliver, eagerly. "But I was thinking that I am ungrateful now."

"To whom?" inquired the young lady.

"To the kind gentleman, and the dear nurse, who took so much care of me before," rejoined Oliver. "If they knew how happy I am, they would be pleased, I am sure."

"I am sure they would," rejoined Oliver's benefactress. "Mr Losberne has already promised that when you are strong enough, he will carry you to see them."

"Has he, ma'am?" cried Oliver, his face brightening. "I don't know what I shall do when I see their kind faces once again!"

In a short time Oliver was sufficiently recovered to undergo the fatigue of this expedition. One morning he and Mr Losberne set out in a little carriage which belonged to Mrs Maylie. When they came to Chertsey Bridge, Oliver turned pale, uttering a loud exclamation. "What's the matter with the boy?" cried the doctor. "Do you see anything – here anything – feel anything – eh?"

"That house, sir," cried the boy, pointing out the carriage window.

"What of it? Stop, coachman. Pull up here," cried the doctor. "What of the house, my man; eh?"

"The thieves – the house they took me to!" whispered Oliver.

"The devil it is!" cried the doctor. "Halloa, there! Let me out!"

But, before the coachman could dismount from his box, he had tumbled out of the coach and, running down to the deserted tenement, began kicking at the door like a madman.

"Halloa?" said a little ugly hump-backed man opening the door so suddenly, that the doctor nearly fell forward into the passage. "What's the matter here?"

"Matter!" exclaimed the other, collaring him without a moment's thought. "A good deal. Robbery is the matter."

"There'll be murder the matter, too," replied the hump-backed man, coolly, "if you don't take your hands off. Do you hear me?"

"I hear you," said the doctor, giving his captive a hearty shake. "Where's – what's his rascally name – Sikes. Where's Sikes?"

The hump-backed man stared in amazement and indignation then twisted from the doctor's grasp. Before he could shut the door, however, the doctor had passed into the parlour, without a word of pardon. He looked anxiously round. Not an article of furniture or even the position of the cupboards answered Oliver's description!

"Now!" said the hump-backed man, watching him keenly. "What do you mean by coming into my house in this violent way? Do you want to rob me, or to murder me? Take yourself off, before I do you a mischief?"

"As soon as I think proper," said Mr Losberne, looking into the other parlour which, like the first, bore no resemblance whatever to Oliver's account of it. "I shall find you out, some day, my friend."

"Will you?" sneered the ill-favoured cripple. "If you ever want me, I'm here. I haven't lived here for five-and-twenty years to be scared by you." And so saying, he set up a yell, and danced as if wild with rage.

"The boy must have made a mistake," muttered the doctor. "Here! Put that in your pocket, and shut yourself up again." He flung the hunchback a piece of money, and returned to the carriage.

The man followed, uttering the wildest curses all the way. He continued to curse until the driver had resumed his seat. When they were once more on their way, they could see him, beating his feet upon the ground in transports of real or pretended rage.

"I am an ass!" said the doctor, after a long silence. "Did you know that before, Oliver?"

"No, sir."

"Then don't forget it another time."

"An ass," said the doctor again, after a further silence. "Even if it had been the right place, and they had been there, what could I have done, single-handed? And if I had had assistance, I see no good that I should have done, except to show how I have hushed up this business. That would have served me right, though. I am always involving myself in some scrape or other, by acting on impulse. It might have done me good."

As Oliver knew the name of the street in which Mr Brownlow lived, they were able to drive straight there. When the coach turned into it, his heart beat so violently, he could scarcely breathe.

"Now, my boy, which house is it?" inquired Mr Losberne.

"That!" replied Oliver, pointing eagerly from the window. "The white house. Oh! Pray make haste! I feel as if I should die!"

"Come, come," said the good doctor, patting him on the shoulder. "You will see them directly, and they will be overjoyed to find you safe and well."

"Oh! I hope so!" cried Oliver. "They were so very good to me."

The coach rolled on. It stopped. No, not that one, that, next door. It went on a few paces, and stopped again. Oliver looked up at the windows, with tears of happy expectation coursing down his face.

Alas! The house was empty. There was a notice – "To Let."

"Knock at the next door," cried Mr Losberne, taking Oliver's arm. "Ask what has become of Mr Brownlow, who used to live in the adjoining house."

The servant went to inquire. She presently returned, saying that Mr Brownlow had sold off his goods, and gone to the West Indies, six weeks before. Oliver clasped his hands, and sank backward.

"Has his housekeeper gone, too?" inquired Mr Losberne.

"Yes, sir," replied the servant. "The old gentleman, housekeeper, and a gentleman who was a friend of Mr Brownlow's, all went."

"Turn towards home again," said Mr Losberne to the driver, "and don't stop till you get out of this confounded London!"

"The bookseller, sir?" said Oliver. "I know the way there. See him, pray, sir!"

"My poor boy, this is disappointment enough for one day," said the doctor. "If we go to the bookseller's, we shall certainly find that he is dead, or he's run away. No; home again straight!" And in obedience to the doctor, home they went.

This bitter disappointment caused Oliver much sorrow, even in the midst of his happiness. Many times during his illness, he had thought of Mr Brownlow and Mrs Bedwin. The delight it would be to tell them how many long days and nights he had passed in reflecting on what they had done for him, and in bewailing his cruel separation from them. The hope of eventually clearing himself with them and explaining how he had been forced away, had buoyed him up and sustained him. Now, the idea that they should have gone so far, believing that he was an impostor and a thief – a belief which might remain uncontradicted to his dying day – was almost more than he could bear.

There was no change however, in the behaviour of his benefactors. After another fortnight, when the fine warm weather had fairly begun, they made preparations for quitting the house at Chertsey, for some months. Sending the plate, which had so excited Fagin, to the bank and leaving Giles and another servant in care of the house, they departed to a cottage at some distance in the country, and took Oliver with them.

Who can describe the pleasure and delight, the peace of mind and soft tranquillity the sickly boy felt in the balmy air! Men who have lived in crowded, pent-up streets, through lives of toil, and who have never wished for change have been known to yearn for one short glimpse of Nature's face.

It was a lovely spot to which they repaired. Oliver, whose days had been spent among squalid crowds, and in the midst of noise and brawling, seemed to enter on a new existence there. The rose and honeysuckle clung to the cottage walls, the ivy crept round the trunks of the trees, and the garden flowers perfumed the air with delicious odours. Hard by was a little churchyard not crowded with tall unsightly gravestones, but full of humble mounds, covered with fresh turf and moss. Oliver often wandered here and, thinking of the wretched grave in which his mother lay, would sometimes sit him down and sob unseen.

It was a happy time. The days were peaceful and serene; the nights brought with them neither fear nor care. Every morning he went to a white-headed old gentleman, living near the little church, who taught him to read better, and to write. And he spoke so kindly, and took such pains, that Oliver could never try enough to please him. Then, he would walk with Mrs Maylie and Rose, and hear them talk of books; or perhaps sit near them, in some shady place, and listen whilst the young lady read. When evening came, the ladies would walk out again, and he with them, listening with such pleasure to all they said. When it became quite dark, and they returned home, the young lady would sit down to the piano, and play some pleasant air, or sing, in a low and gentle voice, some old song which it pleased her aunt to hear. There would be no candles lighted at such times as these; and Oliver would sit by one of the windows, listening to the sweet music, in a perfect rapture.

And when Sunday came, how differently the day was spent from any way in which he had ever spent it yet! There was the little church, in the morning, with the green leaves fluttering at the windows: the birds singing without: and the sweet-smelling air stealing in at the low porch, and filling the homely building with its fragrance. Then, there were the walks as usual and at night, Oliver read a chapter or two from the Bible, which he had been studying all the week.

By six every morning, Oliver would be roaming the fields, plundering the hedges far and wide, for nosegays of wild flowers. These were arranged to the best advantage on the breakfast-table.

So three months glided away. With the purest and most amiable generosity on one side and the truest, warmest, soul-felt gratitude on the other, it is no wonder that, by the end of that short time, Oliver Twist had become completely domesticated with the old lady and her niece.

CHAPTER 32

Spring flew swiftly by, and summer came. If the village had been beautiful at first it was now in the full glow and luxuriance of its richness. The great trees, which had looked shrunken and bare in the earlier months, had now burst into strong life and health. The earth had donned her mantle of brightest green and shed her richest perfumes abroad. All things were glad and flourishing.

Still, the same quiet life went on at the little cottage, and the same cheerful serenity prevailed among its inmates. Oliver had long since grown stout and healthy, but health or sickness made no difference in his warm feelings to those about him, though they do in the feelings of a great many people. He was still the same gentle, affectionate creature that he had been when pain and suffering had wasted his strength, and when he was dependent for every slight attention and comfort on those who tended him.

One beautiful night, they had taken a longer walk than was customary with them, for the day had been unusually warm, and there was a brilliant moon, and a light wind had sprung up, which was unusually refreshing. Rose had been in high spirits, too, and they had walked on, in merry conversation, until they had far exceeded their ordinary bounds. Mrs Maylie being fatigued, they returned more slowly home. The young lady merely throwing off her simple bonnet, sat down to the piano as usual. After running abstractedly over the keys for a few minutes, she fell into a low and very solemn air and as she played it, they heard a sound as if she were weeping.

"Rose, my dear!" said the elder lady.

Rose made no reply, but played a little quicker, as though the words had roused her from some painful thoughts.

"Rose, my love!" cried Mrs Maylie, rising hastily, and going to her. "What is this? In tears! My dear child, what distresses you?"

"Nothing, aunt," replied the young lady. "I don't know what it is. I can't describe it, but I feel – "

"Not ill, my love?" interposed Mrs Maylie.

"No, no! Not ill!" replied Rose, shuddering as though some deadly chill passed over her. "I shall be better presently. Close the window, pray!"

Oliver hastened to comply with her request. The young lady, making an effort to recover her cheerfulness, strove to play some livelier tune but her fingers dropped powerless on the keys. Covering her face with her hands, she sank upon a sofa, and gave vent to the tears that she was now unable to repress.

"I would not alarm you if I could avoid it," rejoined Rose. "But indeed I have tried very hard, and cannot help this. I fear I am ill, aunt."

She was, indeed; for, when candles were brought, they saw that in the very short time since their return home, her skin had changed to a marble whiteness. There was an anxious, haggard look about the gentle face, which it had never worn before. Another minute and it was suffused with a crimson flush and a heavy wildness came over the soft blue eye. Again this disappeared, and she was once more deadly pale.

Oliver, who watched the old lady anxiously, observed that she was alarmed by these appearances and so in truth, was he. Seeing that she tried to make light of them, he endeavoured to do the same. When Rose was persuaded by her aunt to retire for the night, she was in better spirits and appeared even in better health. She assured them that she should rise in the morning, quite well.

"I hope," said Oliver, when Mrs Maylie returned, "that nothing is the matter? She don't look well tonight, but – "

The old lady motioned to him not to speak and sitting down remained silent for some time. At length, she said, in a trembling voice, "I hope not, Oliver. I have been very happy with her for some years, too happy, perhaps. It may be time that I should meet with some misfortune but I hope it is not this. She is very ill now and will be worse, I fear. My dear Rose! Oh, what should I do without her!"

She gave way to such great grief, that Oliver, suppressing his own emotion, ventured to remonstrate with her and to beg, that, for the sake of the dear young lady herself, she would be more calm.

"And consider, ma'am," said Oliver, as tears came into his eyes, despite his efforts to the contrary. "How young and good she is, and what pleasure and comfort she gives to all about her. I am quite certain – that, for your sake, who are so good yourself and for the sake of all she makes so happy she will not die. Heaven will never let her die so young."

"Hush!" said Mrs Maylie, laying her hand on Oliver's head. "You think like a child, poor boy. But you teach me my duty. I had forgotten it for a moment, Oliver, but I hope I may be pardoned, for I am old, and have seen enough of illness and death to know the agony of separation from the objects of our love. God's will be done! I love her and He knows how well!"

Oliver was surprised to see that as Mrs Maylie said these words, she drew herself up and became composed and firm. He was still more astonished to find that this firmness lasted and that, under all the care and watching which ensued, Mrs Maylie was ever ready and collected. She performed all her duties steadily, and, to all external appearance, even cheerfully. But he was young, and did not know what strong minds are capable of under trying circumstances. How should he, when their possessors so seldom know themselves?

An anxious night ensued. When morning came, Mrs Maylie's predictions were confirmed. Rose was in the first stage of a high and dangerous fever.

"We must be active, Oliver, and not give way to useless grief," said Mrs Maylie, laying her finger on her lip as she looked at him. "This letter must be sent, with all speed, to Mr Losberne. Take it to the market town by the footpath across the fields. Thence dispatched, by an express on horseback, straight to Chertsey. The people at the inn will do this and I can trust to you to see it done, I know."

Oliver made no reply, but looked ready to go.

"Here is another letter," said Mrs Maylie, pausing to reflect. "But whether to send it now, or wait until I see how Rose goes on, I scarcely know. I would not forward it, unless I feared the worst."

"Is it for Chertsey, too, ma'am?" inquired Oliver, impatient to leave, holding out his trembling hand for the letter.

"No," replied the old lady, giving it to him mechanically. Oliver glanced at it, and saw that it was directed to Harry Maylie, Esquire, at some great lord's house in the country.

"Shall it go, ma'am?" asked Oliver, looking up, impatiently.

"I think not," replied Mrs Maylie, taking it back. "I will wait."

With these words, she gave Oliver her purse, and he started off, without more delay, at the greatest speed he could muster.

Swiftly he ran across the fields, and down the little lanes which sometimes divided them. Nor did he stop once, save now and then, for a few seconds, to recover breath, until he came, in a great heat, and covered with dust, to the market-place of the town.

Here he paused, and looked about for the inn. In one corner there was a large house, with all the wood about it painted green, before which was the sign of "The George." To this he hastened.

He spoke to a postboy dozing under the gateway, who referred him to the ostler. The landlord was a tall gentleman in a blue neckcloth, a white hat, drab breeches, and boots.

This gentleman walked with much deliberation into the bar to make out the bill. A horse then had to be saddled, and a man to be dressed, and this took up ten good minutes more. Oliver was in such a state of impatience that he felt as if he could have jumped upon the horse and galloped to the next stage. At length, all was ready and the little parcel having been handed up with many entreaties for its speedy delivery, the man set spurs to his horse. Rattling over the paving of the market-place, he was out of the town, galloping along the turnpike-road, in a couple of minutes.

Feeling certain that assistance was sent for, and that no time had been lost, Oliver hurried up the inn-yard with a somewhat lighter heart. He was turning out of the gate when he by chance stumbled against a tall man wrapped in a cloak, coming out of the inn door.

"Hah!" cried the man, fixing his eyes on Oliver, and suddenly recoiling. "What the devil's this?"

"I beg your pardon, sir," said Oliver. "I was in a great hurry and didn't see you were coming."

"Death!" muttered the man to himself, glaring at the boy with his large dark eyes. "Who would have thought it! Grind him to ashes! He'd start up from a stone coffin, to come in my way!"

"I am sorry," stammered Oliver, confused by the strange man's wild look. "I hope I have not hurt you!"

116

"Rot you!" murmured the man, between clenched teeth. "If I had only had the courage to say the word, I might have been free of you in a night. Curses on your head! What are you doing here?"

The man shook his fist, as he advanced towards Oliver, as if intending to aim a blow at him. But then he fell violently on the ground, writhing and foaming, in a fit.

Oliver gazed, for a moment, at the struggles of the madman (for such he supposed him to be) and then darted into the house for help. Having seen him safely carried into the hotel, he turned his face homewards, running as fast as he could.

The meeting did not dwell on his mind long, however, for when he reached the cottage, there was enough to occupy him. Rose Maylie had rapidly grown worse and before midnight she was delirious. A medical practitioner living close by was in constant attendance upon her and after first seeing the patient, had taken Mrs Maylie aside, and pronounced her disorder to be one of a most alarming nature. "In fact," he said, "it would be little short of a miracle, if she recovered."

How often did Oliver start from his bed that night, and stealing out, with noiseless footsteps, to the staircase, listen for the slightest sound from the sick chamber! How often did a tremble shake his frame, and cold drops of terror start upon his brow, when a sudden trampling of feet caused him to fear that something too dreadful to think of, had even then occurred! And what had been the fervency of all the prayers he had ever uttered, compared with those he poured forth, now, in the agony and passion of his supplication for the life and health of the gentle creature, who was tottering on the deep grave's verge!

Morning came and the little cottage was lonely and still. People spoke in whispers. Anxious faces appeared at the gate, from time to time – women and children went away in tears. All the livelong day, and for hours after it had grown dark, Oliver paced softly up and down the garden, raising his eyes every instant to the sick chamber, and shuddering to see the darkened window. Late at night, Mr Losberne arrived. "It is hard," said the good doctor, turning away as he spoke. "So young, so much beloved, but there is very little hope."

Another morning. The sun shone brightly as if it looked upon no misery or care. With every leaf and flower in full bloom about her, with life, and health, and sounds and sights of joy, surrounding her on every side, the fair young creature lay, wasting fast. Oliver crept away to the old churchyard, and sitting down on one of the green mounds, wept and prayed for her, in silence.

There was such peace and beauty in the scene, that, when the boy looked about, the thought instinctively occurred to him, that this was not a time for death. Rose could surely never die when humbler things were all so glad and gay. Graves were for cold and cheerless winter, not for sunlight and fragrance.

Oliver turned homeward, thinking on the many kindnesses he had received from the young lady, and wishing that the time could come over again, that he might never cease showing her how grateful and attached he was.

When he reached home Mrs Maylie was sitting in the little parlour. Oliver's heart sank at sight of her; for she had never left the bedside of her niece and he trembled to think what change could have driven her away. He learnt that she had fallen into a deep sleep, from which she would waken, either to recovery and life, or to bid them farewell, and die.

They sat, listening, and afraid to speak, for hours. The uneaten meal was removed, with looks which showed that their thoughts were elsewhere, they watched the sun as it sank lower, and, at length, cast over sky and earth those brilliant hues which herald its departure. Their quick ears caught the sound of an approaching footstep. They both involuntarily darted to the door, as Mr Losberne entered.

"What of Rose?" cried the old lady. "Tell me at once! I can bear it, anything but suspense! Oh, tell me! In the name of Heaven!"

"You must compose yourself," said the doctor, supporting her. "Be calm, my dear ma'am, pray."

"Let me go, in God's name! My dear child! She is dead! She is dying!"

"No!" cried the doctor, passionately. "As He is good and merciful, she will live to bless us all, for years to come."

The lady fell upon her knees, and tried to fold her hands together; but the energy that had supported her so long, fled up to Heaven with her first thanksgiving; and she sank into the friendly arms that were extended to receive her.

CHAPTER 33

It was almost too much happiness to bear. Oliver felt stunned by the news – he could not weep, or speak, or rest. It wasn't until after a long ramble in the quiet evening air that a burst of tears relieved him, and he seemed to awaken to a full sense of the joyful change that had occurred, and the load seemed lifted from his heart.

The night was fast closing in as he returned homeward, laden with flowers for the sick chamber. As he walked briskly along the road, he heard behind him, the noise of a post-chaise, driven at great speed. The horses were galloping, and the road was narrow, so he stood leaning against a gate until it passed him.

As it dashed on, Oliver caught a glimpse of a man in a white nightcap, whose face seemed familiar to him. In another second or two, the nightcap was thrust out of the chaise-window, and a stentorian voice bellowed to the driver to stop. Then, the nightcap once again appeared and the same voice called Oliver by his name.

"Here!" cried the voice. "Oliver, what's the news? Miss Rose!"

"Is it you, Giles?" cried Oliver, running up to the chaise-door.

Giles popped out his nightcap again when he was suddenly pulled back by a young gentleman who occupied the other corner of the chaise, who eagerly demanded the news.

"In a word!" cried the gentleman. "Better or worse?"

"Better – much better!" replied Oliver, hastily.

"Thank Heaven!" exclaimed the gentleman. "You are sure?"

"Quite, sir," replied Oliver. "The change took place only a few hours ago and Mr Losberne says that all danger is at an end."

The gentleman opened the chaise-door, leaped out, and taking Oliver hurriedly by the arm, led him aside. "You are quite certain? There is no possibility of any mistake, is there?" he demanded in a tremulous voice. "Do not deceive me, by awakening hopes that are not to be fulfilled."

"I would not, sir," replied Oliver. "Mr Losberne's words were that she would live to bless us for many years to come. I heard him say so."

The gentleman turned his face away for some minutes. Oliver thought he heard him sob but stood apart, feigning to be occupied with his nosegay.

"I think you had better go on to my mother's in the chaise, Giles," said the gentleman. "I would rather walk slowly on, so as to gain a little time before I see her. You can say I am coming."

"I beg your pardon, Mr Harry," said Giles. "But I should be very much obliged if you would leave the postboy to say that. It wouldn't be proper for the maids to see me this way, sir. I should never have authority with them if they did."

"Well," rejoined Harry Maylie, smiling. "Let him go on with the luggage, if you wish, and follow with us. Only first change that nightcap, or we shall be taken for madmen."

Mr Giles, swiftly substituted a hat, of grave and sober shape. This done the postboy drove off. Giles, Mr Maylie, and Oliver, followed at their leisure.

As they walked along, Oliver glanced occasionally with much curiosity at the newcomer. He seemed about five-and-twenty years of age, and was of the middle height. His countenance was frank and handsome and his demeanour easy and prepossessing. He bore so strong a likeness to the old lady, that Oliver would have had no great difficulty in imagining their relationship, if he had not already spoken of her as his mother.

Mrs Maylie was anxiously waiting to receive her son when he reached the cottage.

"Mother!" whispered the young man. "Why did you not write before?"

"I did," replied Mrs Maylie. "But, on reflection, I kept the letter until I had heard Mr Losberne's opinion."

"But why," said the young man, "why run the chance of that occurring which so nearly happened? If Rose had – I cannot utter that word now – if this illness had ended differently, how could you ever have forgiven yourself! How could I ever have known happiness again!"

"If that had been the case, Harry," said Mrs Maylie, "I fear your happiness would have been blighted, and that your arrival here, a day sooner or later, would have made very little difference. I know that she deserves the best and purest love the heart of man can offer. I know that the devotion and affection of her nature require no ordinary return, but one that shall be deep and lasting."

"This is unkind, mother," said Harry. "Do you suppose that I am a boy ignorant of my own mind, and mistaking the impulses of my own soul?"

"I think, my dear son," returned Mrs Maylie, laying her hand upon his shoulder, "that youth has many generous impulses which do not last and that among them are some, which, being gratified, become only the more fleeting. Above all, I think," said the lady, fixing her eyes on her son's face, "that if an enthusiastic, ardent, and ambitious man marries a wife on whose name there is a stain, although it originates in no fault of hers, if he is made the subject of sneers, and his wife and children also, no matter how generous and good his nature, he may one day repent of this marriage. And she may have the pain of knowing that he does so."

"Mother," said the young man, impatiently. "He would be a selfish brute."

"You think so now, Harry," replied his mother.

"And ever will!" said the young man. "The mental agony I have suffered, during the last two days, wrings from me the avowal to you of a passion which, as you well know, is not one of yesterday, nor one I have lightly formed. On Rose, sweet, gentle girl! My heart is set, as firmly as ever heart of man was set on woman. I have no thought, no view, no hope in life, beyond her; and if you oppose me in this great stake, you take my peace and happiness in your hands, and cast them to the wind. Mother, think better of this, and of me, and do not disregard the happiness of which you seem to think so little."

"Harry," said Mrs Maylie. "It is because I think so much of warm and sensitive hearts, that I would spare them from being wounded. But we have said enough, and more than enough, on this matter."

"Let it rest with Rose, then," interposed Harry. "You will not press these opinions of yours, as to throw any obstacle in my way?"

"I will not," rejoined Mrs Maylie. "but consider – "

"I have considered!" was the impatient reply. "Mother, I have considered, years and years. I have considered ever since I have been capable of serious reflection. My feelings remain unchanged. No! Before I leave this place, Rose shall hear me."

"She shall," said Mrs Maylie.

"There is something in your manner, which would almost imply that she will hear me coldly, mother," said the young man.

"Not coldly," rejoined the old lady, "far from it."

"How then?" urged the young man. "She has formed no other attachment?"

"No, indeed," replied his mother. "You have, or I mistake, too strong a hold on her affections already. What I would say," resumed the old lady, stopping her son as he was about to speak, "is this. Before you stake your all on this chance, before you suffer yourself to be carried to the highest point of hope, reflect for a few moments, my dear child, on Rose's history, and consider what effect the knowledge of her doubtful birth may have on her decision. Devoted as she is to us, that perfect sacrifice of self which, in all matters, has always been her characteristic."

"What do you mean?"

"That I leave you to discover," replied Mrs Maylie. "I must go back to her. God bless you!"

"I shall see you again tonight?" said the young man, eagerly.

"By and by," replied the lady; "when I leave Rose."

"You will tell her I am here?" said Harry.

"Of course," replied Mrs Maylie.

"And say how anxious I have been, and how much I have suffered, and how I long to see her. You will do this, mother?"

"I will tell her all," said the old lady. And pressing her son's hand affectionately, she hastened from the room.

Mr Losberne and Oliver were at the other end of the room while this hurried conversation took place. The former now held out his hand to Harry Maylie and hearty salutations were exchanged between them. The doctor then communicated, in reply to multifarious questions from his young friend, a precise account of his patient's situation. It was quite as full of promise, as Oliver's statement had encouraged him to hope, and Mr Giles, who affected to be busy about the luggage, listened with greedy ears.

"Have you shot anything particular, lately, Giles?" inquired the doctor, when he had concluded.

"Nothing particular, sir," replied Mr Giles, colouring.

"Well," said the doctor, "I am sorry to hear it, because you do that sort of thing admirably. Pray, how is Brittles?"

"The boy is very well, sir," said Mr Giles, recovering his usual tone of patronage, "and sends his respectful duty, sir."

The remainder of the evening passed cheerfully away, for the doctor was in high spirits and however fatigued or thoughtful Harry Maylie might have been at first, he was not proof against the worthy gentleman's good humour. The good doctor came forth with a great variety of sallies and professional recollections, and an abundance of small jokes, which struck Oliver as being the drollest things he had ever heard. He laughed to the evident satisfaction of the doctor, who laughed immoderately at himself, and made Harry laugh almost as heartily, by the very force of sympathy. So, they were as pleasant a party as, under the circumstances, they could well have been and it was late before they retired.

Oliver rose next morning in better heart, and went about his usual early occupations with more hope and pleasure than he had known for many days.

It is worthy of remark, and Oliver did not fail to note it at the time, that Harry Maylie joined him for his morning expeditions. After the very first morning when he met Oliver coming laden home, he was seized with such a passion for flowers, and displayed such a taste in their arrangement, as left his young companion far behind. Oliver knew where the best flowers were to be found and morning after morning they scoured the country together, and brought home the fairest that blossomed. The window of the young lady's chamber was opened now; for she loved to feel the rich summer air stream in, and there always stood in water, just inside the lattice, one particular little bunch, which was made up with great care every morning. Oliver could not help noticing that the withered flowers were never thrown away, although the little vase was regularly replenished. The days were flying by and Rose was rapidly recovering.

Nor did Oliver's time hang heavy on his hands. He applied himself, with redoubled assiduity, to the instructions of the white-headed old gentleman, and laboured so hard that his quick progress surprised even himself. It was while he was engaged in this pursuit, that he was greatly startled and distressed by a most unexpected occurrence.

The little room in which he sat when busy at his books, was on the ground floor, at the back of the house. It looked into a garden, whence a wicket-gate opened into a small paddock. Beyond, was fine meadowland and wood. There was no other dwelling nearby.

One beautiful evening, when the first shades of twilight were beginning to settle upon the earth, Oliver sat, intent upon his books. The day had been uncommonly sultry, and he fell asleep.

Oliver knew perfectly well that he was in his own little room, his books were lying on the table before him, and the air was stirring the plants outside. And yet he was also asleep. Suddenly, the scene changed

– the air became close and confined, and he thought, with a glow of terror, that he was in the Jew's house again. There sat the hideous old man, in his usual corner, pointing at him, and whispering to another man, who sat beside him.

"Hush, my dear!" he thought he heard the Jew say. "It is he, sure enough. Come away."

"He!" the other man seemed to answer. "Could I mistake him? If you buried him fifty feet deep, and took me across his grave, I'd know, if there wasn't a mark to say that he lay buried there!"

The man said this with such dreadful hatred, that Oliver awoke with a start.

Good Heaven! What was that, which deprived him of his voice and power to move! There – there – at the window – close before him – so close, that he could have almost touched him – there stood the Jew! And beside him, white with rage or fear, or both, were the scowling features of the very man from the inn-yard.

It was but an instant, a flash before his eyes and they were gone. But they had recognised him, and he them. He stood transfixed for a moment then, leaping from the window into the garden, called loudly for help.

CHAPTER 34

When the inmates of the house, attracted by Oliver's cries, hurried to him, they found him, pale and agitated, pointing in the direction of the meadows behind the house, and barely able to say the words, "The Jew! The Jew!"

Mr Giles was at a loss but Harry Maylie, who had heard Oliver's history from his mother, understood it at once.

"What direction did he take?" he asked, catching up a heavy stick.

"That," replied Oliver, pointing. "I missed them in an instant."

"Then, they are in the ditch!" said Harry. "Follow! And keep as near me, as you can." So saying, he sprang over the hedge, and darted off at a speed difficult for the others to keep up.

Giles followed as well as he could and Oliver followed too. A minute or two later, Mr Losberne, who had been out walking, tumbled over the hedge after them, and struck into the same course at no contemptible speed, shouting all the while to know what was the matter.

The search was in vain. There were not even the traces of recent footsteps to be seen. They stood now, on the summit of a little hill, commanding the open fields in every direction for three or four miles. There was the village in the hollow on the left. A thick wood skirted the meadows in another direction, but they had not had enough time to reach that cover.

"It must have been a dream, Oliver," said Harry Maylie.

"Oh no, indeed, sir," replied Oliver, shuddering at the very recollection of the old wretch. "I saw them both, as plainly as I see you now."

"Who was the other?" inquired Harry and Mr Losberne, together.

"The very same man I told you of, who came so suddenly upon me at the inn," said Oliver. "We had our eyes fixed full upon each other. I could swear to him."

"They took this way?" demanded Harry: "Are you sure?"

"As sure as I am that the men were at the window," replied Oliver, pointing down, as he spoke, to the hedge that divided the cottage garden from the meadow. "The tall man leaped over, just there, and the Jew ran a few paces to the right, to creep through the gap."

The two gentlemen watched Oliver's earnest face as he spoke, and looking then to each other, seemed satisfied of the accuracy of what he said. Still, the grass was long, but it was trodden down nowhere, save where their own feet had crushed it. The sides of the ditches were of damp clay, but nowhere could they see the print of men's shoes.

"This is strange!" said Harry.

"Strange?" echoed the doctor. "Blathers and Duff, themselves, could make nothing of it."

Even though the search seemed pointless, they did not stop until the coming of night and even then, they gave up reluctantly. Giles was despatched to the alehouses in the village, with the best description Oliver could give of the strangers. The Jew was, at all events, sufficiently remarkable to be remembered but Giles returned with no further intelligence to lessen the mystery.

The following day, a fresh search was made, and inquiries renewed but with no better success. On the day after, Oliver and Mr Maylie went to the market town, in the hope of seeing or hearing something of the men there, but this effort was equally fruitless. After a few days, the affair began to be forgotten.

Meanwhile, Rose was rapidly recovering. She had left her room and able to go out, was mixing once more with the family, carrying joy into the hearts of all.

But, although this happy change had a visible effect on the little circle, there was at times, an unwonted restraint upon some there. Mrs Maylie and her son were often closeted together for a long time and more than once Rose appeared with traces of tears upon her face. After Mr Losberne had fixed a day for his departure, these symptoms increased; and it became evident that something was upsetting the young lady, and somebody else besides.

One morning, when Rose was alone in the breakfast parlour, Harry Maylie entered and, with some hesitation, begged permission to speak with her for a few moments.

"A few – a very few – will suffice, Rose," said the young man, drawing his chair towards her. "What I shall have to say, has already presented itself to your mind. The most cherished hopes of my heart are not unknown to you, though you have not yet heard them from my lips."

Rose had been very pale from the moment of his entrance but that may have been due to her recent illness. She bowed, and bending over some plants, waited in silence for him to proceed.

"I – I – ought to have left here, before," said Harry.

"You should, indeed," replied Rose. "Forgive me for saying so, but I wish you had."

"I was brought here, by the most dreadful fear of losing the one dear being on whom my every wish and hope are fixed," he said. "You were dying, trembling between earth and heaven. We know that when the young, the beautiful and good are ill, their pure spirits turn towards heaven. We know, Heaven help us, that the best and fairest of our kind, too often fade in blooming."

There were tears in the eyes of the gentle girl, as these words were spoken. One fell upon the flower over which she bent, and glistened brightly in its cup.

"A creature," continued the young man, passionately, "a creature as fair and innocent as one of God's own angels, fluttered between life and

126

death. Rose, Rose, to know that you were passing away like some soft shadow, to have no hope that you would be spared to those who linger here and yet to pray, that you might be restored to those who loved you – these were distractions almost too great to bear. They were mine, by day and night; and with them, came such a rushing torrent of fears, and apprehensions, and selfish regrets, lest you should die, and never know how devotedly I loved you. You recovered. Day by day, and almost hour by hour, some drop of health came back. I have watched you change almost from death, to life, with eyes that turned blind with their eagerness and deep affection. Do not tell me that you wish I had lost this; for it has softened my heart to all mankind."

"I did not mean that," said Rose, weeping. "I only wish you had left here, that you might have returned to high and noble pursuits, to pursuits well worthy of you."

"There is no pursuit more worthy of me than the struggle to win such a heart as yours," said the young man, taking her hand. "Rose, my own dear Rose! For years – for years – I have loved you, hoping to win my way to fame, and then come proudly home and tell you it had been pursued only for you to share. That time has not arrived, but here, with no fame won, and no young vision realised, I offer you the heart so long your own."

"Your behaviour has ever been kind and noble," said Rose, mastering her emotions. "So hear my answer."

"It is, that I may endeavour to deserve you. It is, dear Rose?"

"It is," replied Rose, "that you must endeavour to forget me – not as your old and dearly attached companion, for that would wound me deeply, but, as the object of your love. Instead I will be the truest, warmest, and most faithful friend you have."

There was a pause, during which Rose, who had covered her face with one hand, gave free vent to her tears. Harry held the other.

"And your reasons, Rose," he said, at length, in a low voice, "for this decision?"

"You have a right to know them," rejoined Rose. "You can say nothing to alter my resolution. It is a duty that I must perform. I owe it to myself, that I, a friendless, portionless girl with a blight upon my name, should not give your friends reason to suspect that I had sordidly yielded to your first passion, and fastened myself to all your hopes and projects. I owe it to you and yours, to prevent you from opposing, in the warmth of your generous nature, this great obstacle to your progress in the world."

"If your inclinations chime with your sense of duty – " Harry began.

"They do not." replied Rose, colouring deeply.

"Then you return my love?" said Harry. "Say but that, dear Rose, say but that, and soften the bitterness of this hard disappointment!"

"If I could have done so, without doing heavy wrong to him I loved," rejoined Rose. "I could have – "

"Have received this declaration very differently?" said Harry. "Do not conceal that from me, at least, Rose."

"I could," said Rose. "Stay!" she added, disengaging her hand, "why should we prolong this painful interview? Farewell, Harry! As we have met today, we meet no more; but in other relations than those in which this conversation would have placed us, we may be long and happily entwined. May every blessing that the prayers of a true heart can call down, cheer and prosper you!"

"Another word, Rose," said Harry. "Your reason in your own words. From your own lips let me hear it!"

"The prospect before you," answered Rose, firmly, "is a brilliant one. All the honours to which great talents and powerful connections can help men in public life, are in store for you. But those connections are proud and I will neither mingle with such as may hold in scorn the mother who gave me life nor bring disgrace or failure on the son of her who has so well supplied that mother's place. In a word," said the young lady, turning away, as her temporary firmness forsook her, "there is a stain upon my name, which the world visits on innocent heads. I will carry it into no blood but my own and the reproach shall rest alone on me."

"One word more, Rose. Dearest Rose! One more!" cried Harry, throwing himself before her. "If I had been less – less fortunate, the world would call it – if some obscure and peaceful life had been my destiny – if I had been poor, sick, helpless – would you have turned from me then?"

"Do not press me to reply, answered Rose. "The question does not arise, and never will. It is unfair, almost unkind, to urge it."

"If your answer be what I almost dare to hope it is," retorted Harry, "it will shed a gleam of happiness upon my lonely way. Oh, Rose! In the name of my ardent and enduring attachment; in the name of all I have suffered for you, and all you doom me to undergo, answer me this one question!"

"Then, if your lot had been differently cast," rejoined Rose. "If you had been even a little, but not so far, above me; if I could have been a help and comfort to you in any humble scene of peace and retirement, and not a drawback in ambitious and distinguished crowds; I should have been spared this trial. I have every reason to be very happy, now; but then, Harry, I should have been happier."

Recollections of old hopes, cherished as a girl, crowded into her mind, while making this avowal. But they brought tears with them.

"I cannot help this weakness, and it makes my purpose stronger," said Rose, extending her hand. "I must leave you now, indeed."

"I ask one promise," said Harry. "Once, and only once more – say within a year, but it may be much sooner – I may speak to you again on this subject, for the last time."

"Not to press me to alter my right determination," replied Rose, with a melancholy smile, "it will be useless."

"No," said Harry; "to hear you repeat it, if you will – finally repeat it! I will lay at your feet, whatever of station or fortune I may possess, and if you still adhere to your present resolution, will not seek, by word or act, to change it."

"Then let it be so," rejoined Rose. "It is but one pang the more, and by that time I may be able to bear it better."

She extended her hand again. But the young man caught her to him and imprinting one kiss on her beautiful forehead, hurried from the room.

CHAPTER 35

"So you are resolved to be my travelling companion this morning; eh?" said the doctor, as Harry Maylie joined him and Oliver at the breakfast table. "Why, you are not in the same mind or intention two half-hours together!"

"You will tell me a different tale one of these days," said Harry, colouring without any perceptible reason.

129

"I hope I may have good cause to do so," replied Mr Losberne. "Only yesterday morning you had made up your mind, to stay here, and to accompany your mother to the seaside. Before noon, you announce that you are going to do me the honour of accompanying me as far as I go, on your road to London. And at night, you urge me, with great mystery, to start before the ladies are stirring; which means that young Oliver here is pinned down to this breakfast when he ought to be ranging the meadows after botanical phenomena of all kinds. Too bad, isn't it, Oliver?"

"I should have been very sorry to have missed you and Mr Maylie leaving, sir," rejoined Oliver.

"That's a fine fellow," said the doctor. "You shall come and see me when you return. But, to speak seriously, Harry – has any communication from the great nobs produced this sudden anxiety on your part to be gone?"

"The great nobs," replied Harry, "by whom I take you mean my most stately uncle, have not communicated with me at all, since I have been here. Nor, at this time of the year, is it likely that anything would occur to render necessary my immediate attendance among them."

"Well," said the doctor, "you are a queer fellow. But of course they will get you into parliament at the election before Christmas, and these sudden shiftings and changes are no bad preparation for political life. There's something in that. Good training is always desirable, whether the race be for place, cup, or sweepstakes."

Harry Maylie looked as if he could have made one or two remarks that would have staggered the doctor not a little; but he contented himself with saying, "We shall see," and pursued the subject no farther. The post-chaise drove up to the door shortly afterwards, and Giles coming in for the luggage, the good doctor bustled out, to see it packed.

"Oliver," said Harry Maylie, in a low voice, "let me speak a word with you."

Oliver walked into the window-recess to which Mr Maylie beckoned him.

"You can write well now?" said Harry, laying his hand upon his arm.

"I hope so, sir," replied Oliver.

"I shall not be at home again, perhaps for some time. I wish you would write to me – say once a fortnight – every alternate Monday: to the

General Post Office in London. Will you?"

"Oh! Certainly, sir, I shall be proud to do it," exclaimed Oliver greatly delighted with the commission.

"I should like to know how – how my mother and Miss Maylie are," said the young man. "You can tell me what walks you take, and what you talk about, and whether she – they, I mean – seem happy and quite well. You understand me?"

"Oh! Quite, sir," replied Oliver.

"I would rather you did not mention it to them," said Harry, hurrying over his words, "because it might make my mother anxious to write to me oftener. Let it be a secret between you and me. Tell me everything! I depend upon you."

Oliver, quite elated and honoured by a sense of his importance, faithfully promised to be secret and explicit in his communications. Mr Maylie took leave of him, with many assurances of his regard and protection.

The doctor was in the chaise. Giles, who was to stay behind, held the door open in his hand. Harry cast one slight glance at the latticed window, and jumped into the carriage.

"Drive on!" he cried. "Nothing short of flying will keep pace with me today."

The vehicle wound its way along the road, almost hidden in a cloud of dust: now wholly disappearing, and now becoming visible again. It was not until even the dusty cloud was no longer to be seen, that the gazers dispersed.

And there was one looker-on that remained with eyes fixed upon the spot where the carriage had disappeared, long after it was many miles away. Behind the white curtain that had kept her from view when Harry looked towards the window, sat Rose.

"He seems in high spirits and happy," she said, at length. "I feared for a time he might be otherwise. I was mistaken. I am very glad."

Tears are signs of gladness as well as grief; but those which ran down Rose's face, as she sat at the window, seemed to tell more of sorrow than of joy.

CHAPTER 36

Mr Bumble sat in the workhouse parlour, with his eyes moodily fixed on the cheerless grate.

A great change had taken place in his affairs. The laced coat, and the cocked hat, where were they? He still wore knee breeches and dark cotton stockings but they were not *the* breeches. The coat was wide-skirted, and in that respect like *the* coat, but, oh, how different! The mighty cocked hat had been replaced by a modest round one. Mr Bumble was no longer a beadle.

Mr Bumble had married Mrs Corney, and was master of the workhouse. Another beadle had come into power. On him the cocked hat, gold-laced coat, and staff, had all three descended.

"And tomorrow two months it was done!" said Mr Bumble, with a sigh. "It seems a age."

Mr Bumble might have meant that he had concentrated a whole existence of happiness into the short space of eight weeks. But the sigh – there was a vast deal of meaning in the sigh.

"I sold myself," said Mr Bumble, pursuing the same train of reflection. "For six teaspoons, a pair of sugar-tongs, and a milk-pot; with a small quantity of second-hand furniture, and twenty pound in money. I went very reasonable. Cheap, dirt cheap!"

"Cheap!" cried a shrill voice. "You would have been dear at any price. Dear enough I paid for you, Lord knows!"

Mr Bumble turned, and encountered the face of his interesting consort, who, misunderstanding the few words she had overheard, had hazarded her response.

"Mrs Bumble, ma'am!" said Mr Bumble, with a sentimental sternness.

"Well!" cried the lady.

"Have the goodness to look at me," said Mr Bumble, fixing his eyes upon her. "If she stands such a eye as that," thought Mr Bumble, "she can stand anything. It is a eye I never knew to fail with paupers. If it fails with her, my power is gone."

The matron was in no way overpowered by Mr Bumble's scowl, but, on the contrary, treated it with great disdain, even laughing.

On hearing this unexpected sound, Mr Bumble looked, first incredulous, and then amazed. He went back to meditating.

"Are you going to sit snoring there, all day?" asked Mrs Bumble.

"I am going to sit here, as long as I think proper, ma'am," rejoined Mr Bumble. "And although I was not snoring, I shall snore, gape, sneeze, laugh, or cry, as I wish; as is my prerogative."

"Your prerogative!" sneered Mrs Bumble, with contempt.

"The prerogative of a man, ma'am," said Mr Bumble, "is to command."

"And what's the prerogative of a woman, in the name of Goodness?" cried the relict of Mr Corney deceased.

"To obey, ma'am," thundered Mr Bumble. "Your late unfortunate husband should have taught you. Perhaps, he might be alive now. I wish he was, poor man!"

Mrs Bumble, realising that the decisive moment had now arrived, no sooner heard this allusion to the dead and gone, than she dropped sobbing into a chair, screaming that Mr Bumble was a hard-hearted brute.

But tears would not find their way to Mr Bumble's soul; his heart was waterproof. He eyed his good lady with looks of great satisfaction, and begged that she cry her hardest – the exercise being looked upon as good for one's health.

"It opens the lungs, exercises the eyes, and softens down the temper," said Mr Bumble. "So cry away."

Mr Bumble then took his hat from a peg, and putting it on, thrust his hands his pockets, and sauntered towards the door.

Now, Mrs Corney that was, had tried the tears, but was prepared to try a more physical approach, as Mr Bumble soon found.

The first proof he had was the hollow sound of his hat flying to the opposite end of the room. The expert lady then clasped him tightly round the throat with one hand and inflicted a shower of blows upon it with the other. This done, she scratched his face, and tore his hair. Having inflicted as much punishment as she deemed necessary for the offence, she pushed him over a chair, and defied him to talk about his prerogative again, if he dared.

"Get up!" said Mrs Bumble, in a voice of command. "And take yourself away from here, or I shall do something desperate."

Mr Bumble rose, wondering what something desperate might be. Picking up his hat, he looked towards the door.

"Are you going?" demanded Mrs Bumble.

"Certainly, my dear, certainly," rejoined Mr Bumble, making a quicker motion towards the door. "I'm going, my dear! You are so very violent, that really I – "

At this instant, Mrs Bumble stepped hastily forward to replace the carpet, which had been kicked up in the scuffle. Mr Bumble darted out of the room.

Mr Bumble was fairly taken by surprise, and fairly beaten. He had a decided propensity for bullying and, consequently, was a coward.

But, the measure of his degradation was not yet full. After making a tour of the house, Mr Bumble came to a room where some female paupers were usually employed in washing parish linen. The sound of voices came to him.

"Hem!" said Mr Bumble, summoning all dignity. "These women at least shall continue to respect the prerogative. Hallo there! What do you mean by this noise, you hussies?"

With these words, Mr Bumble opened the door, and walked in with a very fierce and angry manner. This became a most humiliated and cowering air, as his eyes unexpectedly rested on the form of his lady wife.

"My dear," said Mr Bumble, "I didn't know you were here."

"Didn't know I was here!" repeated Mrs Bumble. "Why are you here?"

"I thought they were talking rather too much to be working properly, my dear," replied Mr Bumble, glancing at a couple of old women at the wash tub.

"You thought they were talking too much?" said Mrs Bumble. "What business is it of yours?"

"Why, my dear – " urged Mr Bumble submissively. "It's very true, you're matron here, my dear, but I thought you weren't around."

"I'll tell you what, Mr Bumble," returned his lady. "you're too fond of poking your nose into things that don't concern you. Everybody in the house laughs the moment your back is turned. You make yourself look a fool every hour in the day. Be off!"

Mr Bumble, seeing with excruciating feeling, the delight of the two old paupers, hesitated for an instant. Mrs Bumble, whose patience brooked no delay, caught up a bowl of soapsuds, and motioning him towards the door, ordered him instantly to depart, on pain of receiving the contents upon his portly person.

What could Mr Bumble do? He looked round, and slunk away and, as he reached the door, the titterings of the paupers broke into a shrill chuckle of delight. He was degraded in their eyes, he had lost station before the paupers, he had fallen from the height of beadleship to the lowest depth of henpeckery.

"All in two months!" said Mr Bumble, dismally. "Two months! I was not only my own master, but everybody else's, so far as the porochial workhouse was concerned, and now! – "

It was too much. Mr Bumble boxed the ears of the boy who opened the gate for him and walked, distractedly, into the street.

He walked up one street, and down another, until exercise had abated the first passion of his grief. He passed a great many public houses, finally pausing before one in a by-way, whose parlour had just one solitary customer. It then began to rain heavily. This determined him. Mr Bumble stepped in and ordered something to drink.

The man seated there was tall and dark, and wore a large cloak. He had the air of a stranger; and seemed, by the dust on his dress, to have travelled some distance. He eyed Bumble askance, as he entered, but hardly deigned to nod his head.

Mr Bumble had dignity enough for two, so he drank his gin-and-water in silence, and read the paper.

It so happened that Mr Bumble felt, every now and then, a strong urge to look at the stranger. But whenever he did so, he withdrew his eyes in confusion, as the stranger was at the same time stealing a look at him. Mr Bumble's awkwardness was enhanced by the very remarkable expression of the stranger's eye, which was keen and bright and repulsive to behold.

After several glances in this way, the stranger, in a harsh, deep voice, broke silence. "Were you looking for me when you peered in at the window?"

"Not that I am aware of, unless you're Mr – " Here Mr Bumble stopped short, curious to know the stranger's name, and thought he might supply the blank.

"I see you were not," said the stranger, an expression of quiet sarcasm playing about his mouth, "or you would have known my name. You don't know it. I would recommend you don't ask."

"I meant no harm, young man," observed Mr Bumble.

"And have done none," said the stranger.

Another silence followed, again broken by the stranger.

"I have seen you before, I think?" said he. "You were differently dressed at that time. I only passed you in the street. You were beadle here, were you not?"

"I was," said Mr Bumble, in some surprise.

"Just so," rejoined the other, nodding. "What are you now?"

"Master of the workhouse," rejoined Mr Bumble, slowly.

"You have the same eye to your own interest that you always had, I doubt not?" resumed the stranger, looking keenly into Mr Bumble's eyes, as he raised them in astonishment. "You can answer freely, man. I know you pretty well, you see."

"I suppose, a married man," replied Mr Bumble, surveying the stranger from head to foot, "is no more averse to turning an honest penny when he can, than a single one. Porochial officers are not so well paid that they can afford to refuse a little extra fee, when it comes in a proper way."

The stranger smiled, and nodded his head again, as if to say, he had not mistaken his man. He then rang the bell.

"Fill this glass again," he said, handing Mr Bumble's empty tumbler to the landlord. "Let it be strong and hot. You like it so?"

"Not too strong," replied Mr Bumble, with a delicate cough.

"You understand what that means, landlord!" said the stranger.

The host smiled, disappeared and shortly returned with a steaming glass. The first gulp brought tears to Mr Bumble's eyes.

"Now listen to me," said the stranger, after closing the door. "I came here today, to find you; and, by one of those odd chances, you walked into the very room I was sitting in. I want information from you. I don't ask you to give it for nothing. Take this, to begin with." He pushed a couple of sovereigns across the table to his companion. When Mr Bumble had scrupulously examined the coins, and put them in his waistcoat-pocket, he went on:

"Carry your memory back – let me see – twelve years, last winter."

"It's a long time," said Mr Bumble. "But I've done it."

"The scene, the workhouse. And the time, night."

"Yes."

"And the place, the crazy hole, in which miserable drabs gave birth to children for the parish to rear, and hid their shame, rot 'em, in the grave!"

"The lying-in room, I suppose?" said Mr Bumble, not quite following the stranger's excited description.

"Yes," said the stranger. "A boy was born there. I speak of one – a meek-looking, pale-faced boy, who was apprenticed to a coffin-maker. I wish he had made his coffin, and screwed his body in it. He afterwards ran away to London, as it was supposed."

"Why, you mean Oliver Twist!" said Mr Bumble. "I remember him, of course. There wasn't a obstinater young rascal – "

"It's not of him I want to hear. I've heard enough of him," said the stranger, stopping Mr Bumble. "It's of a woman – the hag that nursed his mother. Where is she?"

"It would be hard to tell," said Mr Bumble. "There's no midwifery wherever she's gone, so she must be out of a job."

"What do you mean?" demanded the stranger, sternly.

"That she died last winter," rejoined Mr Bumble.

The man stared at him for some moments, his gaze gradually becoming vacant and abstracted; and he seemed lost in thought. Then he rose, as if to depart.

But Mr Bumble was cunning and saw an opportunity for the lucrative disposal of some secret in the possession of his better half. He well remembered the night of old Sally's death, and although Mrs Corney had never confided to him what had happened, he had heard enough to know it had something to do with the old woman's attendance upon the young mother of Oliver Twist. Hastily calling this circumstance to mind, he informed the stranger, with an air of mystery, that one woman had been with the old woman as she died, and that she might be able to throw some light on the subject of his inquiry.

"How can I find her?" said the stranger, plainly showing that all his fears were aroused afresh by the news.

"Only through me," rejoined Mr Bumble.

"When?" cried the stranger, hastily.

"Tomorrow," rejoined Bumble.

"At nine in the evening," said the stranger, producing a scrap of paper, and writing down upon it, an obscure address by the waterside; "bring her to me there. I needn't tell you to be secret."

With these words, he led the way to the door, after stopping to pay for the liquor that had been drunk. Shortly remarking that their roads were different, he departed.

On glancing at the address, the parochial functionary observed there was no name. The stranger had not gone far, so he made after him to ask.

"What do you want?" cried the man, turning quickly as Bumble touched him on the arm. "Following me?"

"What name am I to ask for?" said the other, pointing to the paper.

"Monks!" rejoined the man, and strode, hastily, away.

CHAPTER 37

It was a dull, close, overcast summer evening. The clouds, which had been threatening all day, spread out in a dense and sluggish mass of vapour and seemed to presage a violent thunderstorm. Mr and Mrs Bumble, turning out of the main street, went towards a scattered little colony of ruinous houses, a mile and a-half, or thereabouts away, bordering upon the river.

They were both wrapped in shabby outer garments, to protect them from the rain as well as to shelter them from observation. The husband carried a lantern, from which, however, no light yet shone; and trudged on, a few paces in front.

This place was a collection of mere hovels, jumbled together without any attempt at order or arrangement, and planted, for the most part, within a few feet of the river's bank.

In the heart of this cluster of huts stood a large building, formerly used as some kind of factory. It had, in its day, probably furnished employment to the inhabitants of the surrounding tenements. But it had long since gone to ruin. A considerable portion of the building had already sunk down into the water, while the remainder seemed to wait the opportunity of completing the task.

The worthy couple paused before this ruin, as the first peal of distant thunder reverberated in the air, and the heavy rain began.

"It is somewhere here," said Bumble, consulting the paper.

"Halloa there!" cried a voice from above.

Following the sound, Mr Bumble raised his head, to see a man looking out of a door, breast-high, on the second story.

"Stand still, a minute," cried the voice. "I'll be with you directly." With which the head disappeared, and the door closed.

"Is that the man?" asked Mr Bumble's good lady.

Mr Bumble nodded.

"Then, mind what I told you," said the matron. "Say as little as you can, or you'll betray us at once."

Mr Bumble, eyeing the building with rueful looks, was about to express some doubts relative to the advisability of proceeding any further when Monks appeared, having opened a small door, near which they stood. He beckoned them inwards.

"Come in!" he cried impatiently. "Don't keep me here!"

The woman walked boldly in, without any other invitation. Mr Bumble followed, obviously ill at ease and with scarcely any of that dignity which was usually his chief characteristic.

Monks turned upon the matron, and stared at her, till even she, who was not easily cowed, had to turn her eyes to the ground. "This is the woman, is it?" he demanded.

"Hem! That is the woman," replied Mr Bumble, mindful of his wife's caution.

"You think women never can keep secrets, I suppose?" said the matron, returning, as she spoke, the searching look of Monks.

"I know they will always keep *one* till it's found out," said Monks.

"And what may that be?" asked the matron.

"The loss of their own good name," replied Monks. "So, by the same rule, if a woman's party to a secret that might hang her, I'm not afraid of her telling it to anybody, not I! Do you understand?"

"No," rejoined the matron, slightly colouring as she spoke.

"Of course you don't!" said Monks. "How should you?"

Beckoning his two companions to follow him, the man hastened across the apartment. He was preparing to ascend a steep staircase, leading to another floor when a bright flash of lightning streamed in and a peal of thunder followed, shaking the crazy building.

"Hear it!" he cried, shrinking back. "Rolling and crashing as if it echoed through caverns where the devils were hiding! I hate the sound!"

He remained silent for a few moments; and then, removing his hands suddenly from his face, showed, to the discomfort of Mr Bumble, that it was much distorted and discoloured.

"These fits come over me, now and then," said Monks, observing his alarm. "Thunder sometimes brings them on. Don't mind me."

He led the way up the ladder and hastily closed the window of the room. There sat an old table and three chairs.

"Now," said Monks, when they had all three seated themselves, "the sooner we come to our business, the better. The woman knows what it is, does she?"

The question was addressed to Bumble; but his wife anticipated, intimating that she was perfectly acquainted with it.

"He is right in saying that you were with this hag the night she died and that she told you something – "

"About the mother of the boy you named," replied the matron, interrupting him. "Yes."

"The first question is, of what nature was her communication?" said Monks.

"That's the second," observed the woman. "The first is, what may all this be worth?"

"Who can tell, without knowing what it is?" asked Monks.

"Nobody better than you, I feel," answered Mrs Bumble.

"Humph!" said Monks significantly, and with a look of eager inquiry. "There may be money's worth to get, eh?"

"Perhaps there may," was the composed reply.

"Something that was taken from her," said Monks. "Something that she wore."

"You had better bid," interrupted Mrs Bumble. "I have heard enough, to know that you are the man I should talk to."

Mr Bumble, still unaware of his wife's secret, listened to this dialogue with outstretched neck and distended eyes.

"What's it worth to you?" she asked, as collectedly as before.

"It may be nothing, it may be twenty pounds," replied Monks. "Speak out, and let me know which."

"Add five pounds to the sum you have named; give me five-and-twenty pounds in gold," said the woman. "I'll tell you all I know."

"Five-and-twenty pounds!" exclaimed Monks, drawing back.

"I spoke as plainly as I could," replied Mrs Bumble. "It's not a large sum, either."

"Not a large sum for a paltry secret, that may be nothing when it's told!" cried Monks impatiently. "And which has been lying dead for twelve years past or more!"

"Such matters keep well, and, like good wine, often double their value in course of time," answered the matron.

"What if I pay it for nothing?" asked Monks, hesitating.

"You can easily take it away again," replied the matron. "I am but a woman; alone here; and unprotected."

"Not alone, my dear, nor unprotected neither," submitted Mr Bumble, in a voice tremulous with fear: "I am here, my dear."

"You are a fool," said Mrs Bumble, in reply. "Hold your tongue."

"So! He's your husband, eh?" said Monks grimly. "I thought as much, when you came in. So much the better. I have less hesitation in dealing with two people, with only one will between them."

He thrust his hand into a side-pocket and counted out twenty-five sovereigns from a canvas bag. He pushed them to the woman.

"Now," he said, "let's hear your story."

The thunder subsided, and Monks bent forward to listen to what the woman should say. The faces of the three nearly touched, as the two men leant over the small table in their eagerness to hear.

"When this woman, that we called old Sally, died," the matron began, "she and I were alone."

"Was there no one by?" asked Monks. "No one to hear, who might, possibly understand?"

"Not a soul," replied the woman. "I stood alone beside the body when death came over it."

"Good," said Monks, attentively. "Go on."

"She spoke of a young creature," resumed the matron, "who had brought a child into the world some years before, in the same bed, in which she then lay dying."

"Ay?" said Monks, with quivering lip. "How things come about!"

"The child was the one you named to him," she continued, nodding towards her husband. "The mother this nurse had robbed."

"In life?" asked Monks.

"In death," replied the woman, with something like a shudder. "She stole from the dead mother that which she had prayed her, with her last breath, to keep for the infant's sake."

"She sold it?" cried Monks, desperately. "Did she sell it? Where? To whom? When?"

"She told me, with great difficulty, that she had done this," said the matron, "then fell back and died."

"Without saying more?" cried Monks, even more furiously. "It's a lie! She said more. I'll tear the life out of you both. Tell me!"

"She didn't say another word," said the woman, to all appearances unmoved by the strange man's violence. "But she clutched my gown, with one hand. When I saw that she was dead, and removed the hand by force, I found it held a scrap of dirty paper."

"Which contained – " interposed Monks, stretching forward.

"Nothing," replied the woman. "It was a pawnbroker's duplicate."

"For what?" demanded Monks.

"In good time I'll tell you," said the woman. "I judge that she had kept the trinket, for some time. She then pawned it, but managed to scrape together enough money to pay the broker's interest each year to prevent its running out so that it could still be redeemed. The time was out in two days; I thought something might one day come of it too; and so redeemed the pledge."

"Where is it now?" asked Monks quickly.

"There," replied the woman. And, as if glad to be relieved of it, she hastily threw upon the table a small kid bag, which Monks pounced upon and tore open with trembling hands. It contained a little gold locket, in which were two locks of hair, and a plain gold wedding ring.

"It has the word 'Agnes' engraved on the inside," said the woman. "There's a blank left for the surname and then follows the date – within a year before the child was born. I found out that."

"And this is all?" said Monks, after a close scrutiny of the bag.

"All," replied the woman.

Mr Bumble drew a long breath, relieved the story was over, and that no mention was made of taking the five-and-twenty pounds back again.

"I know nothing of the story, beyond what I can guess at," said his wife, addressing Monks after a pause. "And I want to know nothing; for it's safer not. But may I ask two questions?"

"You may ask," said Monks, with some show of surprise, "but whether I answer or not is another question."

"Is that what you expected?" demanded the matron.

"It is," replied Monks. "The other question?"

"What you propose to do with it? Can it be used against me?"

"Never," rejoined Monks. "Nor against me either. See here!" He suddenly pulled the table aside, and pulling an iron ring in the boarding,

142

threw back a large trapdoor which opened close at Mr Bumble's feet.

"Look down," said Monks, lowering the lantern into the gulf. "Don't fear me. I could have let you down, quietly enough, when you were seated over it, if that had been my game."

The matron drew near to the brink; and even Mr Bumble himself ventured to do the same. The turbid water, swollen by the heavy rain, was rushing rapidly on below. All other sounds were lost in the noise of its plashing against the green and slimy piles.

"If you flung a man's body down there, where would it be tomorrow?" said Monks, swinging the lantern in the dark well.

"Twelve miles down the river, and cut to pieces besides," replied Bumble, recoiling at the thought.

Monks drew the little bag from his breast, where he had hurriedly thrust it and tied it to a leaden weight. He then dropped it into the stream. It fell straight, and true as a die, clove the water with a scarcely audible splash, and was gone.

The three looked at each other and seemed to breathe more freely.

"There!" said Monks, closing the trapdoor. "If the sea ever gives up its dead, as books say it will, it will keep its gold and silver to itself, and that trash among it. We have nothing more to say, and may break up our pleasant party."

"By all means," observed Mr Bumble, with great alacrity.

"You'll keep a quiet tongue in your head, will you?" said Monks, with a threatening look. "I am not afraid of your wife."

"You may depend upon me, young man," answered Mr Bumble, making gradually towards the ladder.

"I am glad, for your sake, to hear it," remarked Monks. "Light your lantern! And get away from here as fast as you can."

Mr Bumble descended in silence, followed by his wife. Monks brought up the rear, after pausing on the steps to satisfy himself that there were no other sounds to be heard than the beating of the rain without, and the rushing of the water.

The married couple emerged into the wet and darkness outside.

They were no sooner gone, than Monks, who appeared to dislike being left alone, called to a boy hidden somewhere below. Bidding him go first with the light, he returned to the chamber.

CHAPTER 38

Sikes had been ill, and was being looked after by Nancy. As a consequence the housebreaker had been unable to follow his usual employment. Funds were running low, and Nancy had virtually starved to be sure that Sikes was looked after.

The evening that he was feeling a little better and able to get out of bed, Fagin came to the house, bearing rabbit pie and wine.

Sikes demanded money, and Fagin agreed that Nancy should go home with him to collect a sum to take back to Sikes.

The Jew then, taking leave of his affectionate friend, returned homeward, attended by Nancy and the boys.

In due course, they arrived at Fagin's abode, where they found Toby Crackit.

"Has nobody been, Toby?" asked Fagin.

"Not a living leg," answered Mr Crackit, pulling up his collar; "it's been as dull as swipes."

Mr Toby Crackit swaggered out of the room, with much elegance and gentility.

"Dodger! Charley! It's time you were on the lay. Come! It's near ten, and nothing done yet," said Fagin

In obedience to this hint, the boys, nodding to Nancy, took up their hats and left the room.

"Now," said Fagin, when they had left the room, "I'll go and get you that cash, Nancy. Hush!" he said, hastily concealing the key. "Who's that? Listen!"

The girl, who was sitting at the table with her arms folded, appeared in no way interested in the arrival, until the murmur of a man's voice reached her ears. The instant she caught the sound, she swiftly tore off her bonnet and shawl, and thrust them under the table. She muttered a complaint of the heat when Fagin turned back to her.

"Bah!" he whispered, as though nettled by the interruption. "It's a man I expected. Not a word about the money while he's here, Nance. He won't stop long."

Laying his skinny forefinger upon his lip, the Jew carried a candle to the door, as a man's step was heard upon the stairs outside. He reached it at the same moment as the visitor, who, coming hastily into the room, was close upon the girl before he observed her.

It was Monks.

"Only one of my young people," said Fagin, observing that Monks drew back on beholding a stranger. "Don't move, Nancy."

The girl drew closer to the table, and barely glanced at Monks, but as he turned his eyes towards Fagin, she stole another look – keen and searching.

"Any news?" inquired Fagin.

"Great."

"And – and – good?" asked Fagin, hesitating.

"Not bad, any way," replied Monks with a smile. "I have been prompt enough this time. Let me have a word with you."

The girl drew closer to the table, and made no offer to leave the room, although she could see that Monks was pointing to her. The Jew pointed upward, and took Monks out of the room.

Before the sound of their footsteps had ceased to echo through the house, the girl had slipped off her shoes and pulled her gown loosely over her head. She muffled her arms in it, and stood at the door, listening with breathless interest. The moment the noise ceased, she glided from the room and was lost in the gloom above.

The room remained deserted for a quarter of an hour, then the girl glided back with the same unearthly tread. Immediately afterwards, the two men were heard descending. Monks went at once into the street and the Jew crawled up stairs again for the money. When he returned, the girl was adjusting her shawl and bonnet, as if preparing to go.

"Why, Nance," exclaimed the Jew, starting back as he put down the candle, "how pale you are!"

"Pale!" echoed the girl, shading her eyes with her hands, as if to look steadily at him.

"Quite horrible. What have you been doing to yourself?"

"Nothing that I know of, except sitting in this place for I don't know how long," replied the girl carelessly. "Come! Let me get back."

With a sigh for every piece of money, Fagin counted the amount into her hand. They parted without more conversation, merely exchanging a "good night."

When the girl got into the open street, she sat down upon a doorstep, wholly bewildered and unable to pursue her way. Suddenly she arose and hurried on, in a direction quite opposite to that in which Sikes was awaiting her return. After completely exhausting herself, she stopped to take breath and, as if suddenly recollecting herself, and deploring her inability to do something she was bent upon, wrung her hands, and burst into tears.

Her tears may have relieved her, or she felt the full hopelessness of her condition, but she turned back and soon reached the dwelling where she had left the housebreaker.

Mr Sikes did not see her condition, but merely inquired if she had brought the money. Receiving a reply in the affirmative, he uttered a growl of satisfaction; and replacing his head upon the pillow, resumed the slumbers which her arrival had interrupted.

It was fortunate for her that the possession of money meant the next day was spent eating and drinking. Sikes had neither time nor inclination to be very critical upon her behaviour. That she had the nervous manner of one about to take a bold and hazardous step would have been obvious to the lynx-eyed Fagin. But Mr Sikes lacked the niceties of discrimination, and being, also, in an unusually amiable condition, saw nothing unusual about her.

As the day closed in, the girl's excitement increased and, when night came on, and she sat by, watching until the housebreaker should drink himself asleep, there was an unusual paleness in her cheek, that even Sikes observed with astonishment.

Being weak from the fever, he was lying in bed, taking hot water with his gin to render it less inflammatory. He had pushed his glass towards Nancy for the third or fourth time, when he noticed.

"Why, burn my body!" said the man, staring the girl in the face. "You look like a corpse come to life again. What's the matter?"

"Matter!" replied the girl. "Nothing."

"What is it?" demanded Sikes, grasping her by the arm, and shaking her roughly. "What are you thinking of?"

"Of many things, Bill," replied the girl, shivering, pressing her hands upon her eyes. "But, Lord! What odds in that?"

The tone of forced gaiety seemed to produce a deeper impression on Sikes than the wild and rigid look that had preceded them.

"I tell you wot it is," said Sikes. "If you haven't caught the fever, there's something more in the wind, and something dangerous too. You're not a-going to – no, damme! You wouldn't do that!"

"Do what?" asked the girl.

"There ain't," said Sikes, fixing his eyes upon her, "a stauncher-hearted gal going, or I'd have cut her throat months ago. She's got the fever coming on, that's it."

With this assurance, Sikes drained the glass, and then called for his physic. The girl jumped up, poured it quickly but with her back to him, and held the vessel to his lips while he drank.

"Now," said the robber, "come and sit aside of me, and put on your own face or I'll alter it so that you won't know it again when you do want it."

The girl obeyed. Sikes, locking her hand in his, turned his eyes upon her face. They closed; opened again; closed once more; again opened. He shifted restlessly and was suddenly stricken, as it were, into a deep and heavy sleep. His hand relaxed and fell by his side; and he lay like one in a profound trance.

"The laudanum has taken effect at last," murmured the girl, as she rose from the bedside. "I may be too late, even now."

She hastily dressed herself in her bonnet and shawl. Despite the sleeping draught, she expected every moment to feel the pressure of Sikes's heavy hand upon her shoulder. Then, stooping softly over the bed, she kissed the robber's lips. Opening and closing the door with noiseless touch, she hurried from the house.

A watchman was crying half-past nine.

"Has it long gone the half-hour?" asked the girl.

"It'll strike the hour in another quarter," said the man raising his lantern to her face.

"And I cannot get there in less than an hour or more," muttered Nancy, brushing past him, and gliding rapidly down the street.

The clock struck ten, increasing her impatience. She tore along the narrow pavement, elbowing the passengers from side to side.

When she reached the more wealthy quarter of the town, the streets were comparatively deserted and here her headlong progress excited a still greater curiosity in the stragglers whom she hurried past. When she neared her place of destination, she was alone.

It was a family hotel in a quiet but handsome street near Hyde Park. As the brilliant light of the lamp, which burnt before its door, guided her to the spot, the clock struck eleven. She loitered for a few paces as though irresolute; but the sound determined her, and she stepped into the hall. The porter's seat was vacant. She looked round, and advanced towards the stairs.

"Now, young woman!" said a smartly dressed female, looking out from a door behind her. "Who do you want here?"

"A lady who is stopping in this house," answered the girl. "Miss Maylie."

The young woman, who had by this time noted her appearance, summoned a man. To him, Nancy repeated her request.

"What name am I to say?" asked the waiter.

"It's of no use saying any," replied Nancy. "I must see the lady. Won't somebody see a simple message carried for a wretch like me?"

"Take it up for her, Joe, can't you?" said the cook who was looking on.

"Why?" replied the man. "You don't suppose the young lady will see such as her, do you?"

"Do what you like with me," said the girl, turning to the men again. "But do what I ask first, and give this message for God's sake."

The soft-hearted cook added his intercession, and the result was that the man who had first appeared undertook its delivery.

"What's it to be?" said the man, with one foot on the stairs.

"That a young woman earnestly asks to speak to Miss Maylie alone," said Nancy. "If the lady will only hear the first word she has to say, she will know whether to hear her business, or to have her turned out of doors as an impostor."

"I say," said the man, "you're coming it strong!"

"You give the message," said the girl. "Let me hear the answer."

The man ran up stairs. Nancy remained, pale and almost breathless. The man returned, and said the young woman was to walk up stairs.

Nancy followed the man to a small antechamber, lighted by a lamp from the ceiling. Here he left her.

CHAPTER 39

The girl's life had been squandered in the streets and among the most noisome of the stews of London, but there was something of the woman's original nature left in her still. When she heard a light step approaching the door she felt burdened with the sense of her own deep shame, and shrunk as though she could scarcely bear the presence of her with whom she had sought this interview.

But struggling with these better feelings was pride – the vice of the lowest creatures no less than of the high, and self-assured.

She raised her eyes to observe that the figure that presented itself was that of a slight and beautiful girl. Then she tossed her head with affected carelessness as she said: "It's a hard matter to get to see you, lady. If I had taken offence, and gone away, as many would have done, you'd have been sorry for it one day, and not without reason either."

"I am very sorry if any one has behaved harshly to you," replied Rose. "Do not think of that. Tell me why you wished to see me."

The kind tone of this answer, the sweet voice, the gentle manner, the absence of any haughtiness or displeasure, took the girl completely by surprise, and she burst into tears.

"Oh, lady!" she said, clasping her hands passionately before her face. "If there was more like you, there would be fewer like me!"

"Sit down," said Rose, earnestly. "If you are in poverty or affliction I shall be truly glad to relieve you if I can. Sit down."

"Let me stand, lady," said the girl, still weeping. "And do not speak to me so kindly till you know me better. It is growing late. Is – is – that door shut?"

"Yes," said Rose, recoiling a few steps, as if to be nearer assistance in case she should require it. "Why?"

"Because," said the girl, "I am about to put my life, and the lives of others, in your hands. I am the girl that dragged little Oliver back to old Fagin's, the night he left the house in Pentonville."

"You!" said Rose Maylie.

"I, lady!" replied the girl. "I am the infamous creature you have heard of, that lives among the thieves. Do not mind shrinking openly from me, lady. I am younger than you would think to look at me, but I am well used to it. The poorest women fall back, as I make my way along the crowded pavement."

"What dreadful things are these!" said Rose, involuntarily falling from her strange companion.

"Thank Heaven upon your knees, dear lady," cried the girl, "that you had friends to care for and keep you in your childhood, and that you were never in the midst of cold and hunger. For the alley and the gutter will be my deathbed."

"I pity you!" said Rose, in a broken voice. "It wrings my heart to hear you!"

"Heaven bless you for your goodness!" rejoined the girl. "But I have stolen away from those who would surely murder me, if they knew I had been here, to tell you what I have overheard. Do you know a man named Monks?"

"No," said Rose.

"He knows you," replied the girl. "And knew you were here, for it was by hearing him tell the place that I found you out."

"I never heard the name," said Rose.

"Then he goes by some other amongst us," rejoined the girl. "Some time ago, and soon after Oliver was put into your house on the night of the robbery, I – suspecting this man – listened to a conversation between him and Fagin in the dark. I found out, from what I heard, that Monks had seen him accidentally with two of our boys on the day we first lost him, and had known him directly to be the same child that he was watching for, though I couldn't make out why. A bargain was struck with Fagin, that if Oliver was got back he should have a certain sum, but he was to have more for making him into a thief. Monks wanted this for some purpose of his own."

"For what purpose?" asked Rose.

"He caught sight of my shadow on the wall as I listened in the hope of finding out," said the girl. "And there are not many people besides me that could have got out of their way in time to escape discovery. But I did and I saw him no more till last night."

"And what occurred then?"

"I'll tell you, lady. Last night he came again. Again they went up stairs, and I, wrapping myself up so that my shadow should not betray me, again listened at the door. The first words I heard Monks say were these: 'So the only proofs of the boy's identity lie at the bottom of the river, and the old hag that received them from the mother is rotting in her coffin.' They laughed, and talked of his success in doing this. Monks, talking on about the boy, said that though he had got the young devil's money safely now, he'd rather have had it the other way. For, what a game it would have been to have brought down the boast of the father's will, by driving him through every jail in town, and then hauling him up for some capital felony which Fagin could easily manage, after having made a good profit of him besides."

"What is all this!" said Rose.

"The truth, lady, though it comes from my lips," replied the girl. "Then, he said that if he could gratify his hatred by taking the boy's life without bringing his own neck in danger, he would, but, as he couldn't, he'd be upon the watch to meet him at every turn in life. And if he took advantage of his birth and history, he might harm him yet. 'In short, Fagin,' he says, 'Jew as you are, you never laid such snares as I'll contrive for my young brother, Oliver.'"

"His brother!" exclaimed Rose.

"Those were his words," said Nancy, glancing uneasily round, as she had scarcely ceased to do, since she began to speak, for a vision of Sikes haunted her perpetually. "And more. When he spoke of you and the other lady, he said it seemed contrived by Heaven, or the devil, against him, that Oliver should come into your hands. He laughed, and said there was some comfort in that for how many hundreds of thousands of pounds would you not give, if you had them, to know who your two-legged spaniel was."

"You do not mean," said Rose, turning very pale, "to tell me that this was said in earnest?"

"He spoke in hard and angry earnest, if a man ever did," replied the girl, shaking her head. "I know many who do worse things but I'd rather listen to them all a dozen times, than to that Monks once. It is growing late, and I have to reach home without suspicion of having been on such an errand as this. I must get back quickly."

"But what can I do?" said Rose. "To what use can I turn this communication without you? Back! Why do you wish to return? If you repeat this information to a gentleman whom I can summon in an instant from the next room, you can be taken to safety without half an hour's delay."

"I wish to go back," said the girl. "I must go back, because – how can I tell such things to an innocent lady like you? – because among the men there is one, the most desperate among them all, that I can't leave. Not even to be saved from the life I am leading now."

"Your having interfered in this dear boy's behalf before," said Rose; "your coming here, at so great a risk, leads me to believe that you might be yet reclaimed. Oh!" said the earnest girl, "do not turn a deaf ear to the entreaties of one of your own sex. The first – I do believe, who ever appealed to you in the voice of compassion. Hear my words, and let me save you, for better things."

"Lady," cried the girl, sinking on her knees. "Dear, sweet, angel lady, you are the first that ever blessed me with such words as these, and if I had heard them years ago, they might have turned me from a life of sin and sorrow, but it is too late!"

"It is never too late," said Rose, "for penitence and atonement."

"It is," cried the girl, writhing in the agony of her mind. "I cannot leave him now! I could not be his death."

"Why should you be?" asked Rose.

"Nothing could save him," cried the girl. "If I told others what I have told you, and led to their being taken, he would be sure to die. He is the boldest, and has been so cruel!"

"Is it possible," cried Rose, "that for such a man, you can resign every future hope, and the certainty of immediate rescue? It is madness."

"I don't know what it is," answered the girl. "I only know that it is so, and not with me alone, but with hundreds of others as bad and wretched as myself. I must go back. I am drawn back to him and I should be, I believe, if I knew that I was to die by his hand."

"What am I to do?" said Rose. "I should not let you depart thus."

"You should, lady, and I know you will," rejoined the girl, rising. "You will not stop my going because I have trusted in your goodness, and forced no promise from you, as I might have done."

"Of what use, then, is the communication you have made?" said Rose. "This mystery must be investigated, or how will its disclosure to me benefit Oliver, whom you are anxious to serve?"

"You must have some kind gentleman about you that will hear it as a secret, and advise you what to do," rejoined the girl.

"But where can I find you again when it is necessary?" asked Rose. "I

152

do not ask where these dreadful people live, but where will you be walking at any settled period from this time?"

"Will you promise me that you will have my secret strictly kept, and come alone, or with the only other person that knows it; and that I shall not be watched or followed?" asked the girl.

"I promise you solemnly," answered Rose.

"Every Sunday night, from eleven until the clock strikes twelve," said the girl without hesitation, "I will walk on London Bridge if I am alive."

"Stay another moment," interposed Rose, as the girl moved hurriedly towards the door. "Think once again on the opportunity you have of escaping. Will you return to this gang of robbers, and to this man, when a word can save you?"

"When ladies as young, and good, and beautiful as you are," replied the girl steadily, "give away your hearts, love will carry you all length – even such as you, who have home, friends, other admirers, everything, to fill them. When such as I, who has no certain roof but the coffin-lid, and no friend in sickness or death but the hospital nurse, set our rotten hearts on any man, who can hope to cure us? Pity us, lady – for having only one womanly feeling left, and for having that turned, from a comfort, into a new means of suffering."

"Do not close your heart against all my efforts to help you," said Rose, stepping gently forward. "I wish to serve you indeed."

"You would serve me best, lady," replied the girl, wringing her hands, "if you could take my life at once – for I have felt more grief to think of what I am, tonight, than I ever did before, and it would be something not to die in the hell in which I have lived. God bless you, sweet lady, and send as much happiness on your head as I have brought shame on mine!"

Thus speaking, and sobbing aloud, the unhappy creature turned away. Rose Maylie, overpowered by this extraordinary interview, which seemed more like a dream than an actual occurrence, sank into a chair, and endeavoured to collect her wandering thoughts.

CHAPTER 40

Rose considered who she should talk with. They were remaining in London only three days, prior to departing for some weeks to the coast. It was now midnight of the first day. What course of action could she determine upon, which could be adopted in eight-and-forty hours? Or how could she postpone the journey without exciting suspicion?

Mr Losberne would be with them for the next two days; but Rose was too well acquainted with this gentleman's impetuosity. She thought of seeking assistance from Harry, but remembered their last parting. It seemed unworthy of her to call him back when – the tears rose to her eyes – he might by now have learnt to forget her, and be happier away.

Rose passed a sleepless and anxious night. After more communing with herself next day, she arrived at the desperate conclusion of consulting Harry.

"If it's painful to him," she thought, "to come back here, how painful it will be to me! But perhaps he will not come; he may write, or he may come himself." And here Rose dropped the pen, and turned away.

She had taken up the same pen, and had considered and reconsidered the first line of her letter without writing a word, when Oliver, who had been walking in the streets with Mr Giles for a bodyguard, entered the room in a breathless state.

"What makes you look so flurried?" asked Rose, advancing to meet him.

"I feel as if I shall choke," replied the boy. "Oh dear! To think that I should see him at last, and you will know that I have told you all the truth!"

"I never doubted you," said Rose, soothing him. "But what is it? Of whom do you speak?"

"I have seen the gentleman," replied Oliver, scarcely able to articulate, "he who was so good to me – Mr Brownlow, that we have so often talked about."

"Where?" asked Rose.

"Getting out of a coach," replied Oliver, shedding tears of delight, "and going into a house. I didn't speak to him – I couldn't speak to him, for he didn't see me. Giles asked for me, whether he lived there, and they said he did. Look here," said Oliver, opening a scrap of paper, "here's where he lives – I'm going there directly! Oh dear me! What shall I do when I see him and hear him again!"

With her attention not a little distracted by these exclamations of joy, Rose read the address, which was Craven Street, in the Strand. She very soon determined upon turning the discovery to account.

"Quick!" she said. "Tell them to fetch a hackney-coach, and be ready to go with me. I will take you there directly. I will tell my aunt that we are going out for an hour. Be ready."

Oliver needed no prompting, and in little more than five minutes they were on their way to Craven Street. When they arrived there, Rose left Oliver in the coach, under pretence of preparing the old gentleman to receive him. Sending up her card by the servant, she requested to see Mr Brownlow on very pressing business. The servant soon returned, to beg that she would walk upstairs; and, following him into an upper room, Miss Maylie was presented to an elderly gentleman of benevolent appearance, in a bottle-green coat. At no great distance from whom, was seated another old gentleman, in nankeen breeches and gaiters: who did not look particularly benevolent, and who was sitting with his hands clasped on the top of a thick stick, and his chin propped thereupon.

"Dear me," said the gentleman, in the bottle-green coat, hastily rising with great politeness. "I beg your pardon, young lady – I imagined it was some importunate person who – I beg you will excuse me. Be seated, pray."

"Mr Brownlow, I believe, sir?" said Rose.

"That is my name," said the old gentleman. "This is my friend, Mr Grimwig. Grimwig, will you leave us for a few minutes?"

"I believe," interposed Miss Maylie, "that at this period of our interview, I need not give this gentleman the trouble of going away. If I am correct, he is cognisant of the business on which I wish to speak to you."

Mr Brownlow inclined his head. Mr Grimwig, who had made one very stiff bow, and risen from his chair, made another very stiff bow, and dropped into it again.

"I shall surprise you very much, I have no doubt," said Rose, naturally embarrassed. "But you once showed great benevolence and goodness to a very dear young friend of mine, and I am sure you will take an interest in hearing of him again."

155

"Indeed!" said Mr Brownlow.

"Oliver Twist you knew him as," replied Rose.

Mr Brownlow drew his chair nearer to Miss Maylie's, and said,

"Do me the favour, my dear young lady, to leave entirely out of the question that goodness and benevolence of which you speak. If you have it in your power to produce any evidence which will alter the unfavourable opinion I was once induced to entertain of that poor child, in Heaven's name, tell me."

"He is a child of a noble nature and a warm heart," said Rose, colouring.

"Miss Maylie, will you let me know what intelligence you have of this poor child. I exhausted every means in my power to find him, and that since I have been absent from this country, my first impression that he had imposed upon me, and had been persuaded by his former associates to rob me, has been considerably shaken."

Rose quickly related all that had happened to Oliver since he left Mr Brownlow's house. She held back Nancy's story to tell him later, and ended with the assurance that his only sorrow was that he had not been able to meet with his former benefactor and friend.

"Thank God!" said the old gentleman. "This is great happiness to me, great happiness. But you have not told me where he is now, Miss Maylie. Why have you not brought him?"

"He is waiting in a coach at the door," replied Rose.

"At this door!" cried the old gentleman. With which he hurried out of the room, down the stairs, up the coach-steps, and into the coach, without another word.

When the door closed behind him, Mr Grimwig lifted his head, and converting one of the legs of his chair into a pivot, described three circles with the aid of his stick and the table. Then he rose and limped as fast as he could up and down the room at least a dozen times, and then stopping suddenly before Rose, kissed her without the slightest preface.

"Hush!" he said, as the young lady rose in some alarm at this unusual proceeding. "Don't be afraid. I'm old enough to be your grandfather. you're a sweet girl. I like you. Here they are!"

In fact, as he threw himself into his former seat, Mr Brownlow returned, accompanied by Oliver.

"There is somebody else who should not be forgotten," said Mr Brownlow, ringing the bell. "Send Mrs Bedwin here, please."

The old housekeeper answered the summons with all dispatch; and dropping a curtsey at the door, waited for orders.

"Why, you get blinder every day, Bedwin," said Mr Brownlow.

"Well, sir," replied the old lady. "People's eyes, at my time of life, don't improve with age, sir."

"I could have told you that," rejoined Mr Brownlow. "Just put on your glasses, and see what you were wanted for, will you?"

The old lady began to rummage in her pocket for her spectacles. But Oliver's patience could not take this and he sprang into her arms.

"God be good!" cried the old lady, embracing him, "it is my innocent boy!"

"My dear old nurse!" cried Oliver.

"He would come back – I knew he would," said the old lady, holding him in her arms. "How well he looks! Where have you been, this long while? Ah! The same sweet face, but not so pale, the same soft eye, but not so sad. I have never forgotten them or his quiet smile." Running on thus, and now holding Oliver from her to see how he had grown, now clasping him to her and passing her fingers fondly through his hair, the good soul laughed and wept upon his neck by turns.

Leaving her and Oliver to compare notes at leisure, Mr Brownlow led the way into another room; and there, heard from Rose of her interview with Nancy, which gave him no little surprise and perplexity. The old gentleman undertook to hold solemn conference with the doctor and it was arranged that he should call at the hotel at eight o'clock that evening. In the meantime Mrs Maylie should be cautiously informed of all that had occurred. Rose and Oliver then returned home.

Nancy's history was no sooner unfolded to the worthy doctor, than he poured forth a shower of threats aimed at her. But he was restrained by the good sense of Mr Brownlow.

"Then what the devil is to be done?" said the impetuous doctor, when they had rejoined the two ladies.

"We must proceed gently and with great care," rejoined Mr Brownlow.

"I'd send them all to – " exclaimed the doctor.

"Never mind where," interposed Mr Brownlow. "Will sending them anywhere attain the object we have in view?"

"What object?" asked the doctor.

"Simply, the discovery of Oliver's parentage, regaining for him the inheritance of which, if the story is true, he has been deprived."

"Ah!" said Mr Losberne, cooling himself with his pocket-handkerchief. "I almost forgot that."

"You see," pursued Mr Brownlow. "It is quite clear that we shall have extreme difficulty in getting to the bottom of this mystery, unless we can bring this man, Monks, to his knees. We can only do that by catching him, when he is not with these people. If he were apprehended, we have no proof against him. He is not, as far as we know, concerned with the gang in any of their robberies. He would either be discharged, or if he were committed to prison as a rogue and vagabond, ever afterwards his mouth would be so obstinately closed that he might as well, for our purposes, be deaf, dumb, blind, and an idiot."

"Then," said the doctor impetuously, "do you think it reasonable that this promise to the girl should be considered binding? A promise made with the best and kindest intentions, but really – "

"Do not discuss the point, my dear young lady, pray," said Mr Brownlow, interrupting Rose as she was about to speak. "The promise shall be kept. I don't think it will interfere with our proceedings. But it will be necessary to see the girl, to see if she will point out this Monks, on the understanding that he is to be dealt with by us, and not by the law. If she will not, or cannot, do that, to gain knowledge of his haunts and description of his person, so that we can identify him. She cannot be seen until next Sunday night. This is Tuesday. I suggest that in the meantime, we remain perfectly quiet, and keep these matters secret, even from Oliver."

Although Mr Losberne hated the idea of a delay of five whole days, he had to admit that no better course occurred to him. Both Rose and Mrs Maylie sided strongly with Mr Brownlow.

Harry Maylie and Mr Grimwig were also added to the committee.

"We stay in town, of course," said Mrs Maylie, "while there remains the slightest prospect of success. I will stay here for twelve months so long as you assure me that hope remains."

"Good!" rejoined Mr Brownlow. "Now, I am sure you wondered why I was not here to corroborate Oliver's tale, having so suddenly left the kingdom. Please ask me no questions until such time I consider it expedient to tell my own story. Believe me, I make this request with good reason, for I might otherwise excite hopes destined never to be realised, and only increase difficulties and disappointments. Come! Supper has been announced, and young Oliver, all alone in the next room, will be thinking that we have tired of him, and are about to thrust him out into the world."

With these words, the old gentleman gave his hand to Mrs Maylie, and escorted her into the supper room. Mr Losberne followed with Rose. The council was, for the present, broken up.

CHAPTER 41

Skilled as she was, in all the arts of cunning, Nancy could not wholly conceal the effect the knowledge of the step she had taken was having upon her. She remembered that both the crafty Jew and the brutal Sikes had confided to her schemes, which had been hidden from all others, in the full confidence that she was trustworthy and beyond their suspicion. Vile those schemes were and bitter were her feelings towards Fagin, who had led her deeper and deeper into an abyss of crime and misery, whence there was no escape. But there were times when, even towards him, she felt some relenting, lest her disclosure should bring him within the iron grasp he had so long eluded, and he should fall at last by her hand.

Her fears for Sikes would have been more powerful inducements to recoil while there was yet time, but she had stipulated that her secret should be kept. She had given no clue that could lead to his discovery and she had refused, even for his sake, a refuge from this life – what more could she do! She was resolved.

Though she came to this conclusion time and time again, the torment was having an effect. She grew pale and thin, even within a few days.

It was Sunday night, and the bell of the nearest church struck the hour. Sikes and the Jew were talking, but they paused to listen. The girl looked up from her low seat and listened too. Eleven.

"An hour this side of midnight," said Sikes, raising the blind to look out. "Dark and heavy it is too. A good night for business, this."

"That's the way to talk, my dear," replied Fagin, venturing to pat him on the shoulder. "It does me good to hear you."

"Does you good, does it!" cried Sikes. "Well, so be it."

"Ha, ha!" laughed Fagin. "you're like yourself to-night, Bill!"

"I don't feel like myself when you lay that withered claw on my shoulder, so take it away," said Sikes, casting off the Jew's hand.

"It makes you nervous, Bill – reminds you of being nabbed, does it?" said Fagin, determined not to be offended.

"Reminds me of the devil," returned Sikes. "There never was another man with such a face as yours, unless it was your father. I suppose he is singeing his grizzled red beard, unless you came straight from the old 'un without any father at all betwixt you."

Fagin made no comment but, pulling Sikes by the sleeve, pointed towards Nancy, who had put on her bonnet, and was now leaving.

"Nance!" cried Sikes. "Where're you going at this time of night?"

"Not far."

"What answer's that?" returned Sikes. "Where are you going?"

"I don't know where," replied the girl.

"Then I do," said Sikes, more through obstinacy than because he objected to the girl going out. "Nowhere. Sit down."

"I want a breath of air," rejoined the girl.

"Put your head out the winder," replied Sikes.

"I want it in the street," said the girl.

"Then you won't have it," replied Sikes. And he rose, locked the door, took the key out. "There," said the robber. "Now stop where you are, will you?"

"You'll drive me to do something desperate," muttered the girl, placing both hands upon her breast, as though to keep in by force some violent outbreak. "Let me go, will you – this minute!"

"No!" said Sikes.

"Tell him to let me go, Fagin. It'll be better for him. Do you hear me?" cried Nancy.

"Hear you!" repeated Sikes turning round in his chair to confront her. "If I hear you half a minute longer, the dog shall tear some of that screaming voice out of your throat. Wot has come over you?"

"Let me go," said the girl and she sat before the door. "Bill, let me go, you don't know what you are doing. Just for an hour – do – do!"

160

"Cut my limbs off one by one!" cried Sikes, seizing her by the arm, "if I don't think the gal's stark raving mad. Get up."

"Not till you let me go – Never – never!" screamed the girl. Sikes suddenly pinioning her hands dragged her, struggling and wrestling with him, into a small room, where he thrust her into a chair and held her down by force. She struggled and implored by turns until twelve o'clock had struck, and then, wearied and exhausted, ceased to struggle. Sikes then left her to recover and rejoined Fagin.

"Whew!" said the housebreaker. "Wot a strange gal that is!"

"You may say that, Bill," replied Fagin thoughtfully.

"Why did she need to go out tonight, do you think?" asked Sikes. "You know her better than me. Wot does it mean?"

"Obstinacy; woman's obstinacy, I suppose, my dear."

"Well, I suppose it is," growled Sikes. "I thought I had tamed her, but she's as bad as ever."

"Worse," said Fagin thoughtfully. "I never knew her like this, for such a little cause."

"Nor I," said Sikes. "I think she's got a touch of that fever in her blood yet, and it won't come out – eh?"

The Jew nodded quietly.

"She was hanging about me when I was stretched on my back," said Sikes. "We was very poor too, and I think, one way or other, it's worried her, and being shut up here so long has made her restless – eh?"

"That's it, my dear," replied the Jew in a whisper. "Hush!"

As he uttered these words, the girl herself appeared, taking her former seat. Her eyes were swollen and red. She rocked to and fro, tossed her head, and after a little, burst out laughing.

"Why, now she's on the other tack!" exclaimed Sikes.

Fagin nodded to him to take no further notice and a few moments later the girl subsided into her accustomed demeanour. Whispering to Sikes that there was no fear of her relapsing, Fagin took up his hat and bade him good night. He paused when he reached the room-door and asked if somebody would light him down the dark stairs.

"Light him down," said Sikes, who was filling his pipe. "It's a pity he should break his neck himself. Show him a light."

Nancy followed the old man down stairs with a candle. When they reached the passage, he laid his finger on his lip, and drawing close to the girl said, in a whisper, "What is it, Nancy, dear?"

"What do you mean?" replied the girl.

"The reason of all this," replied Fagin. "If he" – he pointed with his finger up the stairs – "is so hard with you, why don't you – "

"Well?" said the girl, as Fagin paused, his eyes looking into hers.

"No matter just now. We'll talk of this again. You have a friend in me, Nance, a staunch friend. I have the means at hand. If you want revenge on those that treat you like a dog, come to me. He is the mere hound of a day, but you know me of old, Nance."

"I know you well," replied the girl, emotionlessly. "Good night."

She shrank back as Fagin offered to lay his hand on hers, but said good night again, in a steady voice, and, closed the door.

Fagin walked towards his own home, intent upon his thoughts. He had conceived the idea – not from what had just passed, though that had confirmed it, but slowly and by degrees – that Nancy, wearied of the housebreaker's brutality, had conceived an attachment for some new friend. The object of this new liking was not among his myrmidons. He would be a valuable acquisition with such an assistant as Nancy, and must (thus Fagin argued) be secured without delay.

There was another, and a darker object, to be gained. Sikes knew too much. The girl must know, that if she shook him off, she could never be safe from his fury. "With a little persuasion," thought Fagin, "she may consent to poison him? Women have done such things to secure the same object before now. There would be the dangerous villain, the man I hate, gone. Another secured in his place and my influence over the girl, with a knowledge of this crime to back it, unlimited."

These things passed through the mind of Fagin, during the short time he sat alone, in the housebreaker's room and with them uppermost in his thoughts, he had taken the opportunity afterwards to hint at Nancy.

But perhaps she would recoil from a plot to take the life of Sikes, and that was one of the chief ends to be attained. "How," thought Fagin, creeping homeward, "can I increase my influence with her? What new power can I acquire?"

If he laid a watch, discovered the object of her altered regard, and threatened to reveal the whole history to Sikes (of whom she stood in no common fear), unless she entered into his designs, could he not secure her compliance?

"I can," said Fagin, almost aloud. "She dare not refuse me then. Not for her life! I have it all. The means shall be set to work. I shall have you yet!"

CHAPTER 42

The old man was up, betimes, next morning, and waited impatiently for the appearance of a new boy, one he was hoping to groom for a life of crime.

"I want you," said Fagin, leaning over the table, "to do a piece of work for me, my dear, that needs great care and caution. I want you to dodge a young woman. I need you but to tell me where she goes, who she sees, and, if possible, what she says. Remember the street or the house and bring me back all the information you can."

"Who is she?" inquired the lad.

"One of us. She has found some new friends, my dear, and I must know who they are," replied Fagin.

"Where is she? Where am I to wait for her? Where am I to go?"

"All that, you shall hear from me. I'll point her out at the proper time," said Fagin. "You keep ready, and leave the rest to me."

That night, and the next the spy sat booted and ready to turn out at a word from Fagin. Six nights passed; and on each, Fagin came home with a disappointed face, and briefly shrugged that it was not yet time. On the seventh, he returned earlier, with an exultation he could not conceal. It was Sunday.

"She goes abroad tonight," said Fagin, "She has been alone all day, and the man she is afraid of will not be back much before daybreak. Come with me. Quick!"

The lad started up without a word, for the Jew was in a state of such intense excitement that it infected him. They left the house stealthily, and, hurrying through a labyrinth of streets, arrived before a public house.

It was past eleven o'clock, and the door was closed. It opened softly on its hinges as Fagin gave a low whistle. They entered and the door was closed behind them.

Nancy sat in a room on her own. The candle lit her unsmiling features.

"I see her," cried the spy.

"Plainly?"

"I should know her among a thousand."

The room door opened, and the girl came out. Fagin drew back in a small partition that was curtained off, and they held their breaths as she passed within a few feet of them and left.

"To the left," whispered Fagin. "Keep on the other side."

The lad did so and saw the girl's retreating figure, already at some distance before him. He advanced as near as he considered prudent, and kept on the opposite side of the street, the better to observe her motions. She looked nervously round, twice or thrice. She seemed to gather courage as she advanced, and to walk with a steadier and firmer step. The spy preserved the same relative distance between them, and followed with his eye upon her.

CHAPTER 43

The church clocks chimed three quarters past eleven, as two figures emerged on London Bridge. One advanced with a rapid step – a woman who looked eagerly about her as though in quest of some expected object. The other was a lad, who slunk along in the deepest shadow he could find, following her every footstep. Thus, they crossed the bridge, from the Middlesex to the Surrey shore, when the woman, apparently disappointed in her anxious scrutiny of the foot-passengers, turned back. At nearly the centre of the bridge, she stopped. The lad stopped too.

It was a very dark night and at that hour and place there were few people stirring. A mist hung over the river, and the forest of shipping below bridge, and the thickly scattered spires of churches above, were nearly all hidden from the sight.

The girl took a few restless turns – closely watched by her hidden observer – when the heavy bell of St Paul's tolled for the death of another day. Midnight.

The hour had not struck two minutes, when a young lady, accompanied by a grey-haired gentleman, alighted from a hackney-carriage close to the bridge, and walked straight towards it. They had scarcely set foot upon its pavement, when the girl immediately made towards them.

They walked on looking about them as though they were expecting something that had little chance of happening, when the young woman came up to them. They halted with an exclamation of surprise, but suppressed it immediately. A young lad came close up – rushed against them, indeed – at that precise moment.

"Not here," said Nancy hurriedly, "I am afraid to speak to you here. Come away, down the steps yonder!"

The steps to which the girl had pointed formed landing stairs from the river. To this spot, the lad also hastened unobserved; and after a moment's survey of the place, he began to descend. He found a hiding place with his back to a pillar, and waited, pretty certain that they would come no lower, and that even if he could not hear what was said, he could follow them again, with safety.

The time dragged and he more than once gave the matter up for lost, and persuaded himself either that they had stopped far above, or had chosen a different spot to converse. He was about to emerge from his hiding-place, and regain the road above, when he heard the sound of footsteps and then voices almost at his ear.

He drew himself against the wall, and without a breath listened intently.

"This is far enough," said a voice, evidently the gentleman. "I will not suffer the young lady to go any farther. Many people would have distrusted you too much to have come even so far. For what purpose have you brought us to this strange place? Why not speak to us in the light, instead of this dark and dismal hole?"

"I told you before," replied Nancy. "I was afraid to speak to you there. I have such a dread upon me that I can hardly stand."

"A fear of what?" asked the gentleman, who seemed to pity her.

"I scarcely know," replied the girl. "I wish I did. Horrible thoughts of death, and shrouds with blood upon them."

"Imagination," said the gentleman, soothing her.

"No imagination," replied the girl in a hoarse voice. "They carried a coffin close to me, in the streets tonight."

"There is nothing unusual in that," said the gentleman. "They have passed me often."

"*Real ones*," rejoined the girl. "This was not."

"Speak to her kindly," said the young lady to her companion. "Poor creature! She seems to need it."

"You were not here last Sunday night," he said.

"I couldn't come," replied Nancy. "I was kept by force, by him that I told the young lady of before."

"No one suspects you of communicating with anybody on the subject which brings us here tonight?" asked the old gentleman.

"No," replied the girl, shaking her head. "It's not very easy for me to leave unless he knows why. I couldn't have seen the lady when I did, but that I gave him a drink of laudanum before I came away."

"Did he awake before you returned?" inquired the gentleman.

"No, and neither he nor any of them suspect me."

"Good," said the gentleman. "Now listen to me."

"I am ready," replied the girl, as he paused for a moment.

"This young lady," the gentleman began, "has told me and some other friends who can be trusted, what you told her. I confess to you that I had doubts at first, whether you were to be believed, but now I firmly believe you are."

"I am," said the girl earnestly.

"I repeat that I firmly believe it. To prove to you that I am disposed to trust you, I tell you, that we propose to extort the secret, from the fears of this man Monks. But if – if – " said the gentleman, "he cannot be secured, or, if secured, cannot be acted upon as we wish, you must deliver up the Jew."

"Fagin!" cried the girl, recoiling.

"That man must be delivered up by you," said the gentleman.

"I will not do it! I will never do it!" replied the girl. "Devil that he is, I will never do that."

"You will not?" said the gentleman, who was prepared for this answer.

"Never!" returned the girl.

"Tell me why."

"For one reason," rejoined the girl firmly, "that the lady knows and will stand by me in, for I have her promise. And because as bad a life as he has led, I have led a bad life too. There are many of us who have kept the same courses together, and I'll not turn upon them, when any of them might have turned upon me, but didn't, bad as they are."

"Then," said the gentleman, quickly, "put Monks into my hands, and leave him to me to deal with. This Fagin shall not be brought to justice without your consent. In such a case I believe I could show you reasons that would induce you to consent."

"Have I the lady's promise?" asked the girl.

"You have," replied Rose. "My true and faithful pledge."

"Monks would never learn how you know this?" said the girl, after a short pause.

"Never," replied the gentleman. "He will never even guess."

"I have been a liar, and among liars since a child," said the girl after another interval of silence, "but I will take your words."

She then proceeded to describe by name and situation, the public house whence she had been followed that night. From the manner in which she occasionally paused, it appeared as if the gentleman were making some hasty notes of the information she communicated.

"He is tall," said the girl, "and a strongly made man, but not stout. As he walks, he constantly looks over his shoulder, first on one side, and then on the other. His eyes are sunk in his head so much deeper than any other man's, that you might almost tell him by that alone. His face is dark, like his hair and eyes and he can't be more than six or eight and twenty. His lips are often disfigured with teeth marks for he has desperate fits, and sometimes even bites his hands – why did you start?"

The gentleman replied that he was not conscious of having done so, and begged her to proceed.

"Part of this," said the girl, "I've drawn from other people at the house, for I have only seen him twice, when he was covered in a large cloak. I think that's all. Stay though," she added. "Upon his throat, so high that you can see a part of it below his neckerchief when he turns his face, there is – "

"A broad red mark, like a burn or scald?" cried the gentleman.

"How's this?" said the girl. "You know him!"

The young lady uttered a cry of surprise.

"I think I do," said the gentleman. "By your description. Many people are singularly alike. It may not be the same."

As he said this he took a step or two nearer the concealed spy, who very clearly heard him mutter, "It must be he!"

"Now," he said, returning to where he had stood, "you have given most valuable assistance. I wish I could help you. What can I do to serve you?"

"Nothing," replied Nancy.

"Please don't say that," rejoined the gentleman, kindly. "Think now. Tell me."

"Nothing, sir," rejoined the girl, weeping. "You can do nothing to help me. I am past all hope, indeed."

"You put yourself beyond its pale," said the gentleman. "The past has been a dreary waste with you, of youthful energies mis-spent. I cannot offer you peace of heart and mind. But if you need asylum, either in England, or, if you prefer, in some foreign country, it is not only within our ability but would be our most anxious wish. Before the dawn you could be entirely beyond the reach of your former associates. Come! I would not have you go back there. Quit while there is time and opportunity!"

"She will be persuaded," cried the young lady. "She hesitates."

"I fear not, my dear," said the gentleman.

"No, sir, I do not," replied the girl, after a short struggle. "I am chained to my old life. I loathe and hate it but I cannot leave it. I must have gone too far to turn back. But, this fear comes over me again. I must go home."

"Home!" repeated the young lady, with stress upon the word.

"Home, lady," rejoined the girl. "To such a home as I have raised for myself with the work of my whole life. Let us part. If I have done you any service, all I ask is, that you leave me, and let me go my way alone."

"It is useless," said the gentleman, with a sigh. "We compromise her safety, perhaps, by staying here. We may have detained her longer than she expected already."

"Yes, yes," urged the girl. "You have."

"What," cried the young lady, "can be the end of this poor creature's life!"

"What!" repeated the girl. "Look before you, lady, at that dark water. How many times do you read of such as I who spring into the tide, leaving no living thing to care for them. It may be years hence, or it may be only months, but I shall come to that at last."

"Do not speak thus, pray," returned the young lady.

"It will never reach your ears, dear lady, and God forbid such horrors should!" replied the girl. "Good night, good night!"

The gentleman turned away.

"This purse," cried the young lady. "Take it for my sake, that you may have some resource in an hour of need and trouble."

"No!" replied the girl. "I have not done this for money. And yet – give me something that you have worn: I should like to have something – your gloves or handkerchief – anything that I can keep, as having belonged to you, sweet lady. There. God bless you. Good night!"

The agitation of the girl, and the fear of discovery, seemed to determine the gentleman to leave, as requested. The sound of retreating footsteps was audible and the voices ceased. The figures of the young lady and her companion soon appeared upon the bridge. They stopped at the summit of the stairs.

"Hark!" cried the young lady, listening. "Did she call?"

"No, my love," replied Mr Brownlow, looking sadly back. "She will not move till we are gone."

Rose Maylie lingered, but the old gentleman drew her arm through his, and led her gently away. As they disappeared, the girl sunk down upon the stone stairs, and cried bitter tears.

After a time she arose, and with feeble steps ascended to the street. The astonished listener remained motionless at his post for some minutes afterwards. Having ascertained with cautious glances that he was again alone, he crept slowly from his hiding place.

When he reached the top, the spy darted away at top speed, and made for the Jew's house as fast as his legs would carry him.

CHAPTER 44

It was nearly two hours before day-break and Fagin sat watching in his old lair, with face so distorted and pale, and eyes so red and bloodshot, that he looked less like a man, than like some hideous phantom.

He sat over a cold hearth, wrapped in an old torn coverlet, with his face turned towards a wasting candle that stood upon a table by his side.

Stretched upon a mattress on the floor, lay the young spy, fast asleep. The old man sometimes directed his eyes at him for an instant, and then brought them back again to the candle that plainly showed his thoughts were busy elsewhere.

Indeed they were. Mortified at the overthrow of his notable scheme; hatred of the girl who had dared to palter with strangers; an utter distrust of the sincerity of her refusal to give him up; bitter disappointment at the

169

loss of his revenge on Sikes; fear of detection, ruin, and death, and a fierce and deadly rage; all these followed close upon each other with a ceaseless whirl through the brain of Fagin.

He sat without moving until his quick ear seemed to hear a footstep in the street.

"At last," he muttered, wiping his dry and fevered mouth.

The bell rang gently as he spoke. He crept up to the door, and presently returned accompanied by Sikes.

"There!" Sikes said, laying the bundle on the table. "Take care of that, and do the most you can with it."

Fagin laid his hand upon the bundle, and locking it in the cupboard, sat down again without speaking. But he did not take his eyes off the robber, for an instant. Now they sat face to face, he stared at him, with his lips quivering so violently, that the housebreaker drew back his chair, and gave a look of fright.

"Wot now?" cried Sikes. "Wot do you look at a man so for?"

Fagin raised his right hand, shaking his forefinger, but his passion was so great, that the power of speech was for the moment gone.

"Damme!" said Sikes. "He's gone mad. I must look to myself."

"No, no," rejoined Fagin, finding his voice. "It's not – you're not the person, Bill. I've no – no fault to find with you. I've got that to tell you, Bill," said Fagin, drawing his chair nearer, "will make you worse than me."

"Aye?" returned the robber. "Tell away! Look sharp, or Nance will think I'm lost."

"Lost!" cried Fagin. "She has pretty well settled that, in her own mind already."

Sikes looked with great perplexity at the Jew's face, and reading no satisfactory explanation, clenched his coat collar in his hand and shook him. "Speak, will you!" he said; "Open your mouth and say wot you've got to say in plain words, you thundering old cur!"

"Suppose that lad that's lying there – " Fagin began, pointing to the lad asleep.

Sikes turned round to the boy. "Well?"

"Suppose that lad," pursued Fagin, "was to peach – to blow upon us all – first seeking out the right folks, and then having a meeting with 'em in the street to paint our likenesses. Describes every mark that they might know us by and the crib where we might be most easily taken. Suppose he was also to blow upon a plant we've all been in, more or less – of his own fancy. Not grabbed, trapped, tried, by the parson and brought to it on bread and water – but of his own fancy. Stealing out at nights. Do you hear me?" cried the Jew. "Suppose he did all this, what then?"

"What then!" replied Sikes; with a tremendous oath. "If he was still alive, I'd grind his skull under the iron heel of my boot into as many grains as there are hairs upon his head."

"What if I did it!" cried Fagin almost in a yell. "I, that know so much, and could hang so many myself!"

"I don't know," replied Sikes, turning white at the mere suggestion. "I'd do something that 'ud get me put in irons and if I was tried along with you, I'd fall upon you with them in the open court, and beat your brains out afore the people."

"You would?"

"Would I!" said the housebreaker. "Try me."

"If it was Charley, or the Dodger, or Bet, or – "

"I don't care who," replied Sikes. "I'd serve them the same."

Fagin looked hard at the robber, and, motioning him to be silent, shook the sleeper to rouse him. Sikes leant forward in his chair: looking on with his hands upon his knees.

"Poor lad!" said Fagin, speaking slowly and with marked emphasis. "He's tired – with watching for her so long – Bill."

"Wot d'ye mean?" asked Sikes, drawing back.

Fagin made no answer, but hauled the sleeper upright. The lad rubbed his eyes, yawned and looked sleepily about him.

"Tell me that again – just for him to hear," said the Jew, pointing to Sikes. "That about – *Nancy*. You followed her?" He clutched Sikes by the wrist, as if to prevent his leaving before he had heard enough.

"Yes."

"To London Bridge? Where she met two people?"

"So she did."

"A gentleman and a lady who she went to of her own accord before, who asked her to give up all her pals, and Monks first – and to describe him, which she did – and to tell what house we meet at, which she did – and what time the people went there, which she did. She did all this, told every word without a threat, without a murmur – she did – did she not?" cried Fagin, half-mad with fury.

"That's about it," said the lad.

"What did they say, about last Sunday?"

"I told yer that before!" replied the boy.

"Tell it again!" cried Fagin, tightening his grasp on Sikes.

"They asked her," said the boy, seeming to realise who Sikes was, "why she didn't come, last Sunday, as she promised. She said she couldn't."

"Why – why? Tell him!"

"Because she was forcibly kept at home by Bill, the man she had told them of before," replied the lad. She couldn't easily leave unless he knew where she went, and so the first time she went to see the lady, she said she gave him laudanum."

"Hell's fire!" cried Sikes, breaking fiercely from the Jew. "Let me go!" Flinging the old man from him, he rushed up the stairs.

"Bill, Bill!" cried Fagin, following him hastily. "A word!"

The word would not have been exchanged, if the housebreaker had been able to open the door. The Jew came panting up.

"Let me out," said Sikes. "Don't speak to me; it's not safe. Let me out, I say!"

"Hear me," said Fagin, his hand upon the lock. "You won't be – too – violent, Bill?"

Day was breaking, and it was light enough for the men to see each other. They exchanged one brief glance, fire in their eyes.

"I mean," said Fagin, knowing all disguise was now useless, "not too violent for safety. Be crafty, Bill, and not too bold."

Sikes made no reply, but opened the door and dashed into the silent streets.

Without one pause the robber held on his headlong course, not muttering a word, nor relaxing a muscle, until he reached his own door. He opened it softly, strode lightly up the stairs and entering his own room, double-locked the door. He drew back the bed curtain.

The girl was lying there, half-dressed. He had roused her from her sleep, for she raised herself with a hurried and startled look.

"Get up!" said the man.

"It is you, Bill!" said the girl, smiling at his return.

"It is," was the reply. "Get up."

The man hastily hurled the candle into the grate. Seeing the faint light of dawn, the girl rose to pull the curtain.

"Let it be," said Sikes. "There's light enough for wot I've got to do."

"Bill," said the girl, in the low voice of alarm, "why do you look like that at me!"

The robber sat regarding her, for a few seconds, with heaving breast, and then, grasping her by the head and throat, dragged her into the middle of the room, and looking once towards the door, placed his heavy hand upon her mouth.

"Bill, Bill!" gasped the girl, wrestling with the strength of mortal fear. "I – I won't scream – not once – hear me – speak to me – tell me what I have done!"

"You know, you she devil!" returned the robber. "You were watched tonight, every word you said was heard."

"Then spare my life for the love of Heaven, as I spared yours," rejoined the girl, clinging to him. "Dear Bill, you cannot have the heart to kill me. Think of all I have given up, just tonight, for you. Bill, for dear God's sake, for your own, for mine, stop before you spill my blood! I have been true to you, upon my soul!"

The man struggled violently to free his arms but the girl's were tight round his, and tear as he would, he could not tear them away.

"Bill," cried the girl, trying to lay her head on his chest, "the gentleman and lady told me tonight of a home in some foreign country where I could end my days in peace. Let me see them again, and beg them to show the same goodness to you!"

The housebreaker freed one arm, and grasped his pistol. Knowing, even in his fury that its fire would be heard, he instead beat it twice with all his strength upon her upturned face.

She staggered and fell, nearly blinded from the blood pouring from a deep gash in her forehead. She managed to lift herself, and drew from her bosom a white handkerchief – Rose Maylie's own. She held it high towards Heaven and breathed one prayer for mercy to her Maker.

The murderer, staggering backward to the wall, and shutting out the sight with his hand, seized a heavy club and struck her down.

CHAPTER 45

Of all bad deeds that, under cover of the darkness, had been committed within wide London's bounds since night hung over it, that was the worst.

The bright sun – that brings back, not light alone, but new life and hope – burst upon the crowded city in clear and radiant glory. It lighted up the room where the murdered woman lay. He tried to shut it out. If the sight had been ghastly in the dull morning, what was it now, in brilliant light!

He had not moved, afraid to stir. There had been a moan and motion of the hand and, with terror added to rage, he had struck and struck again. There was the body – mere flesh and blood, no more – but such flesh, and so much blood!

He struck a light, kindled a fire, and thrust the club into it. There was hair upon the end, which blazed and shrunk into a light cinder, and, caught by the air, whirled up the chimney. He held the weapon till it broke, and then piled it on the coals to burn away, and smoulder into ashes. He washed himself, and rubbed his clothes; there were spots that would not be removed, but he cut the pieces out, and burnt them. The very feet of the dog were bloody.

All this time he had never once turned his back upon the corpse, even for a moment. He moved, backward, towards the door, dragging the dog with him, lest he should soil his feet anew and carry out new evidences of the crime into the streets. He shut the door softly, locked it, took the key, and left the house.

He crossed over, and glanced up at the window, to be sure that nothing was visible from the outside. The curtain was still drawn, which she would have opened to admit the light she never saw again.

It was a relief to have got free of the room. He whistled on the dog, and walked rapidly away.

He went through Islington, strode up the hill at Highgate, turned down to Highgate Hill, unsteady of purpose, and uncertain where to go. He headed off to Hampstead Heath. Thence to Highgate, and at North End, he laid himself down under a hedge, and slept.

Soon he was up again, and away – not far into the country, wandering up and down in fields, and lying on ditches' edges to rest, and starting up to ramble on again.

Where could he go, that was near and not too public, to get some meat and drink? Hendon. That was a good place, not far off, and out of most people's way. But when he got there, all the people he met seemed to view him with suspicion. Back he turned again, without purchasing bit or drop; and once more he lingered on the Heath, uncertain where to go.

He wandered over miles and miles of ground; at last heading for Hatfield. It was nine o'clock at night, when the man, quite tired out, and the dog, limping and lame from the unaccustomed exercise, crept into a small public house. There was a fire in the tap-room, and some country-labourers were drinking before it. They made room for the stranger, but he sat down in the furthest corner, and ate and drank alone.

Leaving the bar, he walked out into the street where he recognised the mail from London standing at the little post-office. He almost knew what was to come; but crossed over, and listened.

The guard stood at the door, waiting for the letter-bag.

"Anything new up in town, Ben?" asked the man from the post office.

"No, not that I know," replied the man, pulling on his gloves. "I did hear talk of a murder down Spitalfields way."

"A dreadful murder it was, too," said a gentleman inside, looking out of the window.

"Man or woman, sir?" rejoined the guard, touching his hat.

"A woman," replied the gentleman. "It is supposed – "

"Now, Ben," replied the coachman impatiently. "Time to go."

The horn sounded a few cheerful notes, and the coach was gone.

Sikes remained in the street, apparently unmoved by what he had just heard, and agitated by no stronger feeling than a doubt where to go. At length he went back again, and took the road to St Albans.

He went on doggedly; but as he left the town behind him, he felt a dread creeping upon him that shook him to the core. Every object before him, still or moving, took the semblance of some fearful thing. But these fears were nothing compared to the sense that haunted him of that morning's ghastly figure following. He could trace its shadow in the gloom, and note how stiff and solemn it seemed to stalk along. He could hear its garments rustling in the leaves, and every breath of wind came laden with that last low cry. If he stopped it did the same. If he ran, it followed – not running but like a corpse endowed with the mere machinery of life.

175

There was a shed in a field he passed, that offered shelter for the night. Before the door, were three tall poplar trees, which made it dark within; and the wind moaned with a dismal wail. He could not walk on, till daylight came again; and here he stretched himself close to the wall.

Now he could see those widely staring eyes, so lustreless and so glassy appear in the midst of the darkness. They were everywhere. If he closed his eyes, he saw the room with every well-known object; each in its accustomed place. The body was in its place, and its eyes were as he saw them when he stole away. He got up, and rushed into the field. The figure was behind him. He re-entered the shed, and shrunk down once more.

And here he remained in such terror as none but he can know, trembling in every limb, and the cold sweat starting from every pore.

When daylight broke, he resolved to return to London.

"There's somebody to speak to there, at all events," he thought. "A good hiding-place, too. Why, if I lie by for a week or so, and, force blunt from Fagin, I'll go abroad to France. I'll risk it."

He acted without delay, and chose the least frequented roads, resolving to lie concealed close to the town, to enter it at dusk.

However, if there were any descriptions of the dog out, it would be expected that it had probably gone with him. This might lead to his arrest as he passed along the streets. He resolved to drown him, and walked on, looking about for a pond. He picked up a heavy stone and tied it to his handkerchief.

The animal looked up into his master's face while these preparations were being made and instinct made him cautious. He skulked a little farther in the rear than usual. When his master stopped at a pool, and called him, he stopped outright.

"Do you hear me call? Come here!" cried Sikes.

The animal came up from habit, but as Sikes stooped to attach the handkerchief to his throat, he uttered a low growl and started back.

"Come back!" said the robber, and he whistled.

The dog advanced, retreated, paused, turned, and scoured away at his hardest speed.

The man whistled again and sat down, waited for the dog. But it never appeared, and at length he resumed his journey.

CHAPTER 46

Twilight was closing in, when Mr Brownlow alighted from a hackney coach at his own door, and knocked softly. The door being opened, a sturdy man got out of the coach and stood to one side of the steps, while another man, dismounted too, and stood, upon the other side. At a sign from Mr Brownlow, they helped out a third man, and hurried him into the house. It was Monks.

They walked up the stairs without speaking, and Mr Brownlow led the way into a back room. At this door, Monks, who had ascended with evident reluctance, stopped. The two men looked to the old gentleman as if for instructions.

"He knows the alternative," said Mr Brownlow. "If he hesitates or moves a finger, drag him into the street, call for the police, and impeach him as a felon in my name."

"How dare you say this of me?" asked Monks.

"Will you try it, young man?" replied Mr Brownlow, confronting him with a steady look. "Are you mad enough to leave this house? Unhand him. There, you are free to go, and we to follow. But I warn you, by all I hold most sacred, that the instant you set foot in the street, I will have you apprehended on a charge of fraud and robbery. I am resolute. If you are determined to be the same, your blood be upon your own head!"

"By what authority am I kidnapped in the street, and brought here by these dogs?" asked Monks, looking between the men beside him.

"By mine," replied Mr Brownlow. "Those persons are indemnified by me. If you complain of being deprived of your liberty, throw yourself for protection on the law. I will appeal to the law too – but when you have gone too far to recede, do not ask me for leniency, for the power will be in other hands."

Monks was plainly alarmed. He hesitated.

"You will decide quickly," said Mr Brownlow, with perfect firmness. "If you wish to be dealt with publicly, and to receive a punishment the extent of which, although I can foresee, I cannot control, you know the way. If, however, you appeal to my forbearance, and the mercy of those you have deeply injured, sit yourself quietly in that chair. It has waited for you two days."

Monks muttered some unintelligible words, but wavered still.

"A word from me," said Mr Brownlow, "and the alternative has gone for ever."

Still the man hesitated. "Is there – " demanded Monks with a faltering tongue, "no middle course?"

"None."

Monks looked at the old gentleman with an anxious eye; and then walked into the room, and, shrugging his shoulders, sat down.

"Lock the door on the outside," said Mr Brownlow to the attendants, "and come when I ring."

The men obeyed, and the two were left alone together.

"This is pretty treatment, sir," said Monks, throwing down his hat and cloak, "from my father's oldest friend."

"It is because I was your father's oldest friend, young man," returned Mr Brownlow. "It is because the hopes and wishes of young and happy years were bound up with him, and because he knelt with me beside his only sister's death-bed when he was yet a boy, on the morning that would – but Heaven willed otherwise – have made her my young wife. It is because my seared heart clung to him, from that time forth, through all his trials and errors, till he died. It is because of these things that I am moved to treat you gently now – yes, Edward Leeford, even now – and blush for your unworthiness who bear the name."

"What has the name to do with it?" asked the other, after contemplating, half in silence, and half in dogged wonder. "What is the name to me?"

"Nothing," replied Mr Brownlow, "nothing to you. But it was hers and even at this distance of time brings back to me, an old man, the glow and thrill that I once felt. I am very glad you changed it – very."

"This is all mighty fine," said Monks. "But what do you want with me?"

"You have a brother," said Mr Brownlow, rousing himself, "the whisper of whose name in your ear when I came behind you was, in itself, enough to make you accompany me here."

"I have no brother," replied Monks. "You know I was an only child. Why do you talk to me of brothers?"

"Attend to what I do know, and you may not," said Mr Brownlow. "I shall interest you by and by. I know that of the wretched marriage, into

178

which family pride forced your unhappy father when a mere boy, you were the sole and most unnatural issue. And I also know the misery, the slow torture, the protracted anguish of that ill-assorted union. I know how indifference gave place to dislike, dislike to hate, hate to loathing. Finally they wrenched the clanking bond asunder, and retired a wide space apart. Your mother succeeded in forgetting the marriage. But it ate at your father's heart for years."

"Well, they were separated," said Monks, "and what of that?"

"When they had been separated for some time," returned Mr Brownlow, "and your mother, wholly given up to continental frivolities, had utterly forgotten the young husband ten years her junior, who, lingered on at home, he fell among new friends. This circumstance, at least, you know already."

"Not I," said Monks, looking away, determined to deny all.

"Your manner assures me that you have never forgotten it," returned Mr Brownlow. "I speak of fifteen years ago, when you were not more than eleven years old, and your father but one-and-thirty. He was, I repeat, a boy, when his father ordered him to marry. Must I go back to events which cast a shade upon the memory of your parent, or will you tell me the truth?"

"I have nothing to disclose," rejoined Monks.

"These new friends, then," said Mr Brownlow, "were a naval officer retired from active service, whose wife had died some half-a-year before, and left him with two children. They were both daughters, one a beautiful creature of nineteen, and the other a mere child of two or three years old."

"What's this to me?" asked Monks.

"They resided," said Mr Brownlow, without seeming to hear the interruption, "where your father in his wandering had chosen to live. Acquaintance, intimacy, friendship, fast followed on each other. Your father was gifted as few men are. He had his sister's soul. As the old officer knew him more he grew to love him. I would that it had ended there. His daughter did the same."

The old gentleman paused. Monks was biting his lips, eyes fixed upon the floor. Seeing this, he continued. "The end of a year found him contracted, solemnly contracted, to that daughter."

"Your tale is of the longest," observed Monks, moving restlessly in his chair.

179

"It is a true tale of grief and trial, and sorrow, young man," returned Mr Brownlow. "At length, one of his rich relations died leaving him money. It was necessary that your father should immediately go to Rome, where this man had died, leaving his affairs in great confusion. He went, was seized with mortal illness there, was followed, the moment the news reached Paris, by your mother who carried you with her. He died the day after her arrival, leaving no will – no will – so that the whole property fell to her and you."

Here Monks held his breath, and listened eagerly, though not looking at the speaker.

"Before he went abroad, and as he passed through London on his way," said Mr Brownlow, slowly, "he came to me."

"I never heard that," interrupted Monks.

"He came to me, and left with me, among some other things, a portrait painted by himself – a likeness of this poor girl – which he did not wish to leave behind, and could not carry on his hasty journey. He was worn by anxiety and remorse almost to a shadow; talking in a wild, distracted way, of ruin and dishonour worked by himself. He confided to me his intention of converting his whole property, at any loss, into money, and, having settled on his wife and you a portion of his recent acquisition, to fly the country – I guessed too well he would not fly alone – and never see it more. He promised to write and tell me all, and after that to see me once again, for the last time on earth. Alas! That was the last time. I had no letter, and I never saw him more.

"I went," said Mr Brownlow, after a short pause. "When all was over, to the scene of his – of his guilty love, resolved that if my fears were realised that erring child should find one heart and home to shelter her. The family had left a week before, by night. Why, or where to, none can tell."

Monks drew breath more freely, and gave a smile of triumph.

"When your brother," said Mr Brownlow, drawing nearer to the other's chair, "a feeble, ragged, neglected child, was cast in my way by a stronger hand than chance, and rescued by me from a life of vice and infamy – "

"What?" cried Monks.

"I told you," said Mr Brownlow, "I should interest you before long. I see that your cunning associate suppressed my name, although for aught he knew, it would be quite strange to your ears. When he was rescued by me, then, and lay recovering in my house, his strong resemblance to this picture I have spoken of struck me with astonishment. Even when I first saw him in all his dirt and misery, there was a lingering expression in his face that struck me like a glimpse of some old friend flashing on in a vivid dream. I need not tell you he was snared away before I knew his history – "

"Why not?" asked Monks hastily.

"Because you know it well. I lost the boy, and no efforts could recover him. Your mother being dead, I knew that you alone could solve the mystery if anybody could. When I had last heard of you, you were on your own estate in the West Indies – whither you retired upon your mother's death. I made the voyage. You had left it, months before, and were supposed to be in London, but no one could tell where. I returned. Your agents had no clue to your residence. You came and went, they said, as strangely as you had ever done. I paced the streets by night and day, but until two hours ago, all efforts were fruitless, and I never saw you for an instant."

"And now you see me," said Monks, rising boldly, "what now? Fraud and robbery are high-sounding words – justified you think, by a fancied resemblance to some young imp of an idle daub of a dead man's. Brother! You don't even know that a child was born."

"I did not," replied Mr Brownlow, rising too. "But within the last fortnight I have learnt all. You have a brother; you know it. There was a will, which your mother destroyed, leaving the secret and the gain to you at her own death. It contained a reference to some child likely to be the result of this sad connection. This child was born and accidentally encountered by you, and your suspicions were first awakened by his resemblance to his father. You went to the place of his birth. There existed proofs – proofs long suppressed – of his birth and parentage. Those proofs were destroyed by you, in your own words to your accomplice, the Jew, 'the only proofs of the boy's identity lie at the bottom of the river, and the old hag that received them from the mother is rotting in her coffin.' Unworthy son, coward, liar, – you, who hold your councils with thieves and murderers in dark rooms, – you, whose plots have brought a violent death to one worth millions such as you, – you, who from your cradle were gall and bitterness to your own father's heart, and in whom all evil passions, and vice, festered. Edward Leeford, do you still brave me?"

"No, no, no!" returned the coward, overwhelmed by these accumulated charges.

"Every word!" cried the old gentleman. "Every word that passed between you and this detested villain, is known to me. Shadows on the wall have caught your whispers, and brought them to my ear. Murder has been done, to which you were morally if not really a party."

"No," interposed Monks. "I – I – know nothing of that; I was going to inquire the truth of the story when you overtook me. I thought it was a common quarrel."

"It was the partial disclosure of your secrets," replied Mr Brownlow. "Will you disclose the whole? Set your hand to a statement of truth and facts, and repeat it before witnesses?"

"I promise."

"Remain quietly here, until such a document is drawn up, and proceed with me somewhere, for the purpose of attesting it?"

"If you insist, I'll do that also," replied Monks.

"You must do more than that," said Mr Brownlow. "Make restitution to an innocent child, for such he is, although the offspring of a guilty and most miserable love. You have not forgotten the provisions of the will. Carry them into execution so far as your brother is concerned, and then go where you please. In this world you need meet no more."

While Monks was pacing up and down, meditating with evil looks on this proposal and the possibilities of evading it: torn by fear on one hand and hatred on the other: the door was hurriedly unlocked, and Mr Losberne entered the room in violent agitation.

"The man will be taken," he cried. "Tonight!"

"The murderer?" asked Mr Brownlow.

"Yes, yes," replied the other. "His dog has been seen lurking about some old haunt, and it seems certain that his master either is, or will be, there, under cover of darkness. Spies are hovering. I have spoken to the men charged with his capture, and they tell me he cannot escape. A reward of a hundred pounds is proclaimed."

"I will give fifty more," said Mr Brownlow, "and proclaim it myself upon the spot, if I can reach it. Where is Mr Maylie?"

"Harry? As soon as he saw your friend here, safe in a coach with you, he hurried off to where he heard this," replied the doctor, "and mounted his horse to join them at some place in the outskirts."

"Fagin," said Mr Brownlow; "what of him?"

"When I last heard, he had not been taken, but he will be soon."

"Have you made up your mind?" asked Mr Brownlow, in a low voice, to Monks.

"Yes," he replied. "You – you – will be secret with me?"

"I will. Remain here till I return. It is your only hope of safety."

They left the room, and the door was again locked.

"What have you done?" asked the doctor in a whisper.

"All that I could hope to do, and more. Coupling the poor girl's intelligence with my previous knowledge, I left him no loophole of escape, and laid bare the whole villainy. Write and appoint the evening after tomorrow, at seven, for the meeting. We shall be there a few hours before, but the young lady may have greater need of firmness than either you or I can quite foresee just now. But my blood boils to avenge this poor murdered creature. Which way have they taken?"

"Drive straight to the office and you will be in time," replied Mr Losberne. "I will remain here."

CHAPTER 47

Near to that part of the Thames at Rotherhithe, where the buildings on the banks are dirtiest, there exists the filthiest, the strangest, the most extraordinary of the many localities that are hidden in London.

To reach this place, the visitor has to penetrate through a maze of close, narrow, and muddy streets, thronged by the roughest and poorest of waterside people. He must walk beneath tottering house-fronts projecting over the pavement, dismantled walls that seem to totter as he passes, chimneys half crushed, half hesitating to fall, windows guarded by rusty iron bars that time and dirt have almost eaten away.

In such a neighbourhood, beyond Dockhead in the Borough of Southwark, stands Jacob's Island, surrounded by a muddy ditch, six or eight feet deep and fifteen or twenty wide when the tide is in. It is a creek or inlet from the Thames, and can always be filled at high water by opening the sluices.

In Jacob's Island, the warehouses are roofless and empty, the walls are crumbling down, the windows are windows no more, the doors are falling into the streets, the chimneys are blackened, but they yield no smoke. Thirty or forty years ago, before losses and chancery suits came upon it, it was a thriving place, but now it is desolate indeed. The houses have no owners; they are broken open and entered by those who have the courage. There they live, and there they die. They must have powerful motives for a secret residence, or be reduced to a desitute condition indeed, who seek a refuge in Jacob's Island.

In an upper room of one of these houses – a detached house strongly defended at door and window, there were assembled three men. They sat for some time in profound and gloomy silence. One of these was Toby Crackit, another Mr Chitling, and the third a robber of fifty years called Kags.

"When was Fagin took then?" asked Toby.

"Just at two o'clock this afternoon. Charley and I made our lucky up the wash'us chimney."

"And Bet?"

"Poor Bet! She went to see the Body, to say who it was," replied Chitling, "and went off mad, screaming and raving. So they put a strait-weskut on her and took her to the hospital – and there she is. Bates'll be here soon. There's nowhere else to go, for the people at the Cripples are all in custody."

"There's more than one will go with this," observed Toby, biting his lips.

"The sessions are on," said Kags. "They'll prove Fagin an accessory before the fact, and get the trial for Friday, and he'll swing in six days from this!"

"You should have heard people groan," said Chitling. "You should have seen how he looked about him, all muddy and bleeding, and clung to the officers as if they were his dearest friends. I can see 'em now, not able to stand upright with the pressing of the mob, and dragging him along amongst 'em. I can see the people jumping up and snarling and making at him. I can see the blood on his hair and beard, and hear the cries of the women who worked themselves into the centre of the crowd, and swore they'd tear his heart out!"

The horror-struck witness of this scene pressed his hands upon his ears, and with his eyes closed paced violently to and fro.

While he did this, and the two men sat in silence, a pattering noise was heard upon the stairs. Sikes's dog bounded into the room. They ran to the window, down stairs, and into the street. The dog had jumped in at an open window; he made no attempt to follow them, nor was his master to be seen.

"What does this mean?" said Toby, when they had returned. "He can't be coming here."

"If he was coming here, he'd have come with the dog," said Kags, stooping down to examine the animal, who lay panting on the floor. "Here! Give him some water, he has run himself faint."

"He's drunk up every drop," said Chitling, after watching the dog some time in silence. "Covered with mud – lame – half-blind – he's come a long way."

"He's been to the other kens, of course!" exclaimed Toby. "And found them filled with strangers. He's been here many a time. But where did he come from, and how comes he alone!"

"He," (none of them named the murderer.) "He can't have made away with himself. What do you think?" said Chitling.

Toby shook his head.

"If he had," said Kags, "the dog 'ud want to lead us to where he did it. No. I think he's got out of the country, and left the dog behind. He's given him the slip somehow, or he wouldn't be so easy."

This solution appeared to them the most probable. The dog, creeping under a chair, coiled himself up to sleep.

It was now dark, the shutter was closed, and a candle lighted and placed upon the table. They drew their chairs closer, starting at every sound. They spoke little, and that in whispers, and were as silent as if the remains of the murdered girl lay in the next room.

They had sat thus, some time, when suddenly was heard a hurried knocking at the door below.

"Young Bates," said Kags, quelling the fear he felt.

The knock came again. No, it wasn't he. He never knocked like that.

Crackit went to the window, and shaking all over, drew in his head. There was no need to say who it was: his pale face was enough. The dog too was on the alert, and ran whining to the door.

"We must let him in," he said, taking up the candle.

"Isn't there any help for it?" asked one in a hoarse whisper.

"None. He must come in."

Crackit went down to the door, and returned, followed by a man with the lower part of his face buried in a handkerchief. Blanched face, sunken eyes, hollow cheeks, beard of three days' growth, wasted flesh, short thick breath; it was the very ghost of Sikes.

He laid his hand upon a chair which stood in the middle of the room, but shuddering, and seeming to glance over his shoulder, dragged it back close to the wall, as close as it would go, and sat down.

No words had been exchanged. He looked from one to another in silence. If an eye met his, it was instantly averted. When his hollow voice broke silence, they all three started.

"How came that dog here?" he asked.

"Alone. Three hours ago."

"Paper says that Fagin's took. Is it true?"

"True."

They were silent again.

"Damn you all!" said Sikes, passing his hand across his forehead. "Have you nothing to say to me?"

There was an uneasy movement among them, but nobody spoke.

Sikes turned to Crackit. "Do you mean to sell me, or to let me lie here till this hunt is over?"

"You can stop here, if you think it safe," Toby replied, hesitantly.

Sikes carried his eyes slowly up the wall behind him and said, "Is – it – the body – is it buried?"

They shook their heads.

"Why not?" he retorted. "Wot do they keep such ugly things above the ground for? Who's that knocking?"

Crackit intimated, by a motion of his hand as he left the room, that there was nothing to fear; and directly returned with Charley Bates behind him. Sikes sat opposite the door, so that the moment the boy entered the room he saw him.

"Toby," said the boy, falling back, as Sikes looked towards him, "why didn't you tell me this downstairs? Let me go into some other room."

"Charley!" said Sikes, stepping forward. "Don't you – don't you know me?"

"Don't come nearer me," answered the boy, retreating, looking with horror in his eyes, upon the murderer's face. "You monster!"

The man stopped half-way, and they looked at each other; but Sikes's eyes sunk gradually to the ground.

"Witness you three," cried the boy, shaking his clenched fist. "Witness – I'm not afraid of him – if they come here after him, I'll give him up – I will. He may kill me for it if he likes, or if he dares, but if I am here I'll give him up. I'd give him up if he was to be boiled alive. Murder! Help! If there's the pluck of a man among you three, you'll help me!"

The boy actually threw himself, single-handed upon the strong man, and in the intensity of his energy and the suddenness of his surprise, brought him heavily to the ground.

The three spectators seemed quite stupefied. They offered no interference and the boy and man rolled on the ground together; the former, never ceasing to call for help with all his might.

The contest, however, was too unequal to last long. Sikes had him down, and his knee was on his throat, when Crackit pulled him back with a look of alarm, and pointed to the window. There were lights gleaming below, voices in loud and earnest conversation, the tramp of hurried footsteps crossing the nearest wooden bridge. One man on horseback seemed to be among the crowd, for there was the noise of hoofs rattling on the uneven pavement. Then, came a loud knocking at the door.

"Help!" shrieked the boy in a voice that rent the air. "He's here! Break down the door!"

"In the King's name," cried the voices without; and the hoarse cry arose again, but louder.

"Break down the door!" screamed the boy. "They'll never open it. Run straight to the room where the light is. Break down the door!"

Strokes, thick and heavy, rattled upon the door and lower window-shutters.

"Find somewhere I can lock this screeching Hell-babe," cried Sikes fiercely, dragging the boy. "That door. Quick!" He flung him in, bolted it, and turned the key. "Is the down-stairs door fast?"

"Double-locked and chained," replied Crackit, who, with the other two men, still remained quite helpless and bewildered.

"The panels – are they strong?"

"Lined with sheet-iron."

"And the windows too?"

"Yes, and the windows."

"Damn you!" cried the desperate ruffian, throwing up the sash and menacing the crowd. "Do your worst! I'll cheat you yet!"

Of all the terrific yells that ever fell on mortal ears, none could exceed the cry of the infuriated throng. Some shouted to those who were nearest to set the house on fire; others roared to the officers to shoot him dead. Among them all, none showed more fury than the man on horseback. He leapt from the saddle, and burst through the crowd as if he were parting water, crying beneath the window, in a voice that rose above all others, "Twenty guineas to the man who brings a ladder!"

The nearest voices took up the cry, and hundreds echoed it. Some called for ladders and some for sledge hammers.

"The tide," cried the murderer, as he staggered back into the room, shutting the faces out, "the tide was in as I came up. Give me a long rope. They're all in front. I'll drop into the Folly Ditch, and clear off that way. Give me a rope, or I shall do three more murders and kill myself."

The men pointed to where they were kept. The murderer, hastily selecting the longest and strongest cord, hurried to the house-top.

All the windows in the rear of the house had been long ago bricked up, except one small trap in the room where the boy was locked, and that was too small even for the passage of his body. But he had never ceased to call on those outside to guard the back. So when the murderer emerged by the door in the roof, a loud shout proclaimed the fact to those in front, who immediately began to pour round.

He planted a board firmly against the door and, creeping over the tiles, looked over the low parapet.

The water was out, and the ditch a bed of mud.

The crowd had been hushed during these few moments, watching his motions and doubtful of his purpose, but the instant they perceived it and knew it was defeated, they raised a cry of triumph. Again and again it rose.

On pressed the people from the front – on, in a strong struggling current of angry faces, with here and there a glaring torch to light them up. The houses on the opposite side of the ditch had been entered by the mob. Sashes were thrown up, there were tiers and tiers of faces in every window. Each little bridge (and there were three in sight) bent beneath the weight of the crowd upon it.

"They have him now," cried a man on the nearest bridge. "Hurrah!"

"I will give fifty pounds," cried an old gentleman at the front, "to the man who takes him alive. I will stay, till he comes for it."

There was another roar. Word was passed that the door was forced at last, and that he who had first called for the ladder had got into the room. The stream of people abruptly turned, as this intelligence ran from mouth to mouth. People at the windows, seeing those upon the bridges pouring back, quitted their stations, and ran into the street, each man striving with his neighbour to get near the door, and look upon the criminal as the officers brought him out. The immediate attention was distracted from the murderer.

The man had shrunk down, thoroughly quelled by the ferocity of the crowd, and the impossibility of escape. Seeing the sudden change he jumped up, determined to make one last effort for his life by dropping into the ditch, and, at the risk of being stifled, endeavouring to creep away in the darkness and confusion.

He set his foot against the stack of chimneys, fastened one end of the rope tightly and firmly round it, and with the other made a strong running noose. He could let himself down by the cord to within less distance of the ground than his own height, and had his knife ready in his hand to cut it then and drop.

At the very instant when he brought the loop over his head prior to slipping it beneath his armpits, the murderer, looking behind him on the roof, threw his arms above his head, and uttered a yell of terror.

"The eyes again!" he cried in an unearthly screech.

Staggering as if struck by lightning, he lost his balance and tumbled over the parapet. The noose was on his neck. It ran up with his weight, tight as a bowstring. He fell for five-and-thirty feet. There was a sudden jerk, a terrific convulsion of the limbs; and there he hung, with the open knife clenched in his stiffening hand.

The old chimney quivered with the shock. The murderer swung lifeless against the wall.

A dog, hidden until now, ran up and down on the parapet with a dismal howl, and collecting himself for a spring, jumped for the dead man's shoulders. Missing the man, he fell into the ditch, and striking his head against a stone, dashed out his brains.

CHAPTER 48

Just two days later Oliver found himself in a carriage rolling fast towards his native town. Mrs Maylie, Rose, Mrs Bedwin, and the good doctor were with him. Mr Brownlow followed in a post-chaise, accompanied by someone not named to him.

They had not talked much; for Oliver was in a flutter of uncertainty that deprived him of the power of collecting his thoughts, and almost of speech. Mr Brownlow had informed Oliver and the two ladies of the admissions forced from Monks. They knew that the object of this journey was to complete the work begun so well, but the whole matter was still shrouded in doubt and mystery.

The same kind friend had, with Mr Losberne's assistance, cautiously prevented them hearing the dreadful occurrences that had so recently taken place. "They must know them before long," he said. "But it might be at a better time than the present, and it could not be at a worse." So, they travelled on in silence.

But now that Oliver was on the road towards his birthplace that he had traversed on foot, a poor, wandering, friendless boy, he found he could not keep quiet.

"See there, there!" cried Oliver, eagerly clasping the hand of Rose, and pointing out at the carriage window; "that's the stile I came over; there are the hedges I crept behind, for fear any one should overtake me and force me back! Yonder is the path across the fields, leading to the old house where I was a little child!"

As they approached the town, and at length drove through its narrow streets, it became matter of no small difficulty to restrain the boy within reasonable bounds. There was Sowerberry's the undertaker's just as it used to be, only smaller and less imposing in appearance than he remembered it. There was the workhouse, the dreary prison of his youthful days, with its dismal windows frowning on the street – there was the same lean porter standing at the gate. There was nearly everything as if he had left it but yesterday and all his recent life had been but a happy dream.

They drove straight to the door of the chief hotel (which Oliver used to stare up at, with awe, but which had somehow fallen off in grandeur and size), and here was Mr Grimwig. There was dinner prepared, and bedrooms ready, and everything arranged as if by magic.

Mr Brownlow did not join them at dinner, but remained in a separate room. Once, Mrs Maylie was called away, and after being absent for nearly an hour, returned with eyes swollen with weeping. All these things made Rose and Oliver, who were not included, nervous and uncomfortable. They sat wondering, in silence or, in whispers, as if they were afraid to hear the sound of their own voices.

At length, when nine o'clock had come, and they began to think they were to hear no more that night, Mr Losberne and Mr Grimwig entered the room, followed by Mr Brownlow and a man whom Oliver almost shrieked with surprise to see. They told him it was his brother – the same man he had met at the market town, and seen looking in with Fagin at the window of his little room. Monks cast a look of hate at the astonished boy, and sat down near the door. Mr Brownlow, papers in hand, walked to a table near to Rose and Oliver.

"This is a painful task," said he, "but these declarations, signed in London before many gentlemen, must be in substance repeated here. I would have spared you the degradation, but we must hear them from your own lips before we part, and you know why."

"Quick," said the person addressed, turning away his face. "I have almost done enough, I think. Don't keep me here."

"This child," said Mr Brownlow, drawing Oliver to him, "is your half-brother; the illegitimate son of your father, my dear friend Edwin Leeford, by poor young Agnes Fleming, who died in giving him birth."

"Yes," said Monks, scowling at the trembling boy. "That is their bastard child."

"The term you use," said Mr Brownlow, sternly, "is a reproach to those who long since passed beyond the feeble censure of the world. It reflects disgrace on no one living, except you who use it. He was born in this town."

"In the workhouse," was the sullen reply. "You have the story there." He pointed to the papers as he spoke.

"I must have it here, too," said Mr Brownlow, looking round upon the listeners.

"Listen then! You!" returned Monks. "His father being taken ill in Rome, was joined by his wife, my mother, from whom he had been long separated. She went from Paris and took me with her – to look after his property, for what I know, for she had no great affection for him, nor he for her. He knew nothing of us, for his senses were gone, and he slumbered on till next day, when he died. Among the papers in his desk, were two, dated on the night his illness first came on. Directed to yourself," he addressed himself to Mr Brownlow; "and enclosed in a few short lines to you, with an intimation on the cover of the package that it was not to be forwarded till after he was dead. One of these papers was a letter to this girl Agnes, the other, a will."

"What of the letter?" asked Mr Brownlow.

"The letter? – A sheet of paper crossed and crossed again, with a penitent confession, and prayers to God to help her. He had palmed a tale on the girl that some secret mystery – to be explained one day – prevented his marrying her just then. She had gone on trusting patiently to him, until she trusted too far, and lost what none could ever give her back. She was, at that time, within a few months of her confinement. He told her all he had meant to do – to hide her shame, if he had lived, and prayed her, if he died, not to curse his memory, or think the consequences of their sin would be visited on her or their young child, for all the guilt was his. He reminded her of the day he had given her the little locket and the ring with her name engraved upon it and a blank left for that which he hoped one day to have bestowed upon her. He prayed her yet to keep it, and wear it next her heart, as she had done before – and then ran on, wildly, in the same words, over and over again, as if he had gone distracted. I believe he had."

"The will," said Mr Brownlow, as Oliver's tears fell fast. Monks was silent.

"The will," said Mr Brownlow, speaking for him, "was in the same spirit as the letter. He talked of miseries which his wife had brought upon him; of the rebellious disposition, vice and malice of you his only son, who had been trained to hate him; and left you, and your mother, each an annuity of eight hundred pounds. The bulk of his property he divided into two equal portions – one for Agnes Fleming, and the other for their child, if it should be born alive, and ever come of age. If it were a girl, it was to inherit the money unconditionally. But if a boy, it was on the stipulation that in his minority he should never have stained his name with any public act of dishonour, meanness, cowardice, or wrong. He did this, he said, to mark his confidence in the mother, and his conviction that the child would share her gentle heart, and noble nature. If he were disappointed in this expectation, then the money was to come to you. For only then, when both children were equal, would he recognise your prior claim upon his purse."

"My mother," said Monks, in a louder tone, "did what a woman should have done. She burnt this will. The letter never reached its destination. The girl's father had the truth from her with every aggravation that her violent hate – I love her for it now – could add. Goaded by shame and dishonour, he fled with his children into a remote corner of Wales, changing his name so that his friends might never know, and here, not long afterwards, he was found dead in his bed. The girl had left home, in secret, some weeks before. He had searched for her in every town and village near. It was the night he returned home, convinced that she had destroyed herself, to hide her shame and his, that his old heart broke."

There was a short silence here. Mr Brownlow again took up the thread of the narrative.

"Years after this," he said, "this man's – Edward Leeford's – mother came to me. He had left her, at eighteen, robbed her of jewels and money, gambled, squandered and fled to London. Here for two years he had associated with the lowest outcasts. She was sinking under an incurable disease, and wished to find him before she died. Inquiries were set on foot, and strict searches made. They were ultimately successful; and he returned with her to France."

"There she died," said Monks, "after a lingering illness. On her deathbed, she bequeathed these secrets to me, together with her unquenchable hatred of all involved – though she need not have left me that, for I had inherited it long before. She would not believe that the girl had destroyed herself, and the child too, but was convinced that a male child had been born, and was alive. I swore that if ever it crossed my path, I would hunt it down, pursue it with the bitterest and most unrelenting animosity and vent upon it the hatred that I deeply felt. I would spit upon that insulting will by dragging it, if I could, to the very gallows-foot. She was right. He came in my way at last. I began well, and would have finished if I could!"

The villain folded his arms tight together, and muttered curses, while Mr Brownlow turned to the terrified group beside him, and explained that the Jew, an old accomplice and confidant, had a large reward for keeping Oliver ensnared.

"The locket and ring?" said Mr Brownlow, turning to Monks.

"I bought them from the man and woman I told you of, who stole them from the nurse, who stole them from the corpse," answered Monks. "You know what became of them."

Mr Brownlow nodded to Mr Grimwig, who, disappearing briefly, returned, pushing in Mrs Bumble along with her unwilling consort.

"Do my hi's deceive me!" cried Mr Bumble, with ill-feigned enthusiasm, "or is that little Oliver? Oh, if you know'd how I've been a-grieving for you – "

"Hold your tongue, fool," murmured Mrs Bumble.

"But I always loved that boy as if he'd been my – my own grandfather," said Mr Bumble, halting for an appropriate comparison. "Master Oliver, my dear, you remember the blessed gentleman in the white waistcoat? Ah! he went to heaven last week, in a oak coffin with plated handles, Oliver."

Mr Brownlow, had stepped up to within a short distance of the respectable couple. He inquired, as he pointed to Monks, "Do you know that person?"

"No," replied Mrs Bumble flatly.

"Perhaps *you* don't?" said Mr Brownlow, addressing her spouse.

"I never saw him in all my life," said Mr Bumble.

"Nor sold him anything, perhaps?"

"No," replied Mrs Bumble.

"You never had, perhaps, a certain gold locket and ring?" said Mr Brownlow.

"Certainly not," replied the matron. "Why are we brought here to answer such nonsense?"

Again Mr Brownlow nodded to Mr Grimwig. This time, he led in two palsied women, who shook and tottered as they walked.

"You shut the door the night old Sally died," said the foremost one, "but you couldn't shut out the sound, or stop the chinks."

"No, no," said the other, looking round and wagging her toothless jaws.

"We heard her try to tell you what she'd done, and saw you take a paper from her hand, and watched you too, next day, to the pawnbroker's shop," said the first.

"Yes," added the second, "and it was a 'locket and gold ring.' We found out that, and saw it given you. We were by."

"And we know more than that," resumed the first. "She told us often, long ago, what the young mother had told her. She felt she should never get over it and was on her way, when she was taken ill, to die near the grave of the father of the child."

"Would you like to see the pawnbroker himself?" asked Mr Grimwig with a motion towards the door.

"No," replied the woman; "if he" – she pointed to Monks – "has been coward enough to confess, as I see he has, and you have sounded all these hags till you have found the right ones, I have nothing more to say. I did sell them, and they're where you'll never get them. What then?"

"Nothing," replied Mr Brownlow, "except we will ensure that neither of you is employed in a situation of trust again. You may leave."

"I hope," said Mr Bumble, ruefully, as Mr Grimwig led away the two old women. "I hope that this unfortunate little circumstance will not deprive me of my porochial office?"

"Indeed it will," replied Mr Brownlow. "You may consider it done, and think yourself well off besides."

"It was all Mrs Bumble. She *would* do it," urged Mr Bumble; first checking that his partner had left the room.

"That is no excuse," replied Mr Brownlow. "You were present when these trinkets were destroyed, and therefore may be considered the guiltier, as the law supposes that your wife acts under your direction."

"If the law supposes that," said Mr Bumble, squeezing his hat in both hands, "the law is a ass – a idiot. If that's the eye of the law, the law is a bachelor. And I wish the law may have his eye opened by experience – by experience."

Laying great stress on the repetition of these two words, Mr Bumble fixed his hat on very tight, and followed his helpmate down stairs.

"Young lady," said Mr Brownlow, turning to Rose, "give me your hand. Do not tremble. You need not fear to hear the few remaining words we have to say."

"I do not know how they can, but if they have – any reference to me," said Rose, "pray let me hear them some other time."

"Nay," returned the old gentleman, drawing her arm through his. "You have more fortitude, I am sure. Do you know this young lady, sir?"

"Yes," replied Monks.

"I never saw you before," said Rose faintly.

"I have seen you often," returned Monks.

"The father of the unhappy Agnes had two daughters," said Mr Brownlow. "What was the fate of the other – the child?"

"When her father died in a strange place," replied Monks, "without a letter, book, or scrap of paper to yield the faintest clue of how his friends or relatives could be traced – the child was taken by some wretched cottagers, who reared it as their own."

"Go on," said Mr Brownlow, signing to Mrs Maylie to approach.

"You couldn't find the spot where these people went," said Monks, "but hatred finds a way. My mother found it, after a year of cunning search – ay, and the child."

"She took it, did she?"

"No. The people were poor and began to sicken – so she left it with them, giving them a small present of money that would not last long, and promised more, which she never meant to send. She didn't entirely rely on their discontent and poverty for the child's unhappiness, so told them the story of the sister's shame. She altered the story as it suited her, bade them take good heed of the child, for she came of bad blood and was sure to go wrong at one time or other. The people believed it and there the child dragged on an existence, miserable enough to satisfy us, until a widow lady, residing then at Chester, saw the girl by chance. She pitied her, and took her home. There was some cursed spell, I think, against us; for in spite of all our efforts she remained there and was happy. I lost sight of her two or three years ago, and saw her no more until a few months back."

"Do you see her now?"

"Yes. Leaning on your arm."

"But not the less my niece," cried Mrs Maylie, folding the fainting girl in her arms. "My dearest child! I would not lose her now, for all the treasures of the world. My own dear girl!"

"The only friend I ever had," cried Rose, clinging to her. "The kindest, best of friends. My heart will burst. I cannot bear all this."

"You have borne more, and have been through all, the best and gentlest creature that ever shed happiness," said Mrs Maylie, embracing her tenderly. "Come, come, my love – remember who this is who waits to hold you, poor child!"

196

"Not aunt," cried Oliver, throwing his arms about her neck. "I'll never call her aunt. My own dear sister! Something taught my heart to love her so dearly from the first! Rose, dear, darling Rose!"

A father, sister, and mother, were gained, and lost, in that one moment. Joy and grief were mingled in the cup.

They were a long time alone. A soft tap at the door at length announced that someone waited. Oliver opened it, glided away, and gave place to Harry Maylie.

"I know it all," he said, taking a seat beside the lovely girl. "Dear Rose, I know it all."

"I am not here by accident," he added after a lengthened silence; "I was told all this only yesterday. You know I have come to remind you of a promise?"

"Stay," said Rose. "You *do* know all?"

"All. You gave me leave, at any time within a year, to renew the subject of our last discourse."

"I did."

"Not to press you to alter your determination," pursued the young man, "but to hear you repeat it, if you would. I was to lay whatever of station or fortune I might possess at your feet, and if you still adhered to your former determination, I pledged myself, by no word or act, to seek to change it."

"The same reasons which influenced me then, will influence me now," said Rose firmly. "If I ever owed a strict and rigid duty to her, whose goodness saved me from a life of suffering, when should I ever feel it, as I should tonight? It is a struggle but one I am proud to make; it is a pang, but one my heart shall bear."

"The disclosure of tonight, – " Harry began.

"The disclosure of tonight," replied Rose softly, "leaves me in the same position, with reference to you, as that in which I stood before."

"You harden your heart against me, Rose," urged her lover.

"Oh, Harry, Harry," said the young lady, bursting into tears. "I wish I could, and spare myself this pain. Harry, we have said enough."

"Not yet, not yet," said the young man, detaining her as she rose. "My hopes, my wishes, prospects, feeling: every thought in life except my love for you: have undergone a change. I offer you, now, no distinction among a bustling crowd; no mingling with a world of malice and detraction, but a home – a heart and home – yes, dearest Rose, and those, and those alone, are all I have to offer."

"What do you mean!" she faltered.

"I mean but this – that when I left you last, I left you with a firm determination to level all fancied barriers. I would make your world mine; that no pride of birth should curl the lip at you, for I would turn from it. This I have done. Those who have shrunk from me because of this, have shrunk from you, and proved you so far right. Such power and patronage, such relatives of influence and rank as smiled upon me then, look coldly now. But there are smiling fields and waving trees in England's richest county; and by one village church there stands a rustic dwelling which you can make me prouder of, than all the hopes I have renounced. This is my rank and station now, and here I lay it down!"

"It's a trying thing waiting supper for lovers," said Mr Grimwig, waking up, and pulling his pocket-handkerchief from over his head.

Truth to tell, the supper had been waiting a most unreasonable time. Neither Mrs Maylie, nor Harry, nor Rose, who all came in together, could offer a word in extenuation.

"I'll take the liberty, if you'll allow me, of saluting the bride that is to be," said Grimwig.

He lost no time in carrying this notice into effect upon the blushing girl and the example, being contagious, was followed both by the doctor and Mr Brownlow.

CHAPTER 49

The court was paved, from floor to roof, with human faces. Inquisitive and eager eyes peered from every inch of space. All looks were fixed upon one man – Fagin.

He stood there, one hand resting on the wooden slab before him, the other held to his ear, and his head thrust forward to enable him to catch with greater distinctness every word that fell from the presiding judge, who was delivering his charge to the jury. At times, he turned his eyes to observe the effect of the slightest featherweight in his favour; and when the points against him were stated with terrible distinctness, looked towards his counsel. Beyond this, he stirred not hand or foot. He had scarcely moved since the trial began.

A slight bustle in the court recalled him to himself. Looking round, he saw that the jurymen had turned together, to consider of their verdict. As his eyes wandered to the gallery, he could see in not one face – not even among the women, of whom there were many there – the faintest sympathy with himself, or any feeling but one of all-absorbing interest that he should be condemned.

As he saw all this in one bewildered glance, the death-like stillness came again, and looking back, he saw that the jurymen had turned towards the judge. Hush!

They only sought permission to retire.

He looked, wistfully, into their faces, one by one, when they passed out, as though to see which way the greater number leant. The jailer touched him on the shoulder. He followed mechanically and sat down on a chair.

He looked up into the gallery again. Some of the people were eating and some fanning themselves with handkerchiefs. There was one young man sketching his face in a little notebook. He wondered what it was like, and looked on when the artist broke his pencil-point, and made another with his knife.

In the same way, when he looked towards the judge, his mind began to busy itself with the fashion of his dress, and what it cost. He pursued this train of careless thought until some new object caught his eye and roused another.

Not that his mind was, for one instant, free from an oppressive overwhelming sense of the grave that opened at his feet – it was ever present to him. But he could not yet fix his thoughts upon it. Thus, even while he trembled, he fell to counting the iron spikes before him, and wondering how the head of one had been broken off. Then, he thought of all the horrors of the gallows and the scaffold – and stopped to watch a man sprinkling the floor to cool it – and then went on to think again.

At length there was a cry of silence. The jury returned, and passed him close. He could glean nothing from their faces. Perfect stillness ensued – not a rustle – not a breath – Guilty.

The building rang with a tremendous shout, and another, and another, and then it echoed loud groans, then gathered strength as they swelled out, like angry thunder. It was a peal of joy from the populace outside, greeting the news that he would die on Monday.

The noise subsided, and he was asked if he had anything to say why sentence of death should not be passed upon him. He looked intently at his questioner while the demand was made; but it was twice repeated before he seemed to hear it, and then he only muttered that he was an old man and was silent again.

The judge assumed the black cap. The address was solemn and impressive – the sentence fearful to hear. But he stood, like a marble figure. His haggard face still thrust forward, his under-jaw hanging down, and his eyes staring out before him, when the jailer put his hand upon his arm, and beckoned him away. He gazed stupidly about him for an instant, and obeyed.

They led him through a paved room under the court, where some prisoners were waiting till their turns came, and as he passed, the prisoners fell back to render him more visible to the people who were clinging to the bars. His conductors hurried him on, through a gloomy passage lit by a few lamps, into the interior of the prison.

Here, he was searched, that he might not have about him the means of anticipating the law. He was led to one of the condemned cells, and left alone.

He sat down on a stone bench opposite the door, which served for seat and bedstead; and casting his blood-shot eyes upon the ground, tried to collect his thoughts. After awhile, he began to remember a few disjointed fragments of what the judge had said. To be hanged by the neck till he was dead.

As it came on very dark, he began to think of all the men he had known who had died upon the scaffold; some of them through his means. He had seen some of them die, – and had joked too, because they died with prayers upon their lips. With what a rattling noise the drop went down; and how suddenly they changed, from strong and vigorous men to dangling heaps of clothes!

Some of them may have inhabited that very cell – sat upon that very spot. It was very dark; why didn't they bring a light? The cell had been built for many years. Scores of men must have passed their last hours there.

At length, two men appeared – one bearing a candle, the other dragging in a mattress on which to pass the night, for the prisoner was to be left alone no more.

Then came night – dark, dismal, silent night. The boom of every clock strike came laden with the one, deep, hollow sound – Death.

The day passed off. Day? There was no day; it was gone as soon as come – and night came on again. So long, and yet so short; long in its dreadful silence, and short in its fleeting hours. Venerable men of his own persuasion came to pray beside him, but he drove them away with curses. They renewed their charitable efforts, and he beat them off.

Saturday night. He had only one night more to live. And as he thought of this, day broke – Sunday.

It was then that a withering sense of his helpless, desperate state came in its full intensity upon his soul. He had never held any defined or positive hope of mercy, but he had been unable to consider more than the dim probability of dying so soon. He had sat there, awake, but dreaming. Now, he started up, every minute, and with gasping mouth and burning skin, hurried to and fro, in such a paroxysm of fear and wrath that even they – used to such sights – recoiled with horror. He grew so terrible in all the tortures of his evil conscience that the two kept watch together.

He cowered down upon his stone bed, and thought of the past. He had been wounded with some missiles from the crowd on the day of his capture, and his head was bandaged with a linen cloth. His red hair hung down upon his bloodless face; his beard was torn, and twisted into knots; his eyes shone with a terrible light; his unwashed flesh crackled with the fever that burnt him up.

From early in the evening until nearly midnight, little groups of two and three presented themselves at the lodge-gate, and inquired, with anxious faces, whether any reprieve had been received. These being answered in the negative, communicated the welcome intelligence to clusters in the street. By degrees they fell off, one by one; and, for an hour, in the dead of night, the street was left to solitude and darkness.

The space before the prison was cleared, and a few strong barriers, painted black, had been already thrown across the road to break the pressure of the expected crowd, when Mr Brownlow and Oliver appeared at the wicket. They had an order of admission to the prisoner, signed by one of the sheriffs. They were immediately admitted into the lodge.

"Is the young gentleman to come too, sir?" said the man to conduct them. "It's not a sight for children, sir."

"It is not indeed, my friend," rejoined Mr Brownlow. "But my business with this man is intimately connected with him. As this child has seen him at the height of his success and villainy, I think it as well – even at the cost of some pain and fear – that he should see him now."

These few words had been said apart, unheard by Oliver. The man touched his hat, and glancing at Oliver with some curiosity, opened another gate and led them on, towards the cells.

"This," said the man, stopping in a gloomy passage where a couple of workmen were making some preparations, "this is the place he passes through. If you step this way, you can see the door he goes out at."

He led them into a stone kitchen, fitted with coppers for dressing the prison food, and pointed to a door. There was an open grating above, through which came the sound of voices, mingled with the noise of hammering, and the throwing down of boards. They were putting up the scaffold.

From this place, they passed through several strong gates, and, having entered an open yard, ascended a flight of narrow steps, and came into a passage with a row of strong doors. The turnkey knocked at one of these with his bunch of keys. The two attendants, after a little whispering, came out into the passage, stretching themselves as if glad of the temporary relief, and motioned the visitors to follow the jailer into the cell. They did so.

The condemned criminal was seated on his bed, rocking, with a countenance like that of a snared beast. His mind was evidently wandering to his old life, for he continued to mutter.

"Good boy, Charley – well done – " he mumbled. "Oliver, too, ha! Oliver too – quite the gentleman now – take that boy away to bed!"

The jailer took the other hand of Oliver; and, whispering him not to be alarmed, looked on without speaking.

"Take him away to bed!" cried Fagin. "Do you hear me, some of you? He has been the – the – somehow the cause of all this."

"Fagin," said the jailer.

"That's me!" cried the Jew, falling, instantly, into the attitude of listening he had assumed upon his trial. "An old man, my Lord!"

202

"Here," said the turnkey, laying his hand upon his breast to keep him down. "Here's somebody to see you. Fagin! Are you a man?"

"I shan't be one long," he replied, looking up with a face of rage and terror. "Strike them all dead! What right have they to butcher me?"

He caught sight of Oliver and Mr Brownlow and shrank to the furthest corner, demanding to know what they wanted there.

"Steady," said the turnkey, still holding him down. "Now, sir, tell him what you want. Quick, if you please, for he grows worse."

"You have some papers," said Mr Brownlow advancing, "given to you, for better security, by a man called Monks."

"It's all a lie together," replied Fagin. "I haven't one – not one."

"For the love of God," said Mr Brownlow solemnly, "do not say that now – tell me where they are. You know that Sikes is dead, that Monks has confessed. There is no hope of any further gain. Where are those papers?"

"Oliver," cried Fagin, beckoning to him. "Here! Let me whisper."

"I am not afraid," said Oliver in a low voice, releasing Mr Brownlow's hand.

"The papers," said Fagin, drawing Oliver towards him, "are in a canvas bag, in a hole a little way up the chimney in the top front-room. I want to talk to you, my dear."

"Yes, yes," returned Oliver. "Let me say one prayer. Say only one, upon your knees, with me, and we will talk till morning."

"Outside, outside," replied Fagin, pushing the boy before him towards the door, and looking vacantly over his head. "Say I've gone to sleep – they'll believe you. You can get me out, if you take me."

"Oh! God forgive this wretched man!" cried the boy.

"Have you nothing else to ask him, sir?" inquired the turnkey.

"No other question," replied Mr Brownlow. "If I hoped we could recall him to a sense of his position – "

"Nothing will do that, sir," replied the man, shaking his head. "You had better leave him."

The door of the cell opened, and the attendants returned.

"Press on, press on," cried Fagin. "Softly, but not so slow. Faster, faster!"

The men laid hands upon him, and disengaging Oliver from his grasp, held him back. He struggled with the power of desperation, then sent up cry upon cry that penetrated even those massive walls, ringing in their ears until they reached the open yard.

Day was dawning when they again emerged. A great multitude had already assembled – the crowd were pushing, quarrelling, joking. Everything told of life and animation, but one dark cluster of objects in the centre of all – the black stage, the cross-beam, the rope, and all the hideous apparatus of death.

CHAPTER 50

Before three months had passed, Rose Fleming and Harry Maylie were married in the village church that was henceforth to be the scene of the young clergyman's labours – on the same day they entered into possession of their new and happy home.

Mrs Maylie took up her abode with her son and daughter-in-law, to enjoy, during the tranquil remainder of her days, the contemplation of the happiness of those on whom the warmest affections and tenderest cares of a well-spent life have been unceasingly bestowed.

It appeared, after careful investigation, that if property remaining in the custody of Monks (which had never prospered either in his or his mother's hands) were equally divided between himself and Oliver, it would yield little more than three thousand pounds to each. By the provisions of his father's will, Oliver was entitled to the whole; but Mr Brownlow, unwilling to deprive the elder son of the opportunity of retrieving his former vices and pursuing an honest career, proposed this mode of distribution, to which his young charge joyfully acceded.

Monks, still bearing that name, retired with his portion to a distant part of the New World. Here he quickly squandered the money and once more fell into his old courses. After a long confinement for some fresh act of fraud and knavery, he died in prison.

Mr Brownlow adopted Oliver as his son. He moved with him and the old housekeeper to within a mile of the parsonage-house, where his dear friends resided.

Soon after the marriage, the worthy doctor returned to Chertsey, bereft of the presence of his old friends. Finding that the place really no longer was, to him, what it had been, he settled his business on his assistant and took a bachelor's cottage outside the village of which his young friend was pastor. Here, he took to gardening, planting, fishing and various other pursuits of a similar kind, all with his characteristic impetuosity.

Before his removal, he had managed to contract a strong friendship for Mr Grimwig, which that eccentric gentleman cordially reciprocated. He is accordingly visited by Mr Grimwig a great many times in the course of the year. On all such occasions, Mr Grimwig plants, fishes, and carpenters, with great ardour; doing everything in a very singular and unprecedented manner, but always maintaining that his mode is the right one. On Sundays, he never fails to criticise the sermon to the young clergyman's face: always informing Mr Losberne, in strict confidence afterwards, that he considers it an excellent performance, but deems it as well not to say so.

Mr and Mrs Bumble, deprived of their situations, finally became paupers in that very same workhouse in which they had once lorded it over others.

As to Mr Giles and Brittles, they still remain in their old posts, although the former is bald, and the last-named boy quite grey. They sleep at the parsonage, but divide their attentions equally among its inmates, and Oliver, and Mr Brownlow, and Mr Losberne.

Master Charles Bates, appalled by Sikes's crime, wondered whether an honest life was not, after all, the best. Arriving at the conclusion that it certainly was, he turned his back upon the scenes of the past. Having a contented disposition, and a good purpose, he succeeded in the end; he is now the merriest young grazier in all Northamptonshire.

Within the altar of the old village church there stands a white marble tablet, which bears as yet but one word "AGNES". There is no coffin in that tomb; and may it be many years, before another name is placed above it! But, if the spirits of the Dead ever come back to earth, to visit spots hallowed by the love – the love beyond the grave – of those whom they knew in life, I believe that the shade of Agnes sometimes hovers round that solemn nook.